P9-DNV-997

Crete Public Library
305 East 13th St
WITHDRAWN
Crete, NE 68333
Established 1878

SHOW AND PROVE

Also by Sofia Quintero

Efrain's Secret

SHOW AND PROVE

SOFIA QUINTERO

ALFRED A. KNOPF

New York

THIS IS A BORZOI BOOK PUBLISHED BY ALFRED A. KNOPF

This is a work of fiction. Names, characters, places, and incidents either are the product of the author's imagination or are used fictitiously. Any resemblance to actual persons, living or dead, events, or locales is entirely coincidental.

Text copyright © 2015 by Sofia Quintero
Jacket art copyright © 2015 by Getty Images

All rights reserved. Published in the United States by Alfred A. Knopf, an imprint of Random House Children's Books, a division of Penguin Random House LLC, New York.

Knopf, Borzoi Books, and the colophon are registered trademarks of Penguin Random House LLC.

Visit us on the Web! randomhouseteens.com

Educators and librarians, for a variety of teaching tools, visit us at RHTeachersLibrarians.com

Library of Congress Cataloging-in-Publication Data
Quintero, Sofia.
Show and prove / Sofia Quintero. — First edition.
p. cm.
Summary: "Friends Smiles and Nike spend the summer of 1983 in the South Bronx working a job at a summer camp, chasing girls, and breakdancing."— Provided by publisher
ISBN 978-0-375-84707-3 (trade) — ISBN 978-0-375-94707-0 (lib. bdg.) — ISBN 978-0-375-89777-1 (ebook)
[1. Summer employment—Fiction. 2. Camps—Fiction. 3. Friendship—Fiction. 4. Dating (Social customs)—Fiction. 5. Hispanic Americans—Fiction. 6. Bronx (New York, N.Y.)—History—20th century—Fiction.] I. Title.
PZ7.Q44Sho 2015
[Fic]—dc23
2014042544

The text of this book is set in 11-point Sabon.

Printed in the United States of America
July 2015
10 9 8 7 6 5 4 3 2 1
First Edition

Random House Children's Books
supports the First Amendment and celebrates the right to read.

YA.
Quintero

For all the young people everywhere
creating something from nothing

SMILES

The vintage postcard with the photograph of the Champs-Elysées is wedged between Pop's union newsletter and a bill from Bronx-Lebanon Hospital addressed to Mama. I flip it over and read it.

Dear Ray,

This is the view from my window. Impressed? Don't be. I'm bored out of my skull. I racked up some cool points though playing that tape you made me, since kids here hadn't heard of Run-D.M.C. yet. How's your summer going? Write me back at this address. Maybe I'll bring you back a French girlfriend, ha, ha, ha.

Eric G.

Eric said he would write me from Paris, but I never believed he would. Not after what I overheard him telling Sean Donovan when he lost that final debate to me. Maybe I

1

should write him back, and perpetrate a fraud like everything is copacetic. Like Don Corleone in *The Godfather* said: *Keep your friends close, but your enemies closer.*

I tuck the postcard into my back pocket and head out the building to Nike's to listen to Eddie Murphy's album again.

On my stoop rocking his white kufi and flowing like Kool Moe Dee, Kevin—I mean, Qusay is politicking with Booby, Pooh, and some other homeboys while they follow along with carbon copies in their hands. Save a few wrinkles about his eyes, you'd think Q was an older brother even though he came up with Pop. The man's the epitome of *Black don't crack.*

"What's up, y'all?" I say. I lower myself onto the step beside Pooh to put on my roller skates and sneak peeks at his sheet, glimpsing a word here and there. *Knowledge. Wisdom. Freedom.* Funny how it feels like home to sit here when it's been months since I hung out with these cats. I used to chill with them all the time, but then Nike moved to the neighborhood, I enrolled at Dawkins, and Mama died. Even if Booby and Pooh be frontin' to impress Junior, who's got beef with Nike, I miss hanging out with them on the stoop like this.

Q says, "Peace, G." Everyone else welcomes me to the cipher with a nod. He offers me a carbon copy.

Before I can tell him I can't stay long, my grandmother throws open the kitchen window of our fifth-floor apartment. "Raymond!" I swear Nana must've been a bat in a previous life and is gonna be a dolphin in the next.

Qusay looks up and waves to her. "Good afternoon, Queen Beatrice."

"That's Mrs. Hastings to you!" Then Nana looks back to

2

me and busts out with the patois. "Raymond, tek weh yuh self."

The homeboys laugh, and I can't blame them. "Nana." I shrug, playing the role. "No ting nah gwan!" But she has already slammed the window shut.

"The Nana has spoken," says Boob. I laugh along with the homeboys. No static so long that's *all* he says about my grandmother.

I say to Q, "Sorry 'bout that."

"Ain't no thing but a chicken wing." Just like Nana with her patois, Qusay sometimes breaks out with slang to prove that despite his conversion to Islam, he's no stick-in-the-mud.

"Now wait a minute. You might want to hold on to that wing." I'm not going to be outdone on my own stoop. "Seeing as Allah forbids you to dine on the swine and all."

Qusay and the homeboys laugh. "That's a good one, G. You inherited your mother's good looks and your father's quick wit. Do me a favor and give Derrick my regards, will you?"

"Will do, Q."

Nana throws open the window again. "Raymond!" She flings her gold, black, and green coin purse through the window guard. "Go to see Father Davis now." The purse hits the pavement with a loud slap. With only one skate on, I hobble to pick it up. In the purse is a folded check made out to St. Aloysius. On the memo line it says "Ethiopian children." Nana done just concocted an errand to get me away from Q. The lecture she's going to give me when I come back from the church is already running through my head. *That Qusay can tun duck off a nest,* Nana'll say. *When that man come roun', you see and blin', hear and deaf. Understand?*

She'll get over it, though. What Nana says about Five Percenters she used to say about b-boys. She swore Nike was a thug and that Rock Steady, the Dynamic Rockers, and all the b-boy crews were just gangs in disguise. I thought that was hilarious and made the mistake of telling Nike, underestimating how sensitive he still is about his so-called image. Was he POed! Then I started imitating a b-boy uprocking his way through a bodega robbery and sticking up people while rhyming, *What people do for moneeey?* Once I had him rolling on the floor, Nike forgot all about my grandmother's cockamamie theories.

I had explained to Nana that Afrika Bambaataa was a former Black Spade who left the gang after making his own pilgrimage to Africa. "He's like a hip-hop Malcolm," I had said. "And now he throws jams to bring gangs together in peace. They battle now with their feet instead of their fists." Trying to build my case, I almost told her about the time that Nike and I went to a party at the Fever and some Five Percenters broke up a fight. Lucky I came to my senses.

Nana stopped fussing for a while, but now she's anti-Nike again. I never should've told her about the crack he made about Dawkins, but just like Mama, my grandmother has a way of getting things out of me. At least Mama liked Nike. She understood that even though he's "status conscious"—one of her social-worker terms, I guess—he's no Savage Nomad.

Qusay asks, "What's the word on the strike, G?"

I shrug and plop onto the ground to put on my other skate. Nana and I follow the news on the negotiations between Pop's union and the MTA, but he won't talk about the possible transit strike. Last week the Con Ed workers went out on strike, and we're all waiting to see how that pans out.

You'd think not talking about it is going to prevent it, but that tactic didn't save Mama.

Qusay motions for me to retake my seat beside Pooh on the step. "Stay and build with us a little."

"Thanks, Q. Some other time." I tie my sneakers together, hang them around my neck, and kick off. Before I hit the curb, however, I think, *Why not ask?* I turn and skate back toward the group. "Actually, I have a question. The men who killed Malcolm were down with the Nation of Islam, right?" With all eyes on me, I choose my next words carefully. "What would you say to those people who believe his killers were also Five Percenters?" I leave out that "those people" also believe Five Percenters are a street gang so no Qusay fanatics bum-rush my grandmother after bingo. If they try it, I'm going to have to fly their heads, and I'm too good-looking to die so young. "Were they?"

"That's a bold question, Mr. King." Qusay motions toward the steps, directing me to have a seat. "Bold but fair." After sneaking a quick glance toward my kitchen window, I skate to the stoop. Qusay says, "Not only was the man who founded the Nation of Gods and Earths himself a pupil of Brother Malcolm, he was excommunicated from the NOI almost two years prior to the assassination." He's back to speaking like a rapper. "Clarence 13X greatly upset the NOI for teaching the people exactly what I'm sharing with the brothers today."

"Word?" I've read everything I can find about Malcolm, but none of the libraries have anything on the Five Percenters. Teaching myself about Black activists from W.E.B. Du Bois to the Black Panther Party left me feeling like I was born too late until Q returned from Sing Sing and started having parliaments around the block. I have to learn more about the

Five Percenters, and what little I've learned so far, I heard on the streets. You know that don't mean squat.

"Furthermore, G, the Nation of Gods and Earths does not preach a doctrine of violence. To have a hand in the assassination of El-Hajj Malik El-Shabazz would be the height of hypocrisy. We can hardly call others to righteousness if we ourselves are not righteous."

"Well, now you sound like Martin Luther King." I didn't mean to crack a joke, but the other guys laugh. I lower myself onto the stoop as Pooh scoots over so I can sit beside him, and just like that, the homeboys accept me into the cipher. No need to fake the funk to fit in, like with the rich white boys at Dawkins, only to find out that they front, too. "C'mon, Q. Make up your mind. The ballot or the bullet."

Qusay laughs and gives me a handout for the lesson. Across the top it reads SUPREME MATHEMATICS. Down the sheet are the numbers one through nine, then a zero. Next to each number is a word followed by a definition. One is *knowledge,* two is *wisdom,* and so on. As I scan the page, Qusay says, "Along with the supreme alphabet, these numbers and the concepts they represent unlock the keys to the universe."

How many times can Nike and I listen to the same comedy album? It won't kill him if I show up a little late. I flip the page over, looking for English translations of the Arabic letters. "Where's the alphabet?"

"One lesson at a time, Brother Raymond," says Qusay, smiling. "Although these are urgent times, one must approach the one hundred and twenty lessons as one would a marathon, not a race. In order to gain knowledge of self, we must master each lesson, one at a time."

NIKE

That rooftop scene in *Five Deadly Venoms* got me inspired, and I've been stifled in this hot apartment waiting on Smiles too long again. Junior and the Barbarians are probably dealing at the park anyways, so better to stay clear of there. I grab my boom box and linoleum and pray there isn't anybody shooting up on the roof of my building.

As usual, Gloria's in the hallway running her mouth on the phone. "When will it end?" I say, imitating Ma Chow, the Scorpion. As I walk past her, I give her a soft kung fu kick to the back of her knee. "She goes on forever."

My sister dips, her bony knees bumping the table. "Stop, Willie!" she whines. "Can't you see I'm on the phone?"

"No crap, Dick Tracy. When aren't you?"

Gloria shoves the receiver in my face. "Nessa wants to talk to you."

Figures she'd be talking to my ex. I debate whether I should speak to her. I put down my radio and mat, then take the receiver. "Yo, when are you giving me back my buckle?"

7

"That's all you have to say to me, Nike? *Where's my buckle?* You're so rude."

"Why I'ma ask you where my buckle is when I know you got it? You best be taking care of it. Don't be cleaning it with no Brillo pad and scratching it all up or you gonna have to buy me a new one."

Before I can add *Call off your brother already,* she yells, "Just put Gloria back on!"

Instead I press the hook, hanging up on Vanessa, and dial Smiles's number. Wonder what excuse he's got this time for leaving me flat. While the phone rings, Gloria curses at me and punches me in the back. "Stop or I'll tell Ma you were acting up while I was on the phone with Smiley's nana. Geez, I'm only gonna be a minute." When Smiles's grandmother answers, I pretend to be some white boy from his bougie school. "Good afternoon. May I please speak to Raymond?"

"Raymond is not here. I expect him soon. Would you like to leave a message?"

She never be that nice to me, man. "No, thank you. Good day." I slam down the phone and grab my stuff. "It's all yours, acheface. Go to town."

"What Ma told you about calling me names?"

"I'm so scared."

When I get to the roof, no one's there, thank God, so I set down my radio and mat and look over the edge. Sure enough, Ma's on the stoop playing dominoes with the rest of the bochincheras. Today's victim is Dee Dee, my ex-ex's mother. Word is she's a crackhead now, thanks to Junior. Ma's going on about how sorry she feels for Blue Eyes and her sister, Sandy, and Sandy's new baby. I almost yell, *Like you Mother of the Year.*

8

I stretch while rewinding the mastermix I recorded from WBLS last Saturday night. *Hip hop, be bop, don't stop.* I flip the cassette over and over, practicing the new flare I learned on my last trip to the Roxy and building a routine around it. Time disappears, and night comes.

Just when I finally master transitioning from the flare into a headstand, Jerry Del Valle races past me, hitting me with his telescope. I crumple to the linoleum. "Get lost, Professor!" I like having the roof to myself, and I'm not sharing it with a ten-year-old know-it-all. I'll snatch him and Donkey Kong his ass down the fire escape if I have to.

But Jerry's soon followed by half the block, including Gloria and Vanessa. I get stupid nervous waiting for Junior and the Barbarians to bust through the door. Then I see that people in other buildings are rushing to their rooftops and fire escapes, pointing at the sky. Finally, I notice the moon. Tonight it looks like someone sliced the head off a quarter and it's bleeding. It reminds me of what Smiles told me about his mother's illness, and I kiss my crucifix in memory of Mrs. King.

"Let me see, Jerry," says Vanessa. The Professor be crushin' on her, so he forks over his precious telescope. You'd think it was official NASA property instead of a plastic toy. Nobody around here who can afford the real thing would spend money on something like that anyways. Even the neighborhood nerd spends his money on fake Pumas with the panther on the logo looking more like a hedgehog and whatnot Vanessa peers through the lens. "Wow, imagine," she says. "Everybody all over the world is watching this right now." She's pretty when she contemplates like that. I move behind her as close as I can without touching her. She rolls her eyes but doesn't move away, because I still got it like that.

But leave it to the Professor to rain on the parade by dropping science. Literally. "No, it's just going to be a partial eclipse," he huffs, all condescending. "And it can only be seen wherever it's night. If it's night over here, it can't be night in, like, Lebanon."

I suck my teeth. "Them A-rab terrorists don't deserve to see no eclipse anyways." I hold out my hand and stare into Vanessa's eyes, hoping she'll give me the telescope—and maybe more when everyone clears out of here.

She gives me a dirty look. "Don't even try it." She slaps the telescope against the Professor's chest. "I'll push you over that ledge."

"It's nighttime in Puerto Rico, too," says Gloria. "So they can see it there, right?"

"The eclipse can be seen all throughout North and South America," says the Professor. "But we have the best view."

"About time the South Bronx got the best of something," I say.

Down on the street, Mister Softee turns the corner playing his song, and folks scatter like roaches in sudden light. Some people can't appreciate anything. On the other side of the world, they can't see this beautiful moon, but these suckers are worried about catching the ice cream man who rolls through here several times a day, every single day. Guess that jingle beats gunshots. Still, these pooh-butts plan on living in this tenement building their whole lives. Not me. Say no go.

"Yo, Professor, lend me your telescope." I snatch it from him anyways and peer at the moon.

"Any babies conceived tonight are going to be born with demons in them," says the Professor. He doesn't sound too scared, though. In fact, he sounds pretty excited by the prospect.

"They in the right neighborhood." These days everywhere you turn, somebody is having a crack baby. That's why no one runs over to coo at some newborn no more. You might go there to find claws hanging outside the crib like in that movie *It's Alive*.

"And did you hear what Columbus did to the natives in Jamaica?"

I didn't even know he went to Jamaica. "Me and history don't mix. I'm a man of the future." I scan the telescope around the block, hoping to catch some chick undressing in front of her window like those frat boys did in *Animal House*. I bite, though, because I bet Smiles don't know that, even though he's part Jamaican and goes to Dawkins and all. "OK, what he do?"

"Columbus got marooned in Jamaica for a few months, and at first, the natives were quite hospitable. They brought his crew food while they waited to be rescued. But Columbus was a jerk, so they stopped helping him."

And then I find what I've been looking for. The prettiest girl I have ever seen is sitting on a fire escape on the third floor of a building across the street and a few doors down from mine. At her bare feet is an open newspaper, but she is looking up at the eclipse as if it is breaking sad news to her.

"So Columbus and his crew are about to starve when he gets an idea. He found an almanac on his ship and realized that a lunar eclipse was going to take place. Columbus told the natives that God would punish them if they didn't feed him and his men, and that there would be an omen in the sky."

11

She has on a long, dark skirt that grazes her ankles and a sailor blouse with long sleeves. At one point, the girl seems to look directly into my lens. She has the darkest almond-shaped eyes. Where did she come from? Probably visiting from Puerto Rico for the summer. Or maybe she moved here for good. All that time messing around with the likes of Vanessa, I missed this new girl.

"Sure enough, the moon went dark, and Columbus went into his cabin, ignoring the natives as they begged him to save them. He waited for an hour and then came back out like, *OK, God said he'll fix it if you keep giving us everything we ask for.* The chief agreed, and lo and behold, the moon emerged from the shadow."

"Yo, that's wack," I say. "If I was the chief, I would've told Codumbus, *Nah, I think God would like it more if we sacrificed your ass instead.* Just call homeboy's bluff. The moon would've reappeared, and I would've had more juice with the tribe than ever!"

"No," says the Professor with that condescending attitude again. "The Taino Indians were peaceful."

"Whatever, clever. Yo, Jerry, who's that girl over there?" I hand him the telescope and point. "The one sitting on the fire escape across the street."

"I don't see anybody."

I snatch back the telescope and look for her, but he's right. She's gone. That's OK. I've got all summer to find her.

SMILES

I'm so deep in sorrow I almost don't hear Qusay call my name. I turn, and he's waving at me while standing outside a storefront. "G, can you help a brother out?" When I reach him, Qusay points to the emblem he has hung in the window. "Is it straight?"

The symbol is a number 7 between a star and a crescent moon against a seven-pointed star surrounded by the words IN THE NAME OF ALLAH. I point and say, "Nah, man, you need to lift it just a little higher on the left."

Qusay gestures for me to stay put, runs inside, and adjusts the sign. When he nails it, I give him the thumbs-up and enter the storefront. There's nothing more than a single filing cabinet, a small desk, a handful of folding chairs, and several boxes of books.

"Why the number seven?" I ask.

"It's the number of perfection. The seventh letter of the alphabet is *G*. *G* stands for God. And that's what we mean when we greet each other with *What's up, G?*"

13

"Word?" I never knew that. "I thought it meant gangster."

Qusay shakes his head. "Unfortunately, you are not the first."

I give it some more thought. Seven is a prime number. Indivisible. There are seven notes on the musical scale. Seven colors in a rainbow. Seven days in the week. Seven continents. Even W.E.B. Du Bois referred to the Black man as the seventh son. "Then why do you call yourselves Five Percenters?"

"Because eighty-five percent of the population has no knowledge of self. They are ignorant of the truth and, as such, are sheep. Another ten percent are evildoers with some knowledge of truth, which they use to control the majority. The remaining five percent—the Nation of Gods and Earths—we are the poor righteous teachers. We know the truth and commit ourselves to liberating the eighty-five by sharing this knowledge with them. What more would you like to know, G?"

The next thing I know, two hours pass as I help Q file papers, unpack books, and give him feedback on his ideas for the neighborhood program he wants to start. He says, "I really want to continue teaching the Universal Language and holding parliaments here, where it's much safer than the park or the streets, but you know no one is going to give me money for speaking the truth." He finishes taping up a poster of Stokely Carmichael shouting before a knot of microphones.

"So how'd you afford this place?"

"The community board gave me enough money for a six-month lease, on the promise of working with the young brothers in the community," Q explains. "You know the saying. *Sell them what they want, but give them what they need.*"

I had never heard of that before, but it reminded me of something my mother once said. She took me to spend the day with her at the agency where she worked. She had a few clients come in to get help with their applications for welfare, housing, Medicaid, whatever. It wouldn't take all that long to complete the applications, but Mama would keep them a half hour, politicking with them. Or more like *to* them. If they came in to apply for Section 8 housing, for example, she'd also tell them about the neighborhood housing coalition and hand them the brochure. If she was helping them get food stamps, Mama would talk about the impact that fast food had on their health as well as their wallet. I couldn't see why Mama wouldn't just zip off the paperwork and send them on their way, especially since I was starving and craving a Happy Meal myself. Mama said, *Meet people where they are and take them someplace better.* Now that I'm older and politicking with Qusay, I get it.

He sighs. "Still, if I want to raise more money to actually do anything, I have to write a full-fledged proposal with a detailed budget. To be honest, G, I don't know where to start. I've gone to one library after the other, and I can't find any examples."

The answer comes to me quickly. "You should talk to my boss Barb," I say. "That's how she started the summer day camp and after-school program at Saint Aloysius."

Qusay snickers. "That's not going to happen."

"Why not?"

"Let's just say Miss Diaz and I have a checkered past," Q says. "I mean Mrs. Cuevas. She's still Mrs. Cuevas, isn't she?"

15

"Yup." I smile for the first time all day. "And Big Lou is bigger than ever. Dish, Q. Between you, me, and our man Stokely here."

"Now where did you learn who this brother was?" Qusay asks.

Obviously, he's trying to change the subject, but since I'm happy that he's impressed, I go with the flow. "On my own. You think they're going to teach me about Black Power at a school like Dawkins?" Actually, they did. In the five minutes my history teacher spent on the Black Panthers, he drove home that they were extremists. *How ironic that their violent radicalism helped sell Martin Luther King Jr.'s better alternative of nonviolent disobedience to white America,* he said, and everyone in the class nodded except me.

"Dawkins that school by the Hub off Third Avenue?"

One moment I'm explaining to Qusay what Dawkins is and how I got there. The next I'm telling him what I have had no one to tell. From the first time a teacher called me eloquent but I couldn't get souped up because it felt more like a dis than a compliment to the debate that made me realize that Eric Grey and Sean Donovan were not my friends. "I had headed back into the locker room to get my books. That's when I overheard this kid Eric complaining to this other guy Sean that it was unfair that I had won." I grab a poster of Marcus Garvey and a chair to put it up on the wall across from Stokely. "Then Sean said, *Yeah, and how's it going to look if the only Black guy on the team doesn't win the debate on whether W.E.B. Du Bois or Booker T. Washington has been proven right?*" This is the first time I ever told the truth about what it's like for me at Dawkins. I tried calling Russell—the Black alum who recruited me—a few times but never heard from him.

I don't want to worry Pop and Nana, and I'm certainly not trying to hear Nike's *I told you so*s.

"Wow," says Q. "Clearly, you could've taken those white boys to task, G. Why didn't you?" His voice has no judgment.

"I promised my mother I would graduate from Dawkins and go on to college." I shrug. "Two years down, one to go."

Qusay points at my face. "That's how you looked when I first saw you out there. And then when you came in and we were building, you lit up like the Empire State Building. And now there you are again."

"Today would've been my mom's birthday." I keep to myself that Pop, Nana, and I have just come from visiting her grave, never saying a word the entire time. It makes losing her that much worse, because if I had my way, I would always talk about her. I'd repeat Mama's jokes, imitate her laugh, and otherwise keep the best of her alive. I joined the debate team at Dawkins because I miss the push-pull of our conversations. She helps me prepare my arguments as I imagine what she might say to propositions and rebuttals. At the end of the debate in my mind, instead of shaking my hand, Mama wraps her arms around me and tells me how proud she is of me.

"Your mom was one of a kind," Qusay says. "You know the moment I knew it?" I shake my head, eager to hear. The pain of listening to people praise my mother is always worth it. "When I asked her out and she said hell no." I laugh so hard I almost fall off the chair. "Be careful, G! And you know who shares a birthday with your mother?" Qusay points to Stokely Carmichael. "Mr. Kwame Ture himself."

17

"Who?"

"He no longer goes by Stokely Carmichael. He's Kwame Ture now."

"Really? I didn't know that. Why?"

And then Qusay and I continue to build way after the sun goes down.

NIKE

This humidity keeps messing with my hair, man. Why did I spend an hour blowing it out last night? *You go to bed looking like Tony Manero and wake up looking like Juan Epstein,* Smiles be saying. *Just rock a Jheri curl and call it a day.* I told him that he was so funny I forgot to laugh. Smiles can snap on my hair, but if I make one little joke about his bougie school, he gets his BVDs in a twist. He lucky I'm keeping our tradition and hanging out with him today. In fact, I finally copied the Eddie Murphy tape I borrowed from him and plan to give it back to him today before he hounds me for it.

I'm in the bathroom putting my DA back in check when my mother barges in. "Willie, you hungry?"

Since she's talking food, I don't go off on her about disrespecting my privacy. "Starvin'."

"How 'bout scrambled eggs and bacon?"

"Nah." I blast some of my sister's Aqua Net on a stray lick and attack it with my comb. "Make sausage."

She finally scrams so I can get fly for the Fourth of July.

19

I waste another fifteen minutes on my hair, though, before I give up. It don't matter, because with the baseball cap I had NIKE airbrushed across the front of, I still look high post.

When I walk into the kitchen to eat, instead of cooking, my mother is clipping coupons from the Sunday paper. She hasn't made a thing—no eggs, sausage, toast, nothing. "Where's breakfast?"

She closes the paper, and on the table are food stamps. Ma pushes them toward me. "Get whatever you want." Then she digs into her pocket for some change to put on the table. "And bring me back four loosies."

Damn, she set me up. No way I'm going to the store with those cupones. "Send Gloria."

Acheface comes into the kitchen on cue, wearing a bata and rubbing sleep from her eyes. "Gloria what? I didn't do nothing!"

"You're already dressed, Willie. If you wanna eat something, you have to go to the supermarket and get it."

"Isn't that your job?"

My mother squints at me in that angry way she has. "You don't think I work enough?"

I almost laugh. Is she serious? "I work. You lounge around here watching telenovelas, reading *People,* and bochinchando on the telephone or the stoop."

"Is that what you think?" I wait for Ma to mention the fire. I wish she would, I swear! Instead she asks, "You think that because I don't leave the house, I don't work? How many nights a week do you make dinner, Willie? And I don't mean heating up a can of ravioli on the stove for yourself."

"You know I don't cook."

20

"Right. I'm the one in this house who cooks, and when I cook, I cook for everyone, right? I don't just make dinner for myself and leave you two to fend for yourselves."

"True," says Gloria.

"This is a conversation between A and B," I tell her, pointing between my mother and me. "C your way out of it."

Ma shuffles the sections of the Sunday paper until she finds the classifieds. She shoves them toward me. "Willie, look through those classifieds and tell me how much a cook gets paid per week."

Finally! I drop into a seat and scan the want ads. One thing I'll give my mother, she's a def cook. I find an opening for one and say, "This one pays a hundred twenty dollars per week."

Ma tells Gloria, "Do me a favor and write that down. *Cook—one hundred twenty dollars.*" Then she turns back to me and says, "As much as I'm on your case to wash your plate instead of just leaving it in the sink, who ultimately does the dishes and cleans the kitchen?" When I refuse to answer, she says, "Gloria, look that up in the classified ads. Let's see how much I would get paid by someone else to do that."

My sister finds an ad for a dishwasher. "Sixty dollars per week."

"Write that down." Ma turns back to me. "And even though you take your jeans to the cleaners, I take everything else you wear to the Laundromat. See if you find any openings for a laundry worker."

"A hundred dollars per week," Glo says excitedly. "Not as much as a cook, but way better than a dishwasher." She adds that figure to the column of numbers she has scribbled in the margin of the paper.

Ma says, "And I don't just clean the kitchen. I clean the entire apartment—including your room, Willie—so let's see what they're paying maids these days."

"Ninety-one dollars," Gloria says.

"And I'm the one who manages the money, pays the bills, and all that. I have to read and answer all your notices from school, not to mention take your telephone messages like a secretary."

"OK, here's an ad for a bookkeeper that pays almost two hundred dollars a week," says Gloria, all eager beaver. "Oh, and this one for an administrative assistant pays two hundred twenty-five."

"So add all that up."

"Seven hundred and ninety-six dollars."

I glare at them, my arms folded across my chest. "Not like you do any of those things for forty hours a week." If this game isn't about finding my mother a job, I don't want to play anymore.

"You want to make sure these numbers are accurate? Run this household for one week. Because I don't want you to think I'm cheating," Ma says, all sarcastic. "And if that's too much for you, we'll make it simple. For one week just do your own housekeeping. You put in the time and shell out the money to shop for your own food, cook your own meals, wash your own clothes—" He interrupts.

"Forget it," I say. "I ain't that hungry." Then I spin out the kitchen and toward the apartment door.

Ma chases after me with the cupones. She even grabs at

my arm and tries to stuff them in my hand. I elbow her off me and open the door. "After you add up the dollars and hours, come back to me. Then we can talk about how much is a fair amount for you to pay me to be your mother, since welfare is not enough." I rush out and through the closed door she yells her usual threats. "One of these days te voy a dar un pescozá if you keep being disrespectful!"

I take the side streets to Moncho's shop. Used to be this was too early for Junior and his crew to be out there hustling. Nowadays, dealers and crackheads hit the street as soon as the sun comes up, searching for each other like star-crossed kids at some twisted prom.

As I walk past the supermarket, I peek into the window, and there's Blue Eyes at a register, staring at her nails. One time, after we were done getting busy at her place, Blue Eyes told me that her older sister Sandy got knocked up on purpose, hoping that welfare would open her own case so she could move out of their mother's apartment. That's when I knew I had to quit Blue Eyes before she trapped me, too.

Moncho's in the barbershop alone. "What's up, Monch!" I slap him five.

"Hey, Willie!"

"Nike." I point to my cap before taking it off. "Can't rap to some biddy with this nest on my head. Cut it close but leave the tail."

Moncho makes a face. "You homeboys wear your hair too damn long." He reaches for an apron and flaps it open. "Tails, cornrows, Jheri curls . . . all that's for girls."

"You too ol'-school, Monch." He's also a businessman. Moncho'll do any style you ask irregardless and do it right.

"Want I should use the razor?"

"What the hell." It's getting hot, and it ain't like it won't grow back like weeds. I sit in his chair, and he ties the apron around my neck.

"Came at the right time. In an hour this place is gonna get packed," says Moncho. "Everyone wants to get fly for the holiday."

"Word." Every year Smiles and I head downtown to watch the Macy's fireworks. When he decided to go to Dawkins, I thought for sure he'd dis me for some rich kid's cookout in the Hamptons, wherever that is. So far Smiles hasn't flaked on me. Yet.

I glance over at the bulletin board above the mirrors. Sure enough, there are at least five flyers for hip-hop concerts going down over the holiday. Maybe Smiles and I should skip the fireworks this year. "Yo, Moncho, let me see that flyer right there." I point to the yellow one with a drawing of a b-boy spinning on his head. Moncho plucks down the flyer and hands it to me. At the T-Connection on White Plains Road tomorrow, Grandmaster Flash and the Furious Five are going to battle the Funky Four Plus One More. "This looks fresh." Even though Smiles likes the harder sound of that new group Run-D.M.C., I bet he'd gladly drop six bucks— only five with the flyer—to watch these crews rhyme. "Can I keep this?"

"Llévatelo," Moncho says as he takes his electric razor to my scalp. The vibration against my head feels like a massage, and I imagine that the clumps of hair falling to the linoleum are shedding my problems with them. "I've got a magazine back there I've been keeping for you, too. They got an article 'bout that place downtown you like to go to."

24

"The Roxy?" I haven't been there since I broke up with Vanessa after she made such a scene. Got to let enough time pass before I show my face there again.

"Eso es." With most of my hair gone, Moncho puts down his razor and pulls out his shears. "Those Rock Steady guys are getting famous."

"They were in that movie *Flashdance*." My stomach kicks with jealousy. "Blink and you missed 'em, 'cause the movie's about the girl dancer anyways."

"I be seeing you dancing out there." Moncho snips around my ears. "You're good."

"I know." Then I spot the flyer with the opportunity of a lifetime. There's a battle at the Roxy—on my birthday no less—judged by none other than Hazardiss of the Rock Steady Crew. A lot of times when I'm dancing, I fantasize about confronting him at a concert at the Bronx River Center. When Afrika Bambaataa spins "Planet Rock," I challenge Haz to a battle, busting my freshest moves and dusting that toy. So impressed with my skills, Rock Steady asks me to join them, and then I'd be off to the next Rap City Tour, traveling to England and France with new homies Fab 5 Freddy and Ramellzee. But this is better than any fantasy. I'll go down to the Roxy and, after taking out all the other suckers, call out the judge for everybody to see. No better way to spend my birthday—going back to the place to be and staking my claim to fame. The only thing I need to bring is a fly routine, some friends, and a fly girl. I grab the flyer, fold it and stick it in my back pocket.

"Look at what the cat done drag in." Junior's ace coom boom Booby and his tail Pooh diddy-bop through the door. "More like drag out, 'cause he's been dodgin' a nigga."

"I ain't dodgin' nobody." I look around for Moncho, who finished my cut and broke out somewhere while I was lost in my daydream. I whip off the apron, pop my cap on my head, and consider breaking out, even though I haven't paid him. He knows I'm good for it, and I can get that magazine anytime.

"He's only messin' with you, Nike," says Pooh, punching me hard in the shoulder. The pain shoots up my neck, but I keep a straight face. "What's up?"

"Nothin' much." I don't trust Pooh, but best to play the role. "You still messin' with that girl on Willis?"

"Nah, man, that crab quit me, and guess who for." Booby laughs and throws himself into a barber chair like it's his couch at home. "That who-ah dumped me for Junior." He waits for me to comment on that, but I know better. "Not for nothing, he's my homeboy and all, but you know how he be acting like he Big Bank Hank or something." True as that is, I'll be damned if I'm gonna agree so he can run tell Junior, *Nike was poppin' shit behind ya back.* Then Pooh asks, "Yo, your homegirl—the Rican chick with the braids—she got a man?"

"Cookie?" I get hot and don't even know why because I ain't even down with her like that no more. "Ask me if I care."

"Yo, Javi was like, 'Nothing could be finer than to be in Carolina in the mooornin','" sings Pooh. Booby cackles, and for a moment I'd like to slug 'em both. I don't want to think of Cookie like that, but she's not my sister, and I told her back then Javi was no good. She ain't listen, and I've got enough problems.

Moncho finally comes back from his office, magazine in hand. "Willie, where you going?"

"He was trying to skip outta here without paying you, but I stopped his ass," says Booby.

"Yo, stop playing, man," I pretend to joke. I want to say, *Quit instigatin'*, but you don't play a Barbarian close like that, even if he's lying like a rug. "Here you go, Moncho," I say as I hold out the cash. He accepts it with one hand while offering me the magazine with the other. I grab it and high-tail it out of there.

I'm three steps out the barbershop when Pooh's right on my heels singing "Beat it, beat it . . ." He's scrawny as he is klutzy, so I can take him in a fair fight, but what's to stop Booby from jumping in? I double up and look over my shoulder. Pooh's on the pay phone, and I know what time it is. Junior and the rest of the Barbarians will be waiting for me in front of my building if I go straight home.

I take the long way, past JD's store, and he waves me inside. Even though I've got no money, I can't resist—he always has the freshest gear. Those Sergio Valentes that JD has in the window would look so def with my shell-toe red-on-white Adidas and my striped Izod shirt.

" 'Member you asked me about the new colors in Lee twills?" He folds a stack of Polo shirts. "They just came in yesterday. Three new shades of blue—sky blue, turquoise, and teal. You a thirty-four, right?"

"Not today, man." I flip through some other designer jeans on a rack. "Definitely next Friday, though." I move on to a rack of mesh shirts. They seem kind of fruity to me, but I may have to get at least one 'cause I got nice arms. It's too

27

hot for sweatshirts, and I don't want to cut off the sleeves on mine after spending fifteen cents a letter to have NIKE, the Playboy bunny, and then FRESH ironed in Gothic letters down one arm and LEO down the other. Now that I think about it, Vanessa still has my sweatshirt, too. Damn, I gave that girl everything! I peep through the window for Junior or any of his hoods.

"Gonna be a tough summer, man," says JD. "Lot of my regulars telling me they've lost their jobs or can't find one. Money problems for y'all means money problems for me."

"I got money." Just never as much as I want. I give in to temptation and cross the store to the Sergios and look through the stack for my size.

"And you should see the folks that be comin' in here. If they're not tryin' to boost my gear, they're tryin' to sell me whatever they stole from elsewhere." JD shakes his head as he walks to the register. "Remember the real pretty lady with the beauty mark on her cheek? Got the Farrah Fawcett hair and the daughters with the pretty eyes?"

"Dee Dee?" That's Blue Eyes and Sandy's mother, and she was so fine she made Farrah look like Miss Piggy. I tried rapping to Dee Dee, but she called me jailbait. I said she can't get in no trouble because she's a woman. It ain't like that pervert who was flashing his thing at the girls on the playground. Cookie done said something to Mrs. King, and she rounded up the grown-ups into a manhunt to find the jerk. Cutter's the one who cornered the sicko under the Willis Avenue Bridge with an aluminum bat. He would've housed that fool, too, if Smiles's mother hadn't talked him out of it while somebody called the cops. Anyways, Dee Dee told me to take a hike, so

I ended up with Blue Eyes. "I used to mess with her daughter. The younger one. A long time ago, though."

"When you see Dee Dee, it's gonna break your heart, man. She's like this now." JD holds up his pinkie finger. "And all those pretty white teeth look like rotting corn."

Ain't gonna break my heart nothing. No one told her to mess with that stuff. Just like no one told Cutter to become a dope fiend. "That's nasty."

"Dee Dee came in here trying to sell me a stack of brand-new baby clothes. She was all, *Oh, I know you have a little boy,* and I was like, *My son's three now,* but she said, *But look, Papa, they brand-new. See how they got the tags from Youngland still? I give you all of 'em for just five dollars.* I had to chase her ass out of here."

"That's messed up, JD. How you gonna steal from your own grandson like that?"

"That's what that crack does to you. Let me catch you messin' with that stuff. I'll clock you so hard you won't land till Wednesday."

I snicker. JD don't care like that, but nice of him to pretend. Mrs. King liked to say that it takes a village to raise a child, but it ain't like that around here no more, if it ever was. Folks too focused on their own survival. "In fact, put these on layaway for me." I bring the jeans to the counter, give JD my last five dollars as a deposit, and break out of the store.

By the time my birthday comes, I'll take the Sergios out of layaway and rock them. And if I get back my buckle and sweatshirt from Vanessa? Yo, whoever's my girl come August is going to be one lucky biddy. I'm going to take her to the

Roxy, dust that toy Hazardiss in the tournament, and finally get my due.

I get so lost in my plans sometimes. Only when I reach my building and find no one on the stoop do I remember about Junior. I make the sign of the cross with my rosary and kiss the crucifix to the sky.

SMILES

Sweat and bacon wake me up. I go to the kitchen and poke my head into the refrigerator. "Mornin', Nana." The Tang is centimeters from my mouth when a hand snatches the pitcher from me.

"Boy, what's wrong with you?" my father yells. He's holding a lardy spatula in one hand and setting the pitcher on the kitchen table with the other. "We raisin' you better than that. Get a glass!"

"What you doing here?" My stomach grinds from a mix of hunger and worry. Pop is only home during the day for two reasons: vacations and strikes. "Y'all stage a walkout?"

That's what happened three years ago. April Fools' Day, to be exact. Except Local 100 was no joke. I was home from school for Easter break, watching the news and hoping to spot my dad in the sea of workers marching across the Brooklyn Bridge. Nana and I cheered the union while Mama paced the living room. Pop was losing two days' pay for every day of

31

the strike because New York has this stupid law that makes it illegal for government workers to walk off the job. He insisted that the union had no choice because the pay increase the MTA offered was an insult, inflation had caused the cost of living in the city to double.

Pop made me too proud to worry. People dropped by the apartment with hot plates and high praises. I'd go to the bodega and strangers would say, *Raymond, tell your father we stand by him.* Even Nike was like, *Yo, your pop's like Martin Luther King Jr. or some shit.* Folks including Cutter and Naim would be in my living room politicking and trading car-pool stories.

Koch can go straight to hell for all I care. . . .

. . . And Reagan can show 'im the shortcut.

Modern-day slavery. That's all these antilabor laws are.

I done lost ten pounds biking to work.

Y'all still on strike come September, my kid's walking to school. He needs to learn how good he got it. Appreciate things.

Whenever someone asked, *Where's Bernadette?* Pop would say, *Somebody around here got to work!* And they'd all bust out laughing because we all knew how much Mama loved her job at the multiservice agency, as thankless as it seemed to most. Although she wasn't a fan, Mama likened her passion for social work to baseball. *You only have to hit it three out of ten times to be considered good, and when you knock it out of the park—help that person everyone wrote off as helpless—there's nothing like it, Ray-Ray.* Pop and his friends laughed that day because they understood—when Mama was healthy, the community was healthy.

"No, no, no," Pop says, placing his hand on my shoulder. "I just decided to take the day off so I can spend the Fourth of July with my better half." Funny—he used to call Mama that. Pop turns off the flame on the stove and slides the bacon onto a plate covered with a paper towel. "I know you want some of this."

"Word." I pull out a chair and flop into a seat.

"Get your ass up and set the table." I jump to my feet and head to the sink. "Boy, this ain't no diner."

I salute and start yanking pairs of utensils out of the dish rack. "Yes, sir!" Pop has a way of busting my chops that cracks me up. He gives it to me straight, no chaser, and sometimes that's the only way to get it.

"Where's Nana?" I lay everything across the kitchen table. "Still asleep?" I go back to the sink for two glasses.

"I fixed her something, then walked her over to the community center. Right now some ol' fool is losing this month's pension check."

"Cool, 'cause I need to rent a tux for the prom." It just comes out my mouth, despite the fact that I've been thinking about not going. Not the senior trip, not the prom, none of it, even if I got the money. But Pop's laughing, so I laugh along with him as we sit to eat. After the first bite, I say, "Man, Pop, this isn't half bad. You could—" Then I clutch my throat and pretend to keel over.

"Smart-ass. You always was a smart-ass, you know that, right? Stop playing around and eat your food before it gets cold. We got things to do today."

Here we go. "Like what? Caulking the bathtub? Roach-bombing the kitchen?" Whatever Pop's scheming, I have to be done in time to go with Nike to the FDR to watch the Macy's fireworks, or he'll never let me hear the end of it.

"Like this." Pop reaches into his pocket and pulls out Yankees tickets. "Your ol' man come through big or what?"

"Yo, that's fresh, Pop!" I grab the tickets, and just like that, I'm eight years old again, like the last time we caught a game together. Then I jump from my seat. "I gotta make a phone call." Nike won't like this, so the sooner I tell him, the quicker he can get over it.

"You can do that later," says Pop. "Finish your breakfast first."

"It'll only take a second, I promise." I dial the number and hope Gloria answers. If I leave a message with her, Nike can't say I just stood him up and I won't have to deal with his whining.

Just my luck, though, he picks up. "Hi, there," he says in the Boom Boom Washington voice he uses in case a girl is on the other end.

"Yo, Nike . . ."

"Smiley Smiles, what's up?" Before I can say anything else, he says, "Yo, man, I was thinking let's skip going downtown today."

"Word?" It can't be this easy. He must have gotten back with Vanessa or the dog already met somebody new.

"Yeah, there's this hip-hop concert over on White Plains Road."

"OK, but depends when it is."

Suddenly Nike yells into the phone. "I knew you was gonna flake!" Pop shoots a look over his shoulder before downing another forkful of scrambled eggs.

"Listen to me, B." I step into the hallway for whatever privacy I can get. "My pop surprised me this morning by taking the day off and getting us tickets to the Yankees game. You know I never see that man in the light of day. I'm the son of Blacula."

Nike calms down some. "So we'll hang out before y'all have to leave." He's stupid excited now, and I can't get a word in edgewise. "Yo, why didn't I think of this before? We can go to Orchard Beach!"

"Orchard Beach?" It's nasty over there! And not nasty-fresh-nasty either. I mean dirty-syringes-and-used-diapers-in-the-water nasty! "You out your mind?"

"Not to swim, dummy! What you take me for? To listen to some fresh music and to rap to the fly girls and all that."

That actually does sound like fun. Then I look down at the tickets. "Nah, I can't go, B. Game starts at two."

"Oh. OK. So how 'bout we check out a concert when you get back. A game's only a couple of hours, right? Guess who's going to be at the T-Connection?"

"Look, man, that sounds def, but I can't make you any promises 'cause you never know when a ball game's gonna end."

"Yeah, you and promises don't mix."

When Nike gets like this, I can't deal with him, and he makes it easy not to. "I'll just call you when we get back," I say, already knowing I won't. "We'll figure it out then."

I hang up on him, any guilt long gone. Like Run-D.M.C. says, *It's like that, and that's the way it is.* I head back to the kitchen, take my seat, and ask Pop, "So who's pitching today?"

NIKE

I've been sitting on this stoop angry, hot, and hungry like some pooh-butt because Smiles left me flat and I want my belt buckle back from Vanessa and she won't just give it to Gloria. If I stood on my rooftop and yelled through a megaphone, *Vanessa and I are quits!* she'd just turn to the chick next to her and say, *Why I still got his buckle then?* As long as Vanessa has my buckle, I got no rap around these parts. She'll run around the neighborhood with it convincing her friends *and* enemies that we're still together until I even believe it. Say no go.

We've been running messages through Gloria for days now. I call them Laverne and Shirley, but truth is they both Laverne-like, all loud and fre'ca. Neither one of 'em perky and sweet like Shirley. Finally, Glo made it sound like she cut a plea bargain for me, like I'm guilty of something and she's that public defender chick on *Hill Street Blues*.

If I turn the corner and don't see your brother waiting for me, I'm going back home, and he'll never see his buckle

36

again, Vanessa told my sister. I almost said forget it just to spite her, but that buckle cost me eleven bucks. The chinos down the block had WILLIE already made for five dollars, but I wanted NIKE. That's five dollars for the frame and then a buck fifty for each letter. I'm getting that sucker back. And Vanessa had better kept the chrome clean with a soft toothbrush like I taught her.

"'We gonna rock down to Electric Avenue.'" Across the street, Cutter stumbles down the block in an ashy Armani suit. It must've cost him at least a grand when he bought it, but now it looks like some polyester rag falling off the hanger at Alexander's. "'And then we'll take it higher!'" Wish I had my boom box to drown out his pathetic ass, but I couldn't risk bringing it down. If Vanessa turns the corner with Junior, I need to book!

I try not to think of all the fun Smiles is having while I just sit here. If I had a father who took a day off to take me to a game, you bet I'd go, and I don't give a damn about baseball anymore. But if I had a homeboy whose father was scarce, I'd ask my pop if we could bring him along. That's the kind of friend I am. I would've bought my own ticket if I had to, but Smiles ain't even think to invite me, and that's the kind of friend he's been.

I check my Swatch. Girls always play this game with me, and the only reason I give 'em one fifteen-minute grace period is because they're usually getting fly for me. But once those fifteen minutes are done, I'm out. My patience is rewarded, because when Vanessa's fourth grace period ends, the Eclipse Cutie suddenly appears. When she walks into Elsie's bodega, I dodge traffic to race across the street.

Inside the bodega Cutter's tapping two quarters on the counter. "More sugar, please. More sugar."

"Ay, bendito, Antonio," says Elsie as she drops another heaping scoop of sugar into a paper cup of coffee. She puts a plastic lid on it and slides it across the counter. Cutter tries to slide over his quarters, but Elsie refuses to accept them.

Cutter looks my way. I suck my teeth and shake my head at him before diddy-bopping down the aisle to look for the Eclipse Cutie. Elsie done made a big mistake letting him have that coffee for free. Cutter's just going to waste the money on dope. The heroin is what makes him crave all that sugar. Over my shoulder, I call, "Mira, Elsie, quiero un sándwich de spiced ham and cheese."

"¿En un rolo?" Elsie pulls out the log of spiced ham from the refrigerator beneath the counter. "¿O quieres un hero?"

"A hero, man. I'm starvin' like Marvin." I swing around the bread rack and crash into her, knocking all the groceries she had in her arms onto the floor. "I'm so sorry!"

"It's OK." We both bend down to pick up her things. "I wasn't looking where I was going."

We carry her groceries to the counter. "Hey, I've seen you before. Just not a lot. You new around here?" What's wrong with me? I'm usually way smoother than this.

"I've seen you before, too," she says, her eyes avoiding mine. I don't hear a Spanish accent, so she's not off the boat from PR. There's something in her voice, though, not from around here. "You were on the roof watching the eclipse through your telescope."

"Yeah!" She noticed me, yo. "I dabble in astronomy."

"That's so cool," she says. "Me, too, because I'm into mythology, and they kind of go together."

In other words, *we* can go together if I rap to her just right. "Yeah, I'm a worldly kinda dude." I stack her groceries onto the counter. Two cans of garbanzo beans, a bag of almonds, and some bottles of spices I've never heard of before called cumin and turmeric. "Your mom's making something special for Independence Day?" How def would it be to get invited to a barbecue or party somewhere. I hope there's plenty of good music and space to break.

"I'm cooking. Nothing special, though. Some fish." Then she remembers something. "And I need rice!"

"Lemme get it," I say as I rush down the aisle. "It be heavy. What kind you want? They got Carolina, Vitarroz . . ."

"Just white rice, right? It's all the same to me. Bring me whatever."

I say, "You should get Vitarroz, though." I like the commercial, and I don't have to bend down to pick it up. I grab a bag, lug it over to the front, and heave it on the counter. "My sister can't cook to save her life," I say. Vanessa can cook, she just won't. Not for me, anyways. Obviously, I don't say that to this girl, seeing as I'm trying to rap to her. "Her rice be like Styrofoam, word."

She laughs. That's good. "Let's see if mine turns out any better." Then she lowers her voice so Elsie can't hear her. "They never have the ingredients I want, so I always have to make substitutions. I hope it comes out OK."

Wow, this girl's a Shirley. How sweet that she didn't want Elsie to hear her complaining about her wack inventory. And so she knows that it's no big thing, I say, "The A&P got everything you need. There's a whole Goya aisle with recaito, sofrito, sazón . . ." She looks like I just spoke Japanese. "I'm sorry." *Damn, Nike, stop doing shit you have*

39

to apologize for. You sound like a doofus. Just chill out. "I forget that not all Puerto Ricans grow up speaking Spanish, you know."

She drops her eyes and opens her purse. "Yeah, I only know a few words here and there." She then asks Elsie how much she owes her and places the exact amount on the counter, down to the penny.

"Don't be embarrassed," I say. "Truth is I don't speak that much of it either." I know all the nasty words, but of course I'm not going to tell her that. "I speak food real good." This time when she laughs, she looks me in the eye. "So what's your name?"

"Sara."

"¡Muchacho, búscame el pan!" Elsie reminds me.

I just snatch a roll and hand it to her. "Y no tan finito."

"Sí, sí, sí." She holds up the roll. "No hero?"

Why couldn't she just play it off? I motion for Elsie to give back the roll, swap it for a hero, and hand it to her. She just snickers, then puts it aside to finish bagging Sara's groceries. Elsie thinks she knows what time it is, since every other week I'm in here trying to rap to some girl. What she doesn't understand is that this Sara is special. I'd pay for her groceries if I hadn't used my last five at JD's to put those Sergios on layaway.

When Elsie slides the bag across the counter toward her, I reach in to grab it. "I got it."

"No, that's OK."

"No, really." I start to follow Sara out of the bodega, calling over my shoulder, "Elsie, revuelvo."

"T'espero, Starvin' Marvin." Then she puts the spiced

ham log back into the refrigerator. Everybody's a comedian these days.

As we walk toward her building, Sara says, "Thank you . . ." Her voice gets lost in her embarrassment again. She doesn't know my name.

At first, I'm like, *Ouch*. Girls usually know who I am before we meet. Still, I play it off. I have to get that buckle back from Vanessa if it's the last thing I do, I swear. "Nike," I say. "That's my tag—"

"I get it!" Sara interrupts. "Because you like to win."

I have no idea what she's talking about. All I can do is just nod and smile, she's so pretty. "Exactly," I say. "I got Pumas, Adidas, Converse, but Nikes are the best kicks."

"And they're named after the goddess of strength and speed."

"Exactly, 'cause I'm athletic and I break and all that." Sara has this smile in her eyes that tells me she knows I'm frontin'. Vanessa would've snapped all over me and told anyone who would listen, *Oh my God, can you believe Nike tagged hisself after a girl?* Instead Sara schooled me without embarrassing me, and if I really were that ignorant, I never would've even known it. "Nike Fresh," I play along. "The original b-girl."

Sara laughs as we pause in front of a building. "This is me." She reaches for the bag.

"I can take this up for you."

"No, you don't have to do that."

"I already walked you all this way, so what's a few flights of stairs?"

She grasps the bag, and her wrist grazes the back of my

41

hand. "My mother would just—" Before she can finish, some kids down the block set off an M-80. *BOOM!* Sara screams and jumps and would've dropped her groceries had I not been holding them, too. Another explosive blows, and Sara throws her hands to her ears and runs up to her steps.

I run behind her, lugging her bag. "Sara, it's OK. They just loud." She's shaking in front of her door, fumbling for her keys. I don't like M-80s either, but they have her trembling so she can barely slip the key into the lock and turn the knob. "Let me do it for you." I take the key from her and unlock the door. Sara rushes into the lobby, her hands pressed to her mouth as she forces back tears. "You OK?" It's like I'm not even there. She leans against the mailboxes. "Can I do something?"

Sara finally looks at me. "I'm so embarrassed."

"Nah, don't be embarrassed. Them M-80s are annoying. Can't stand 'em either." I lift her bag. "You want me to take this upstairs for you?"

"No, no, no!" She reaches for the bag. "Thank you, though."

"Ain't nothing." I watch her go up the stairs. "Sara, listen." She turns around. I don't know what to say. I want to invite her to come to the T-Connection with me, but I already know the answer to that. If she's this sensitive about fireworks, she probably wouldn't care for a hip-hop concert. "Don't be embarrassed—we all afraid of something. And them M-80s are the worst. Whoever got the idea that fun sounds like a big obnoxious *BOOM* must've been some kind of doofus."

"I don't think the guy who invented them was really thinking anyone would use them to celebrate anything," Sara says. "I'll be so glad when this weekend's over."

She seems to want to say more. I'm hoping *Will I see you around?* I wait, but she just hugs her groceries to her chest and starts again up the stairs. So I say it. "See you around?"

"God willing." Then Sara smiles. I can't beat that with a baseball bat. As I diddybop home, I sing "Candy Girl." This must be what Cutter feels like when he's walking the streets high.

When I get to my building, Gloria is on our fire escape. "You're a jerk, Willie!" she yells. "Vanessa saw you with that girl. She says she's going to the Willis Avenue Bridge to throw your buckle into the East River. I said, *Bet. Do it. He deserves it.*"

"Ask me if I care." And I don't. Well, maybe a little, but only because I'm imagining myself walking down the street holding Sara's hand while she's rocking my buckle.

God willing.

SMILES

op and I head out into the mugginess to the Brook Avenue station. He walks over to the token booth and knocks on the glass. The Hispanic lady looks up and smiles at my father like he's Billy Dee Williams. "Derrick!"

"Hey, Sonia. You're looking lovely today." It felt weird watching Pop flirt with Mama, never mind some other woman.

Sonia tugs at the collar of her uniform. "This old thing?" They laugh. "Is that the son you're always bragging about?"

"It sure is." Pop puts his hand on my shoulder. "This is Raymond."

"I was expecting a little thing, and here he is, this tall, handsome young man." I flash her a smile, even though she's stating the obvious.

"Had to give the boy something, and we know it wasn't gonna be smarts. Those he got from his mama." Then Pop launches into his usual spiel whenever he introduces me to someone. "Raymond goes to Dawkins. Full scholarship. They just don't accept anybody. Any school that's good enough for the sons of senators and CEOs is lucky to have my boy."

"You must be so proud," says Sonia. Then she says to me, "And you should be proud of your father."

"Yes, ma'am, I am." The train's coming, thank God. "You hear that, Pop? We gotta go."

"Taking my boy to watch the Yankees put them Sox through the wash."

Sonia laughs. "Have a great time."

Pop reaches for the gate and pulls it open for me. Whenever I'm with my father, we ride the subway for free. If he doesn't know the token clerk personally, he flashes his MTA ID. Being an elected union officer, though, he's always recognized, and the clerks are grinning and nodding as we enter the system through the exit. But Pop warned me that I'd better not ever jump the turnstile. *You beat the fare, I beat your ass.* Funny thing is Dawkins kids do it for kicks, even though seventy-five cents for a token is chump change to them.

In minutes we get to 125th Street and transfer to the uptown 4 train. When the train elevates, I jump to my feet so I can watch the stadium get closer. "You always did that as a kid," laughs Pop. "Soon as we got out that tunnel, you'd be on your knees looking out the window. Now you're big enough to just walk to the door."

At the stadium there are almost as many security guards as there are fans. It takes us a half hour to get through the gate. Pop sprang for some decent terrace-level seats at $8.15 apiece. Then he buys us hot dogs and sodas. "You want a pennant?"

"Pop, I'm too old for that."

"I'ma get you a pennant," he says, and walks over to the

souvenir booth. When Pop comes back with the pennant and two new baseball caps, I'm glad he insisted. I had no idea how worn and filthy with sweat my old cap was until I held it against the crisp new one. Not ready to give it up, though, I stick it in my book bag.

We join the crowd drifting up the ramp toward the terrace. Pop says, "Maybe before the summer's out, we can go to Shea and catch the Mets, too."

"That'd be stupid fresh!"

"Say what now?"

"That's good, Pop," I laugh. "Real good." I almost don't say what I think next. He'll mention her to people like he just did to Sonia, but we never talk about her. "This reminds me of when Mama took me to see *The Wiz*. You know how in *The Wizard of Oz,* the Wicked Witch sends the flying monkeys after Dorothy and her friends? In *The Wiz,* the flying monkeys are a motorcycle gang, and they chase Dorothy and 'em through Shea." It was a special day between just Mama and me. She even kept me home from school to take me.

"Had to work that day, but I remember." Then Pop wanders into a memory of his own that doesn't belong to me. He smiles at me, and I smile back at him. We both hurt, and we both know it. "Did I ever tell you I was covering for a friend at the Coney Island Complex when they were shooting that movie at Astroland?" He chuckles. "Even got a peek at Miss Ross. Almost didn't recognize her without all that hair."

"You got to see Diana Ross in person?" Nike and I were talking about finding some girls and going to her free concert in Central Park in August. If he's still throwing me shade, maybe Pop can take off from work again. If he's not on strike.

"Just a glimpse. Not that I ever told your mother. She would've given me so much jive, and she might not have taken you to see nothing. You owe me." Our hurt smiles turn into pained laughs. "Y'all don't say *jive* anymore, do ya?"

"No, that's some ol' *Sanford and Son* stuff."

"You shut your mouth, boy. That Redd Foxx is a comedic genius. That skinny dude you kids think is so funny? Jerry Murphy? Freddie Murphy?"

"Eddie Murphy, and he's the joint!"

"Your little Eddie Murphy ain't got nothing on no Redd Foxx."

"Nah, Richard Pryor is the deffest one of all."

Pop slaps me on the shoulder. "Well, all right now!" He hooks his arm around my shoulder and hugs me. "There's hope for your generation yet."

We push with the crowd toward our seats, and I get excited when I see the Yankees warming up on the field. "Pop, look, there's Willie Randolph!"

"Yeah, and Dave Winfield's over there."

"Word? Where?"

"Right there."

Nike can stay mad at me forever, and the Sox can murder the Yankees. I'm never going to regret this day. "Could we hang out after the game and see if I can get some Yanks to sign my pennant?"

"Whatever you want."

The announcer asks us to stand for the national anthem. Pop takes off his hat and belts out the words. I just mouth along as Qusay's words about the Black man's plight in this hypocritical country ring in my head. Yet I look at my father singing his heart out, and I wish I could feel that way again. Pop complains about Reagan this and Koch that, but "The Star-Spangled Banner" still means something to him. It would to me, too, if I had never gone to Dawkins, and I don't know if that's a curse or a blessing. Still, today is our day, so I force myself to sing along like I'm a guest star on *Soul Train*.

We retake our seats and wolf down those hot dogs in ten seconds flat. Pop says, "I got this feeling, son, that today's game is going to be a big one. Our boys gonna make the play-offs this year."

"Word."

"You know that today's Georgie Boy's birthday," says Pop, pointing at the owner's box. "And Tricky Dick is right up there with 'im."

"Really?" Not every day the former president comes to the Bronx, never mind Yankee Stadium. "That's why all the security hoopla. I know it's Independence Day and all, but no politics today, OK, Pop?"

"You right, Ray-Ray." Pop hasn't called me that since my eighth-grade graduation, when I announced I was too grown up for such a baby name. He patted me on the back and said, *All right, my little man,* but Mama told me that even when I had a son of my own entering high school, I'd still be her Ray-Ray of sunshine. Before she let go, the last thing she said to me was *I'll always be with you, Ray-Ray.* "So tell me this. You got a squeeze? What happened to that skinny little Puerto Rican girl who lives next door? Why she don't call or come by anymore?"

"Cookie's not my girlfriend!"

Pop is all teeth. "But you like her."

48

"I can't stand that crab."

"That sweet little girl? Used to clean us out, selling those Girl Scout cookies. Who needed crack with them caramel and coconut ones your mama loved so much?"

"The Samoas." Those were my favorites, too. "I don't mean crab cranky, I mean . . ." Knowing that I can talk to my father about these things doesn't make it easy. Since my mother died, we've fallen out of practice.

"Ugly?"

"No."

"Dumb?"

His guesses make me laugh. "No."

"Fast?"

"Yeah, that's it! Cookie's kind of fast. Easy."

"And how do you know that?" Pop's getting salty. "Have you—"

"No!"

"Good. I know you're at that age where the hormones are amok and everything, but let me tell you this. If you get some girl pregnant before you're capable of being a provider so I have to raise that baby, guess what? I'm raising that baby an orphan. Got it?"

"Sheesh." Pop and I have already had this conversation. I had this conversation with Mama, too. Nana tries to have this conversation with me every time a girl calls, which is why I stopped giving out my number.

"So where'd you get the idea that Cookie's fast? Boy, don't believe everything Nike or any of your buddies tell you about what he did with some girl. Nine times out of ten, he's lying. And that tenth time? He's exaggerating!" Before I can tell

Pop about that time in eighth grade when Cookie let Javi walk her home from school and showed up the next day with his hickeys, he says, "Just because a girl shows you interest doesn't mean she's fast." Then he laughs. "You might not be here right now if your mother hadn't made the first move."

"What?"

"You don't know that story? OK, your uncle Nathan and I—"

"Not Nathan. Naim. That's what he wants to be called now, Pop."

"Don't tell me what to call my little brother. He'll always be Nate Baby to me. So anyway, we were playing handball at Clark Playground. They only got that one court over there, right? So your mother and her cousin show up. We're playing, showing out, trying to impress the girls, you know. Eventually, your mama comes up to me and says, *When're you guys gonna cop a breeze, because my cousin and me, we've been waiting for our turn for over an hour, and you dudes don't own the court.*"

"That's cold," I laugh. I love the expressions my parents used when they were my age in the fifties. "And you guys thought they were checking you out."

"So you know how we men are," says Pop. "Got to save face."

"Play the role."

"That's what y'all say now? We were playing the role, all right. Nate and I get to talking smack. *Why don't you girls go play double Dutch or Miss Mary Mack or something. Leave the handball to the men.* Bernadette said, *I don't see any men. All I see is two boys making fools of themselves.* So we challenge the girls to a game. Loser can never show their faces at Clark again. I should've known we were in trouble when your mama hands me the Spaldeen and says, *You serve first.*"

"Y'all lost?" I can't believe it. "No, you let them win."

"As God is my witness, Ray-Ray, your mama and her cousin tanned our hides in front of half the neighborhood."

"Embarrassin'!"

"Yeah, at first." Pop grins from ear to ear. "But after the game, your mama says to me, *I'll let you play on my court if you treat me to White Castle.*"

My father and I sip our overpriced sodas and remember Mama the way she would want to be remembered. Not skin and bones lying in bed but caramel and fire in a black leather jacket. "So Mama was the one with all the moves." Now that I picture her full of life, I'm not surprised.

"And maybe the apple doesn't fall far from the tree," says Pop.

"What do you mean?" Unlike Nike, I don't really rap to girls. For something that's supposed to be fun, it's too much work. When I like a girl, I just become her friend until something clicks. Sometimes I lose out to Nike this way, but then I figure the girl really wasn't for me in the first place. For the most part, I have no problem with the ladies, and because I'm no playboy like Nike, the ladies never have a problem with me. Except for Cookie, who really isn't a lady, no matter what Pop says.

"Maybe the next Mrs. King is going to be a gal a little ahead of her time." Then Pop points to the scoreboard. "Look at that, Ray-Ray. Third inning already and Righetti has yet to give up a hit."

We look at each other, then back at the diamond. I stand up, clapping and yelling, "C'mon, Rags. No batter, no batter, no batter!" Something special is taking place right before our eyes, and we need to pay attention. That's how baseball is. Even when it looks like nothing is going on, something is always happening.

NIKE

I hoist my boom box onto my shoulder and go into the kitchen for something to eat. My mother gets off the couch and follows me. "Willie, when do you get paid?"

Camp hasn't started, and already she's bumming me for money. I'll be damned if she plays la bolita or buys Kools with *my* earnings. Last week when her combination came out, Ma bought Glo a pair of jelly sandals, which she broke three days later playing double Dutch. What'd Nike get? Diddly-squat. "Why you gotta know?"

"What do you mean, why I got to know?" Ma yells. "You like to eat, don't you?" She been running that line into the ground, man. What happened to all the stupid food stamps that just came on the first? "You like to use electricity, right?"

"Totally," says Gloria. My sister's new thing is talking like a Valley girl. As usual, she's got her hair in rolos, her scrawny legs up on the couch, and her face stuck in *People*. That baby prince is on this week's cover. Why people in the U.S. of God

53

Bless America fuss over Princess Diana and all those monarchs? Today they's just figureheads with no real juice in their own country. Like Smiles said, if the English Parliament gave the queen her own death warrant, she'd have to sign it. Not that I have to go to Dawkins to know we done fought a revolution to get rid of those punks. Ma and Gloria, the both of them just sit on the couch all day watching telenovelas and reading bochinche while I go out and work, minding other people's brats. "He be hogging up the bathroom for hours," Gloria says, slipping back to the way she really talks. "Running up the Con Ed bill, blowing out that nappy hair of his."

"Mind your business, 'cause nobody's talking to you," I snap. "You be running your mouth como si fuera la heredera de New York Telephone. And my hair ain't nappy. I got Papi's hair." Still, I reach for the back of my neck, and sure enough, my tail curled up again. That means my DA is now an Afro. "You wish you had hair like me, 'cause yours don't do nothing but hang there like a mop."

"No, you the one jealous 'cause I got hair like a white girl."

My mother blocks my path. "Willie, I'm sick and tired of arguing with you about money."

"Then don't. Gloria's fourteen now. Tell her to get a job."

"I can't get a job, stupid, 'cause I don't have my working papers."

"And whose fault is that?" Just because Gloria is tall and skinny, she thinks she can be a model. She has pictures of Brooke Shields and Gia Carangi taped all over her side of my mother's bedroom and is always on some diet. I done told her they ain't never going to pluck some Puerto Rican girl out the Bronx and make her a supermodel. Now my sister's walking around here saying *gnarly* this and *as if* that, like that's going to fool nobody. Vanessa tried it with all that Valspeak, but I told her that I'd quit her if she didn't stop talking like some airhead on *Square Pegs*. I dumped Vanessa anyway, but she spared herself a few weeks when she quit telling me *Gag me with a spoon!* every two minutes.

And Ma was down with all that modeling crap, too, signing my sister's application for the child model permit or whatever it's called. I told her from the giddyup that agency was bogus. If it weren't for the fact that my mother couldn't pay him with cupones, that sleazeball would've taken us for two hundred dollars for Gloria's so-called head shots.

I say to Gloria, "Ain't nobody tell you to cut school to go to that fake modeling agency instead of seeing the guidance counselor and getting your papers." I put on my Nike cap and Cazal glasses, and head for the door. Some days the best thing about having to work is getting out of here.

SMILES

Barb calls me into work early on the first day to tell me she promoted Cookie Camacho to senior counselor over me. I'm waiting right here until she gets off the phone and gives me an explanation. That is, if I don't get so mad I start crying. I've shed enough tears in this office.

Don't count on that promotion, homeboy, Nike warned me. *Girls be sticking together. Especially those women's lib types like Cookie and Barb.* I didn't believe that and tried to defend Barb without admitting everything to him. Nike, with his one-track mind, read that wrong and started insinuating things. *Yo, you messin' with Barb, Smiley? You can tell me. Yeah, buddy! She fine, though. Like an older, Puerto Rican version of Kelly from* Charlie's Angels. I pretended Nana needed to make a call and hung up on him.

I've been a part of Saint Aloysius since I was five years old. Not only did I go to school here from K through eight, Mama enrolled me in the summer day camp from its start. As soon

56

as I turned fourteen, I came to work for Barb. For the past three years, I've been a counselor during the summer and a youth mentor in the after-school program she runs from September through June. No one is more qualified than me to be Big Lou's assistant.

Barb finally hangs up the telephone. "I don't know what more I can tell you, Smiles. With the last round of budget cuts, we don't have as many kids in the camp. There's no need, never mind money, to hire two senior counselors for each group like we have in the past."

So now I'm Smiles again. Three minutes ago she was all, *Raymond, I had a very tough decision to make, and I hope you'll understand.* "You said all that already. What you didn't explain is why Cookie's going to be the senior counselor for the Champs instead of me." Does Barb think I'm going to let her off that easy because I made the mistake of breaking down that one time? Nah, it's not like that.

Unless the breakdown is the reason she didn't promote me.

"I've been running this camp and the after-school program for seven years, and you're one of the best counselors I've ever had." Barb always used to say that I was *the* best, but now I'm just *one* of the best. "So is Cookie. All things being equal, I had to choose her."

Other than her being a girl, there's only one difference between Cookie and me, and I want her to admit it. "All things being equal, why Cookie?" *Just fess up already, Barb. We both know what Cookie is that I'm not.*

"Look, Smiles, I promise that I'll give you priority consideration for senior counselor next summer."

"Next summer I might be working for Qusay," I bluff.

"Now that he's forming his organization, he wants to create an after-school program."

Barb gets uptight when she hears Qusay's name, and now I know the real deal. The other day when I was skating through Saint Mary's Park, I saw Q parlaying with Booby and some Barbarians about his new storefront until Junior sent Javi to fetch 'em. As we went back to his school, Q admitted that he was the Junior of the block back in his day. At one time he dated Barb, lying about being a hood and otherwise putting her heart through the wringer. Still, everyone swore they'd get married until Qusay got busted. While he was upstate, Big Lou came back from Vietnam, Barb fell for him, and that's all she wrote. I don't get why everyone's throwing Q shade when he came out of prison a better man than he went in. Nike jokes that it's because Qusay no longer eats pork, and no bona fide Puerto Rican is ever going to give up pernil, but it's a lot deeper than that. I would bring it up to Barb in one of our late-afternoon rap sessions in her office, but those days are over.

"You don't want to work for Qusay, Smiles," Barb says. "No good can come to you by associating with the Five Percenters." For a moment, she actually seems jealous of Qusay on my account. That pushes back the tears, but I can't forget that Barb favored Cookie over me for something I can't control. "We're all lucky to have jobs right now," Barb says, "with Reagan cutting programs left and right. . . ."

So the Gipper cut the budget. He's not the one sitting across from me playing favorites. Bottom line: I can't prove that Barb discriminated against me because I'm Black. "Forget it," I say. Then I stand up and break out, ignoring Barb when she calls my name.

NIKE

"**H**ere," I say, handing Smiles his Eddie Murphy tape. No thanks, never mind apologies for flaking out on me yesterday. He just snatches it out of my hand and shoves it in the back pocket of his cutoffs. "Bite my head off, why don't you?" Smiles admits that I was right about Barb, but now I'm too irritated to tell him *I told you so*. Instead I just shrug and say, "So sue 'er."

Homeboy takes me for serious. "I can't sue Barb." A hint of the ol' Smiles peeks through the grin on his face. "Would you testify on my behalf?" Before I can answer, he starts laughing. "The judge would throw me out the courtroom. You're not exactly a reliable witness, yo."

And I was going to say I would, too. "What you mean? If you tell the judge that Barb gave Cookie the promotion over you because she's Puerto Rican, and another Puerto Rican gets on the stand and says it's true, case closed, homeboy." Now I really do want Smiles to sue. Let 'im win a million dollars and remember who helped him.

"Your theory's credible, B, but *you're* not." He starts counting off reasons on his fingers. "One, Big Lou is always docking you, and not once has Barb ever taken your side, so the judge might think you have ulterior motives. . . ."

"But they married, though. That's whatchamacallit? Conflict of interest."

". . . Two, since Big Lou and Barb are also Puerto Ricans, and I'm arguing that they're discriminating against me because I'm not Puerto Rican, drawing attention to the way they treat you actually hurts my case, since they're threatening to fire you every other day. Three, why are they always docking you and threatening to fire you?"

" 'Cause"—I spit on my finger and wipe a smudge off my Adidas—"they wack." I don't want to play this game anymore.

" 'Cause you're always wandering off somewhere with some chick while on the job. So when Barb's lawyer asks you what acts of discrimination against me you've actually witnessed, what evidence are you going to present, Captain Boricua?"

There he goes, pulling out all his debate-team stuff on me. "Fine then." Smiles cracks up. So glad I could cheer him up. "You serious about quitting?"

He shrugs. "She dissed me big-time. And if Qusay's starting his program . . ."

"Yo, later for Q. How you gonna quit camp when he hasn't offered you nothing? Thought you needed the money." Now I got Smiles's attention. "Just chill till Q makes good."

"Word." He gestures toward the Garanimals shrieking about the gym. "Which one is yours?"

"Don't know yet. Cookie taking her sweet ol' time. Probably trying to figure out who the worst ones are so she can assign 'em to me."

"Or assigning all the girl counselors first." Smiles points in Cookie's direction, and the girl she's talking to is none other than Sara. Yeah, buddy! Today she has on the orange camp T-shirt, white shorts, and jelly sandals. She pulls her long dark hair into a ponytail, revealing the knot of a bikini top on her neck. Cookie calls over the twins. Them girls ain't really twins—they look exactly alike but are a year apart—we just call them that. I don't remember their real names. I only got room in my head for breaking routines and girls old enough to give me play.

"Yo, Sara's working here this summer?" I get up and make my way over to her.

Smiles rolls his eyes. "Case in point."

As I cross the gym with my boom box playing "Outstanding," the twins run off to play hopscotch and Sara leans against the wall and opens the *New York Daily News*. I sneak up on her and stand right in front of the paper. Sara's so engrossed in whatever she's reading that she doesn't notice me. I ease up against the newspaper until my sneakers are almost toe to toe with her sandals, and the brim of my cap casts a shadow on the page. Sara looks up and whips the paper away. "Oh," she says. "It's you." She folds the paper and places it between her knees.

"I was just trying to help you out. You know, offering you a little shade so you can see better." Now that the paper is no longer between us, Sara and I are face to face. She's almost as tall as I am, so the brim of my baseball cap sits right about her hairline. I point to the newspaper and crack, "What's the deal? Who got killed now?"

Without missing a beat, she quips, "A fourteen-year-old in Queens got shot on his way to summer school, a kid in the Bronx killed himself playing Russian roulette, and a bunch of children in Lebanon got bombed for being Palestinian."

"Oh!" This girl is quick. I like that. I borrow a line from Smiles. "I guess the cops have the day off." Then I say, "You shouldn't read all that bad news, mami."

Sara folds her arms across her chest. "We're living all that bad news."

"Even more reason we don't need to be reading about it."

"So don't care about what's going on in our world?"

"I care about what I can control in *my* world. Like all the fun you and me are going to have this summer." Sara twists her mouth, trying not to laugh. "You've been assigned to the Champs, right?"

"I think so. My girls are sisters. One's ten, the other eleven."

"Yeah, you in the best group," I lie. I lucked out that Barb didn't put Sara with the Rookies. That's where she usually assigns counselors if they're new to the camp or only fourteen. "The Rookies, they're so young you can't take your eyes off of them, not a second. Too much work."

"Isn't that what we're paid to do, no matter how old they are?"

"And the Famers? Forget about 'em." The twelve- to fourteen-year-olds think they're so big and bad, especially them boy-crazy girls. Blue Eyes was a Famer last summer, and I learned why Barb insists that all the counselors and the crew chief of that group be college kids. "This summer's going to be live! We're going to the Skatin' Palace, Coney Island, Bear Mountain, the Roxy. . . ."

"The Roxy?" Sara bunches her pretty face. "I didn't see that on the camp schedule."

" 'Cause that's where I'm taking you on our first date."

"Nike!" Cock-blocking Cookie skips over. "Here's your assignment." She shoves the copy of the camp registration form into my hand and bounces off before I can even look at it.

I take a quick glance at the name, then yell, "Cookie, I know you're not for real assigning me Shorty Rock this summer."

Cookie spins, then shrugs. "Don't like it? Take it up with Big Lou."

Sara glances at the form in my hand. "What's wrong with Stevie Morales?"

SMILES

Not even an hour with her new title, and Cookie thinks she's all big and bad. After Nike leaves me flat, I make my way across the gym for a quick pickup game. Although I pull my cap low over my eyes and try to creep past Cookie, she still spots me and digs her raggedy nails into my forearm. "Smiles, I have your assignment." She unclips the registration forms and hands them to me. Today she has on a RIDE, SALLY RIDE T-shirt with an iron-on of that lady astronaut on it. So what she's the first woman from the United States in space? The Russians already beat us to it. "You've got Pedro Jimenez. He's ten."

"I can read." I snatch the forms from her, glance at the Woolworth's photographs stapled to them, and look for my kid.

"You're welcome, Raymond!"

This is cold, man. I'm a better counselor than Cookie because I have strong instincts and know how to handle the kids. Most counselors only have one way of dealing with them, and that's not enough to survive the summer. Take Nike. From the get-go, he barks at his kids like Sergeant Snorkel, but that only works for a spell. They'll realize he's all talk and no action, and come August, Nike's kids will be getting over on him left and right.

They call me Smiles because I'm always smiling. This is camp, not juvie. The kids come to have fun, and when they have fun, I have fun. But I know when the kid gloves should come off. Even the counselors know better than to test me. We might be around the same age, but they respect me as much as the kids do. That's why I should have been Big Lou's assistant.

I find Pedro sitting in the bleachers by himself, slowly washing down his blueberry muffin with chocolate milk. Most day camp kids are Saint Aloysius students or at least live in the neighborhood. They come to camp already having friends from school or the block. Since I've never seen him before, and he's alone, I deduce that Pedro must have just moved here.

"Pedro?" He looks up and watches me climb the bleachers toward him. He's a cute kid—dark spiky hair and big brown eyes—but small for ten. I would've guessed eight. Pedro's clothes also set him apart from the other campers. Even the poorest kids try to keep up with the trends, just like Nike did when he first moved to the neighborhood. If they can't afford the Pumas or Lees, they at least get the latest haircut or pull their pennies together to buy some "in" thing like a Rubik's Cube or rubber bracelets. Pedro has on a faded red T-shirt and shorts cut from discount-store jeans, the bluish white threads dangling toward his ashy knees. His sneakers are the fake Adidas with the fourth stripe they sell at Woolworth's, where he probably got his picture taken in the photo booth. I don't know how long he has lived here, but the kids must be crazy teasing him, like they did Nike. For five days a week, though, I'll keep the bullies in check.

"What's up, homeboy?" I sit down next to him. "I'm Smiles, your counselor." He just blinks at me. Although his address is on the registration form, to make conversation I ask, "Where do you live?" He still doesn't answer me. I scan the medical section of his form to see if he has any problems, and it's empty. But in the box labeled NOTES it reads: *ESL*.

I say to Pedro, "No English?" He shakes his head. Cookie trying it, yo!

And just as if she timed the entire scenario, she scampers up the bleachers. "He just moved here from Puerto Rico last month," she says. Then Cookie turns to Pedro and says something in Spanish, including my name and a word that sounds like *counselor*. I take Spanish in school, but she's speaking so fast I can't follow. Probably doing that on purpose, too. Pedro asks her something that makes Cookie laugh. She then says to me as she starts her way back down the bleachers. "In fifteen minutes, we're lining up the kids to take them to the Central Park pool."

"No shit, Sherlock," I say. If the weather's nice, we always take the entire camp to Central Park on the first day. I suggested it to Barb three years ago, and it's now our tradition. It's only four stops on the 6 train with no transfers—a good way to get the kids and counselors used to taking the subway as a group before we start venturing to the pools as far as Astoria, Queens, or even taking the ferry to the one in Staten

Island. On Mondays through Thursdays, each of the three age groups heads someplace different in New York City. On Fridays the entire camp goes on a bus trip to a state park. The last week it's bus trips every day, including Bear Mountain and Coney Island. These kids get a lot for their five-dollar registration fee, including the orange camp T-shirt they have to wear every Friday. "You're not the only one who can read the schedule."

Cookie tells Pedro, "Si él no te trata bien, búscame. Me llamo Carolina." Then she smirks at me, motions toward Pedro, and says, "When you need help, you know where to find me." And then she skips down the steps and back into the crowd.

Pedro asks me something, pointing to her as she crosses the gym to talk to Big Lou. I can't understand his words, but his sad eyes say it all. He'd rather have the crab for a counselor.

All things being equal. I knew it. Barb did give Cookie the promotion because she's Puerto Rican. Just like Barb. Just like her husband Big Lou, the crew chief of the Champs. When push came to shove, Barb gave Cookie the job because she's one of her own. So why shouldn't I go work for Qusay?

Because Qusay doesn't have a job for me yet, that's why. And for all his *Whatever,* Nike would take it as another betrayal, like my decision to transfer to Dawkins. When I realized I could only be Smiles on the block and Raymond at Dawkins, Nike was the one person I thought I could be my whole self with. Now that I'm wondering if going to Dawkins is a mistake, I've got no one to talk to about it.

I can't quit. I don't want to quit, really. I love this camp, man. You'd think after three years, I'd be bored of going to the same places all the time. But every summer there's a Pedro who makes it feel like the first time. Riding the subway, visiting all the different parks and pools, and going to the zoo and movies through his eyes? I'm psyched! And who'll teach the boys to play skully and crack up the girls by playing Chinese jump rope with them? Ain't gonna be Nike.

I tap Pedro on the shoulder and start down the bleachers. "¡Vámanos!" I say like I'm the Rican Mister Rogers. It's corny, but it's the best I can think of now.

Besides, it works. After a second of surprise, Pedro jumps up. "Okai!"

"See!" I put my arm around him, and we head down the bleachers. "I knew you had to know some English."

NIKE

I don't know why we have to take these Garanimals to the Central Park pool on the first day of camp. There be glass in that water! If we're getting on the train, we might as well go to Astoria. It's worth the hour and a half to get there, because the water's always perfect.

At least we're not going to the pool at Saint Mary's Park. Gloria and Vanessa are bound to be there. All I need is for Vanessa to figure out that Sara's going to be my new girl-friend and start trouble before I can even rap to her.

Cookie blows her whistle. "All right, Champions, let's mo-tivate!" We file out of the church, and even though the Cypress Avenue station is only a block away, Big Lou marches us to the next one, on Brook Avenue, chanting like we're in the army.

> Your left, your left
> Your left, right, your left

69

"Dude thinks he's that Black guy in *An Officer and a Gentleman*," I say, taking a sip of my milk. "Sergeant Foley?"

"Nah, he thinks he's Jimmy Snuka." Smiles imitates Superfly, growling and flexing his biceps like the Incredible Hulk. *"You're gonna pay, Don Muraco. I promise you this, my brother. You're gonna pay!"*

I almost spit out my milk, 'cause Big Lou *does* look like Superfly, with all those muscles and that Jheri curl. "Oh, snap!" I wipe stray drops of milk off my chin. "He could go out for the WWF, word." Now that's the Smiles I know.

Shorty Rock gets out of line and tugs at my shirt. "Yo, why we gotta walk all these blocks?"

I shove him back in line. "Some of y'all can stand to burn some energy." If Big Lou thinks I'm such a bad counselor, why did they assign me the camp badass? This demonio traumatized his counselor last year until the sucker quit. Rumor has it the poor kid ended up at Bellevue Hospital, and Big Lou got stuck having to watch Shorty-Rock. Sometimes I think Big Lou likes having excuses to dock me. Maybe the money the camp saves by not paying me a full check for one stupid reason or another goes into *his* pocket. "Stay in line."

"Stop beggin'!" Shorty Rock yells, bouncing out of the line and onto my new shell-toe Adidas.

"Watch it!" I shove him back into place and check my dogs for smudges. This kid don't know how lucky he is he missed me. I stick my finger in his face and say, "Keep it up, and see if you go on the bus trip to Rockland on Friday."

Shorty Rock sucks his teeth but finally stays in line. I elbow Smiles. "Check, buddy. You saw that?" He's not the only one who has a way with kids.

"Yeah, let's see how long that works for you."

We get to the train station, and after Big Lou clears the way with the token clerk, I hold open the exit door so the kids can file onto the platform. Of course, Shorty Rock has to be a clown and leap over the turnstile like he's Mitch Gaylord. Now a whole bunch of other kids want to do it, too. Someone is bound to crack their head open, and then we gonna have some crazy mother in here tomorrow threatening to sue the city, the church, and maybe even me.

Smiles jumps onto the first turnstile to block the rest of the boys from playing monkey see, monkey do. "Y'all know better. Turn ya butts right around and go through the door."

Always quick to copycat, Cookie leaps over the second turnstile and blocks it, too. "Y'all heard Smiley."

Shorty Rock yells, "That's what y'all get for being biters." He sidles up to Cookie like he's her boyfriend.

But she grabs his arm and whips him back through the turnstile like Wonder Woman cracking her golden lasso. "You too. Go back out and come in through the gate, the way you were supposed to in the first place."

Shorty Rock mumbles under his breath but does as he's told. When he comes through the gate, I yell, "Yo, why you did that? Do that again. When you fall and crack your skull, see if I don't laugh."

"You better not laugh if you don't want me to fly that head," says Shorty.

I lift my arm like I'm about to backhand him, and Shorty

71

throws his hands up over his head. "You better learn some respect."

"Why?" Shorty scowls at me over his raised forearm. "You ain't my father!"

"Thank God for that." Man, if everybody weren't looking . . . "If you was my kid, B, you'd be lying across that third rail, and I'd be going to jail!"

Shorty blows a raspberry at me, then runs off down the platform. Only reason I don't chase him and give him an oops upside his head is because Sara walks through the door, holding the hands of the twins.

"Thank you," Sara says.

"Anytime, beautiful," I say. Sara was the only one who thanked me for holding open the gate. All these other poohbutts walked right by me like my name is Benson.

Now Big Lou barges through the gate. "Focus less on the girls and pay more attention to your kid, Nike." With the 6 train pulling into the station, I'm hoping Sara didn't hear him put me in check. In that booming voice of his, Big Lou announces, "Counselors, we're getting off at 110th Street. Four stops."

"Yeah, yeah, yeah," says Smiles. Homeboy's a walking transit map. Mr. King is a motorman for the MTA, so Smiles practically grew up on the subway. He be knowing off the top of his head which trains go to parts of the city he's never even been to.

"Yo, Smiles," I whisper as I nod toward Sara.

"That's Sara," Cookie barks in my ear, "and she's too good for a dog like you."

"Damn, blow out my eardrum, why don't you?" Who

asked her, anyway? "I know Sara. She lives down the street from me."

"We've been like this since she moved here a few weeks ago," Cookie says, crossing her fingers, "and she's never mentioned the likes of you."

"Mind your business, Cookie," says Smiles. I'd give him five for being my backup like he used to, but it ain't about me really. His beef with Cookie's over that dumb promotion I done told him not to get hyped over.

We pile into a car that only has a handful of other passengers on it. The rush of kids annoys a few, but most smile at us. One of the twins climbs onto Sara's lap, even though there are plenty of seats. "I think you might be a little too big for this," Sara says sweetly. The girl smiles and shakes her head. I can't blame her. I'm going to be seventeen next month, and I want to sit on her lap myself. "I don't know. You sure? Are you sure you're not too big for this?"

The girl giggles and sticks a thumb in her mouth.

"Stop that!" her older sister yells. Then she yanks her hand out her mouth. "I'ma tell Mommy you be sucking your thumb."

"Why would you do that?" asks Sara. "It's not *your* thumb."

That's settled. Sara is going to be my camp girl this summer. And who knows? She's so fly I just might make her my block girl, too. We'll just have to keep our thing a secret until Vanessa chills out.

"Yo, Smiles," I say, handing him my boom box. "Hold this for me. I think I got that new jam from Run-D.M.C. off BLS."

"And you know that!" That's Smiles's favorite rap group. He lowers the volume while fast-forwarding the cassette. Meanwhile, I stretch my quads and watch Sara from the corner of my eye. She finally convinces the twin to crawl off her lap and opens up the newspaper. When Smiles reaches the perfect spot, he kicks the volume to ten, and then:

> Bam, bam, bam, bam
> Unemployment at a record high . . .

All the kids and the counselors yell, *Ho!* and bob their heads, rhyming along with Run-D.M.C. Everybody except Sara, who still has her nose in the *Daily News*. She won't for long.

I freestyle until I get a feel of the space. The 6 train be crampin' my style with these stupid narrow cars. That's another reason why I love our trips to Queens. The N train is crazy wide, with plenty of room to do some ill stuff. But everyone is watching me now, and some girl counselors are cheering me on. *Go, Nike, go. Go, Nike, go.* That's def. Nothing gets a girl's attention better than what other girls like. Sara finally looks up from her paper to watch me bust it out.

I uprock my way over to her, but slick—no eye contact—so it doesn't seem like I'm showing off for her benefit. Like instead I'm just in a zone and have no idea that I'm dancing right in front of her, close enough to touch.

But just as I'm in position to break fly, the cheering stops. *Go, Nike, go* becomes *Yo, Nike, look!* Sara taps my knee and points toward the opposite end of the car. Big Lou's arguing with this white dude in a suit while holding tight to Shorty

Rock, who's flouncing about like a fish on a line. And if that weren't bad enough, Smiles shuts off the boom box so everyone can hear what's going down.

"I don't know what more you want me to do," says Big Lou. "I've already apologized three times."

The white guy says, "I don't want an apology." He points to the dusty sneaker print on the shin of his pants. "I want a clean suit."

Big Lou says, "Obviously, you want to be mad, so you know what? Stay mad then. Not like you can't just bend down and wipe it off."

The man in the suit sputters, "That's not the point. . . ."

"Yes, it is the point, because I'm making it the point." And just like that, Big Lou grows another foot and towers over the white guy, who's turning pink. "I said I was sorry he accidentally kicked you and dirtied your suit. I made him say that he was sorry, and then I said I was sorry again. If that's not good enough for you, my heart bleeds."

"What you want him to do?" yells Smiles. "Lick it clean?"

Everybody laughs, and a Black lady nods with approval. Now the white man has gone from pink to red, and I feel bad for him. It even crosses my mind to go over there and offer to pay to clean his suit. The man probably doesn't even want someone to actually do that. He just wants the offer and for it to be sincere instead of defensive. That's all I'd want. But embarrassment has me frozen in place in front of the last person I want to see me humiliated.

Big Lou pulls Shorty away, but Smiles keeps breaking on the man loud enough to hear. "Homeboy's confused," he says. "It's 1983, not 1863. We're free."

"Right!" Cookie says. "This isn't *Roots*." Damn, why can't she mind her own business? Always instigating.

Smiles finally snaps directly on the guy. "Maybe you need to trade that *New York Times* for the Emancipation Proclamation." And now everybody's keeling over with laughter.

"Enough, Smiley. Later for him," says Big Lou. He's cheesin', though.

No one is happier than me when the man gets off at Third Avenue. Bet this ain't his stop neither. Somehow I unglue my shell-toes off the floor and make my way over to Big Lou. Shorty Rock's acting all big and bad now that the man's gone, hollering after him through the window like he's grown. "Later, 'gator! See ya, sucka! Adios, Mr. Morose!"

Big Lou gives his arm a hard yank. "Shut up and sit down! You move from that spot before we get to 110th Street, and you can forget about going to Rockland on Friday." Then he turns to me and says, "You're docked. Two days' pay."

"Two days?" I expected him to dock me, but two days? It's gonna take forever to get my Sergio Valentes off layaway.

"Wanna make it three?" Before I can answer—I mean, do I really need to?—Big Lou points to the bench and says, "You lucky I don't just send you home for the rest of the week. This ain't *Dance Fever,* and you ain't Deney Terrio. We pay you to watch your kid, not to show off your little dance moves."

Big Lou doesn't pay me diddly-squat. The City of New York does, but I stay shut because I'm not trying to get dissed any more in front of Sara. I sit down, sensing all this pity for me in the subway car, sticking to me like a sheet of sweat. I don't need anybody feeling sorry for me. "Smiles, put the music back on."

"Nah, man," he says. "Big Lou—"

I just reach over and hit play myself.

> The next time someone's teaching, why don't
>   you get taught?
> It's like that—what?—and that's the way it is.

Big Lou doesn't say anything about it, but Smiles turns down the volume like, *You ain't the boss of me.*

I glance over at Sara, and she's staring dead at me. The second we catch eyes, she picks up her newspaper and pretends to read. What she needs with the paper now that I've become the bad news of the day? I shoot a look at Shorty Rock, who's knee-deep in a game of rock, paper, scissors with Smiles's kid, Pedro, as if nothing happened. It's gonna take a miracle for me not to kill that kid before summer's end.

SMILES

They thought I was just playing basketball, but from the corner of my eye, I busted those chicks making fun of Pedro. And when I hunt down Cookie, what's she doing when she should be minding her kids? Teaching Sara, the twins, and some other girls how to break-dance. I swear she's a Nike in cornrows. I jet across the gym to tell her off, with Nike on me like a tail, instigating all the way.

"Yo, Cookie!" I reach down and snap off the radio in the middle of "Electric Kingdom." "While you over here trying to be Rokafella, your kids are bullying Pedro."

"My kids?" Cookie picks herself up off the floor, tucks in her Menudo T-shirt, and dusts her jeans. "You sure?"

"You a trip, Cookie!" Nike yells over my shoulder. "You be talking all that women's lib stuff, but homeboy says your kids ain't sugar and spice, and you act all surprised. Girls can be malcria'as, too, you know." Then he turns to Sara. "But not your girls, Sara. The twins are sweethearts, just like you."

78

Unlike Cookie, Sara seems genuinely concerned about Pedro. "What did the girls do?"

"They were teasing him for not knowing English," I say. "And making fun of his clothes."

Nike says, "Yeah, asking him when he got off the boat, calling his pants brincacharcos, and shit like that." At first, I thought Nike was just jumping in because he likes to mess with Cookie and wants Sara to think he cares about the kids. Loyalty to me was the last thing on his mind. But as he repeats what he heard Cookie's kids tell Pedro, I remember when he first moved to the South Bronx.

Nike wasn't Nike then. He was just Willie. Really he was Pedro, with his fake Izod shirts—the crocodile looked more like a snake with legs, and the buttons were plastic instead of pearl—and his high-waters. In a way, Nike probably had it worse than Pedro. He understood every dis, and having moved from Williamsburg, where he was born, he had no defense for not knowing what was in style.

Remembering how the kids on the block used to make fun of Nike just makes me even angrier at Cookie. "Put your kids in check, Cookie."

"Fine!" Cookie looks for the girls and hollers for them. Then she calls over Pedro.

"What you calling him for?"

"You want I take care of this, right?" All three kids look nervous. Pedro shouldn't worry. He didn't do anything wrong, and I'm here to stand up for him. Cookie asks the girls, "You guys bullyin' Pedro?"

The ringleader says, "Like we told Smiles, we was only playin'."

Cookie turns to Pedro and asks, "¿Qué te dijeron?" Pedro repeats in Spanish all the things they said to him. I don't catch most of it.

The sidekick mumbles to Pedro under her breath, "Gosh, why you gotta take us so serious?"

I yell, "Don't talk to him."

"Y'all should be ashamed of yourselves," says Cookie. "Walking around like you going on twenty, only to go pick on a ten-year-old. You should be looking out for Pedro, not making fun of him." Her finger zigs and zags as she puts them in check. "Your mother buys you some Vanderbilt jeans and lets you relax your hair, so now you think you're big and bad? Two weeks ago y'all were running up and down Cypress Avenue with your Skippy sneakers, so stop playing the role."

"Dissed and dismissed!" Nike snorts, and Pedro chuckles.

"Apologize!" The two girls mutter, "Sorry," and Cookie shoos them away. Then she turns to me. "Satisfied?"

"No," I say. "You should've told them they're not going on the bus trip Friday."

"Why you got to be all exaggerated, Smiles? That's two days away, and they said they were sorry."

"Only 'cause you made them." I look over at Nike. Homeboy says he can't take b-girls seriously, but he's teaching Sara and the twins how to six-step. He has his hands on Sara's waist, even though he doesn't need to be doing that to demonstrate anything.

"I'm not going to punish them just for being kids," says Cookie, folding her arms across her chest. "And not for nothin', Smiles, you could teach Pedro how to stand up for himself." Cookie bends over to look Pedro in the eye and says, "La próxima vez que alguien t'está molestando, tu le dice, *Step off!*" Pedro laughs. "Dímelo ahora."

"Eh-step ahff."

"¡Con gana!" orders Cookie. "Step OFF!"

"EH-STEP AHFF!"

Sara giggles. "So cute!"

Now Nike gets into the act. "Yo, Pedro, say, *Step off, B!* y te pare así." Then he demonstrates a b-boy stance.

"Word," Cookie laughs. She cheers on Pedro. "Hágalo, hágalo!"

"Eh-step ahff, B!" Then Pedro cocks his head to the side and wraps his arms around his chest until his hands rest on the opposite shoulder.

Nike yells, "Yeah, buddy!" He gives Pedro a high five. Then Nike finally catches the dirty look I'm giving him. "What?"

I jab my finger in his face. "Forget you." I take Pedro's hand and say, "Venga conmigo." As we walk away, I hear Sara ask Cookie and Nike what's wrong with me now, and they both mumble that they have no idea.

I lead Pedro into the cafeteria. I motion for him to have a seat while I go check to see if we have any leftover breakfast. When we leave for the day, Barb lets in the street people and gives away any remaining food. She says Cutter comes every day. I look inside the box, grab two peaches, and head back to the table. I hand Pedro a peach and take a deep bite from mine. So many things I want to tell him, but I just don't have the vocabulary. We sit in silence for so long that Pedro must wonder if he's in trouble, and I feel bad about that. He did nothing wrong. He didn't even tattle on those girls. I keep thinking, *¿Cómo se dice . . . ?* and *¿Qué quiere decir . . . ?*—the phrases we learned in Spanish 1R to ask the teacher, *How do you say . . . ?* and *What does . . . mean?* The words run repeatedly into each other in my head like a chant. *¿Cómosedicequéquieredecir? ¿Cómosedicequéquieredecir? ¿Cómosedicequéquieredecir?*

And it works like a prayer, because I get an idea. "Pedro . . ." I find the right words and pronunciations in my mind before I continue. "*¿Quiere que yo te enseño un poquito de inglés cada día?*"

A big grin breaks across his face, and he nods. "Yes," he says. "Teash me the English."

"OK, *cada mañana desayuno y la lección del día,*" I say as I tap the table. "*Aquí.*" Then I quickly add, "*¡Pero no malas palabras!*" Pedro wants to learn how to curse? He can see Cookie for that.

He laughs. "Okai."

I offer him my hand, and we shake on it.

NIKE

The phone rings and Glo is on it like white on rice. I pretend to ignore it, but I'm listening. My sister pouts and holds out the receiver. "It's for you."

"Me? Who is it?" It better not be Vanessa.

Gloria sucks her teeth. "I don't know. Some dude."

"Smiles?"

"Just take it already!"

I snatch the phone out of her hand. " 'Lo?"

"Nike, what's up, homeboy?"

Javi. What does he want? "Hey, man."

"Yo, you need to get to the park, like, now. Some dude here poppin' shit about you. Says you can't break to save your life."

"Who?" Can't be a guy from around here, that's for sure. Everyone in this neighborhood knows I'm the real McCoy. No matter. I'll battle any sucker who tries to play me.

"Man, I don't know one b-boy from the next. Especially

83

with those stupid tags y'all be having." Someone behind him feeds him a name. Probably Booby. "Lazarus?"

"Hazardiss?" My heart pounds as I sit up on the sofa. "Where he at?"

"Pulaski Park. He and his crew are there. Booby and me was doing our thing when we heard him call you out. We were like, *Nike's our boy,* 'cause you know what time it is. Even if we beef among ourselves, Mott Haven homeboys gotta stick together and not let no outsider come over here poppin' shit. That's when he started going off on you, and Boob and me, we tol'im, *Why don't you say that to his face, B, you so big and bad?* And he was all, *Where he at?*" Behind Javi, Cutter is singing. " 'Wanna be startin' something, got to be startin' somethin'—' " "Yo, shut up, Cutter! If you ain't got no more dough, take a hike."

I reach for my dogs and slip my feet into them. "Yo, forget about Cutter, and go tell Haz I'm on my way and he better get ready to throw down."

"Ha! You know he's gonna try and leave. Punk."

"Don't let 'im." I hang up the phone and race out the door. I fly down the street toward the Bruckner on pure adrenaline. My chance came sooner than I expected, but I'm ready. Been ready. This is better than I had planned.

When I turn the corner, I crash into Cutter. He falls to the ground like a rag doll. If I weren't quick on my feet, I would've landed right on top of him. "Damn, Cutter, you such a basehead!"

Then I make the mistake of looking him in the eye and see a glimpse of the old Cutter. The guy who coached Little League. The suit-and-tie guy. The family guy. The good Cutter gazes back at me, his shame washing over me and curdling into guilt like spoiled milk. Least I can do is wait until he gets up, make sure he's OK—I mean, as OK as a basehead can be. Cutter is reaching for a hand, but I'll be damned if I touch him. He probably got that AIDS from all his shooting up. When Cutter gets to his feet, he grabs my shoulders and peers into my eyes. " 'Wanna be startin' somethin',' " he sings. " 'Got to be startin' somethin'.' "

"Cutter, you crazy!" I shove him away from me before he can infect me. "It's a freakin' shame."

I start running toward the Bruckner again. Cutter keeps singing at me, his voice fading as I race down the street. Only when I have to stop for a light a block away from the park does it hit me.

Why can't I hear any music?

Hazardiss ain't at the park. Nobody from Rock Steady is. The only dudes at the park besides the baseheads are the people who keep them high.

The Barbarians.

Javi set me up so Junior and his gang can corner me.

Booby spots me just as I'm about to turn around to go back to my building. "Yo, there he goes!"

And fake-ass Javi says, "What's up, homeboy?" He starts to walk toward me, and I break. Now Booby, Javi, and three other Barbarians chase me. Even though I have a good head start, I pray for the traffic on the Bruckner to flow in my favor. I don't think this is what my old principal Father Davis meant when he be telling us to pray with our feet.

My heart is slamming against my rib cage. I'm not going to make it to my building. I have to find someplace to hide.

Forget about any alleys either. If the Barbarians don't own them, a rival street gang does. If I run into a bodega or the game room, they'll corner me for sure. I could head to Moncho's barbershop or JD's clothing store—the Barbarians won't disrespect their places of business—but they'll just wait for me. I have to hide somewhere they won't think to look for me.

I duck into the Laundromat, scrambling through moms and carts toward the bathroom. Someone is locked in there, and I have to make myself scarce before a Barbarian runs past the window and sees me. I rush to the row of arcade games and squeeze myself into the space between Pac-Man and the wall. I listen for kicks pounding concrete outside the Laundromat.

Javi rushes in. "Yo, anybody see a dude with a sky-blue shirt, baseball cap, and navy-blue Nike sneakers? About this big. My complexion?"

A girl says, "Yeah, he actually ran past here." Her voice sounds familiar. "Knocked me down, spilled all my laundry, and didn't even say sorry, the jerk. Now I have to wash everything all over again."

"Which way did he go?"

"That way," says the girl. "Smack him once for me."

I hear Javi rush out and tell the other Barbarians, "He went that way."

"How he go that way and we not see 'im?" asks Booby.

"You askin' me? That's what the girl said."

"Man, Junior's gonna go off when he finds out we lost 'im again."

"We ain't lose 'im!"

I just sink between the game and the wall as Javi and

Booby bicker. They eventually stop, but I'm afraid to crawl out. Even though I can't hear them, they could still be out there. My foot feels like an anthill now.

"You can come out, Willie," says the girl, hovering above me. "They're gone." I look up, and Sara smiles down on me. That Hall and Oates song plays in my head. *Smile awhile for me, Sara.* "Need help?"

I want to take her hand, but I already look like a doofus, cowering behind Blinky, Inky, Pinky, and Clyde. "No, I'm OK." I crawl out and stand. I make a big deal of stomping the numbness out of my foot to avoid looking Sara in the eye. I keep gettin' embarrassed in front of this girl. Still I follow her back to her machine

Sara lays a shirt across the counter and smooths out the wrinkles. "Why is that gang chasing you?" She glances at the TV set sitting on a shelf and showing Wile E. Coyote chasing the Road Runner off a cliff. Then Sara looks at me. Her eyes are the color of tea, and suddenly I'm thirsty.

"Who knows?" I can't tell her about Vanessa. "I'm the victim of the week, I guess." And just so she knows I'm not some punk who tried to get over on the Barbarians, I add, "I'm not down with none of that gang stuff. That's why they don't like me."

Sara nods, adding a shirt to the stack on the counter. I'm not sure if she heard me, because her eyes are fixed on the television, even though now that boring *In the News* just came on. *Israel has agreed to pull its army out of Lebanon, but only if Syrians and Palestinians also leave Lebanon, and they say they won't.*

I stand in her line of sight. "Listen, thanks for helping

me out. And just so you know, I ain't afraid of nobody. I'll whoop any one of 'em one on one in a fair fight. But you see how they rock, wanting to jump somebody."

"I hate bullies." Sara pulls clothes out of another dryer, folding, then stacking them on the counter. The smell of hot fabric softener calms my nerves.

"Word." I'd offer to help her fold the clothes, but I'm not good at that. Besides, I see some panties in there, and I don't want Sara to think I'm getting fresh with her. Instead I say, "Since we're headed the same way, I'll wait until you're finished so I can carry your laundry bag for you."

"That's sweet of you, Willie, but I have a cart." Sara points to it by the window. It already has another bag in it, as well as bottles of detergent and bleach.

Wait. Did she just call me Willie? That has to mean she's been asking Cookie about me. No other way she could know my government name. Yeah, buddy! "Still got to get it up the stairs in front of the building, though." Even if Sara's mother spots her, how can she trip? I'm just being a gentleman.

Sara laughs. "You're so persistent."

"There's no other way to be if you want to have anything in life," I say.

She pulls one of her long skirts from the dryer and shakes it out before folding it. "I have one more load to go, though. Won't be finished for another hour at best."

I reach into the dryer for her orange Saint Aloysius day camp T-shirt. "I've got all the time in the world." I fold the shirt and add it to the pile in the cart. "Besides, it's my fault you got to wash everything all over again, right? Sorry about that."

Sara squints at me. "What?"

"When I ran in here, I knocked over your cart, and your clean clothes got dirty."

"Oh! You didn't do that." Sara laughs and laughs. "Nobody did. I just made that up to get rid of 'em."

SMILES

Perfect day for a bus trip. The kids are excited, singing the military ditties that Big Lou teaches them. It's a miracle that no parents have ever complained about them.

> A ding dong, dong, dong, dong
> A ding dong, dong, dong, dong
> A ding dong
> Your mama don't wear no drawers
> A ding dong
> I saw when she took them off
> A ding dong
> She threw them in the sky
> A ding dong
> Superman refused to fly

Although it's sometimes hard to find the right words, I'm having fun translating for Pedro. When Sara's twins begin to help me out, I take a verse.

90

A ding dong, dong, dong, dong
A ding dong, dong, dong, dong
A ding dong
Your mama don't wear no drawers
A ding dong
I saw when she took them off
A ding dong
She tossed them in a tree
A ding dong
Now all the squirrels got fleas

Oooooh! Not to be outdone, Nike takes the next verse, and he's hamming it up like he's Steve Martin.

A ding dong, dong, dong, dong
A ding dong, dong, dong, dong
A ding dong
Your mama don't wear no drawers
A ding dong
I saw when she took them off
A ding dong
She tossed them on the floor
A ding dong
All the roaches moved next door

And now that Nike has everyone's attention, of course his kid has to steal the show. Stevie changes the words and speeds up the rhythm, and it goes from sounding like a camp song to a church revival.

Ding—dong dong ding—dong
Ding—dong dong ding—dong

Ding—dong dong ding—dong
A ding dong!
Your mama don't wear no drawers
Ding—dong
She took 'em off
Ding—dong
She hung 'em on the line
Ding—dong
The sun refused to shine

He's going so fast and dancing the fila. Just watching him is hilarious. Between Stevie's speed and my laughter, I can't keep up with the translations, but Pedro is cracking up anyway. As the twins scramble to translate between giggles, Stevie sucks in a huge breath and pushes out another verse.

Ding—dong dong ding—dong
Ding—dong dong ding—dong
Your mama don't wear no drawers
Ding—dong
She took 'em off
Ding—dong
She washed them in the sink
Ding—dong
Too bad they still stink

Stevie has the bus in an uproar. *Oh, I ain't never heard that one before!* I'm laughing so hard that my stomach hurts.

"OK, calm down," says Big Lou, but he's grinning from ear to ear. I bet he teaches all his army buddies that one.

Nike puts his hand on Stevie's shoulder. "A'ight, that's

enough. Let someone else get a chance. This ain't *SNL* or *The Shorty Rock Show*."

He just can't share the spotlight. And neither can Stevie. That's why he aims the next verse at Nike.

> Ding—dong dong ding—dong
> A ding dong!
> Your mama don't wear no drawers
> Ding—dong
> She took 'em off
> Ding—dong
> She put them in the bed
> Ding—dong
> Next day your pops was dead

I jump to my feet. I should've seen this coming.

Nike pounces on Stevie. "You little . . ."

"Get off me!" Stevie hollers. "I'ma call the Bureau of Child Welfare on you."

I try to peel Nike's fingers off Stevie's arm, but he won't let go. "You're gonna get docked, B." That makes Nike loosen his grip. Thank God the driver is turning into the parking lot. "C'mon now. He's just messin' with you."

"Nah, man, that little punk shouldn't be talkin' about people's parents." Under his breath, he tells Stevie, "Keep testing me, and you won't be calling child welfare. They gonna be callin' Porto Coeli to plan ya funeral, 'cause I'ma kill you!"

"Step off!" Stevie says, and Nike lunges for him.

From the front of the bus, Cookie yells, "Yo, Smiles, could you put your homeboy in check, puh-leeease?"

Nike is about to yell back at her when I poke him in the

side. "Yo, Sara's watching." He huffs and folds his arms across his chest. The driver stops the bus, so I say, "Help me carry out the food." We head to the back of the bus, where we stacked the three large cardboard boxes of packaged lunches. I notice that the crew chief and counselors of the Rookies are leading them toward the picnic tables, while the Famers are heading straight for the pool, chomping on their sandwiches and sipping their juice as they cross the lot. The Champs always want to copy the older kids, and I say let them unless there's a good reason not to.

Everything's copacetic until Cookie jumps bad after Nike and I get off the bus. When we tear open the boxes and start to hand out lunches to the kids as they step off the bus, she yells, "Why're you doing that?" Cookie rushes over to us. "Wait until we find a place to eat in the park as a group."

"It's lunchtime already," I say. "The kids are going to start acting out if they don't eat." As senior counselor, she should know these things. Cookie reaches for the sandwich I'm handing to one of Sara's twins. I yank it away. Next thing I know, she's scaling my side like I'm a cliff and she's Indiana Jones. Nike laughs as I swat at Cookie with one hand and play keep-away with the sandwich in the other. When she steps on my foot, Nike instigates. "Yo, homey, I know you're not gonna let that girl stomp all over your shell-toes."

Sometimes I wish Nike would just mind his business. There are more important things than a pair of sneakers, but I *can't* let Cookie trample my dogs. "Step off," I warn her.

"Make me."

"Ooh!" yells Nike.

Big Lou comes over. "What the hell is going on here?"

94

"Cookie won't let me feed the kids."

"Don't exaggerate."

"You're the one getting all melodramatic."

"I'm not being melodramatic. I'm being right."

I hiss at her.

"Don't *pssst* me," says Cookie, rolling her eyes and twisting her head.

I imitate her. "Medusa!"

"How old are you guys?" Big Lou says. "You're worse than the kids sometimes."

"This is a big pool, and we need to keep the group intact," says Cookie. "We should find a place in the park and have lunch together. Then when we finish lunch, we go into the pool together. This way when the time comes to go back home, we're not looking for counselors and kids scattered all over the place."

"One," I say, "the kids are hungry. Two, by the time we find a place, have lunch, and round everybody up to go into the pool together, we might as well get back on the bus and—"

"There you go exaggerating again!" interrupts Cookie. "They don't allow food in the pool, so they have to eat first anyway. And really they should wait at least a half hour before going in the water."

"That's an old wives' tale." Humor wins me points when I debate, so I break out the patois. "And ya damn rude!" I turn back to Big Lou, who's trying not to laugh. "If fish deh a river bottom an tell yu seh alligator have gum boil, believe him! Why can't we do like at any city pool? Choose a place and time for everyone to meet, and let everybody do their thing. You want to eat now? Go eat. If you want to skip lunch and go into the pool now and buy something inside later—"

"That food in there is freakin' expensive!" Cookie yells. "What we got free lunch for?"

"Yo, stop cutting me off!" A lot of these kids get money from their parents for the bus trip. After four days of bologna and peanut butter and jelly, they *want* to splurge on a hot dog or hamburger. That's part of what makes the bus trip a different kind of fun. "What do we pay counselors for if we—"

"The both of you shut up!" Big Lou scans the parking lot. "I don't see why we can't just say we'll meet at that tree over—" And then his eyes land on Nike trying to rap to Sara while Stevie is climbing the grille of somebody's Thunderbird. The second his thighs hit the hot metal of the hood, he leaps off of the car, yelling in pain. Then Stevie punches the hood ornament as if the car burned him on purpose. "Nike, look at what your kid is doing!" Big Lou yells. "All we need is for the owner to come out and see that." Then he puts his whistle in his mouth and blows it. "Champs, here's the plan. We're meeting by this tree right now for fifteen minutes to have lunch."

Counselors and kids groan and suck their teeth. "Why do we have to wait?" asks one kid. "We want to go into the pool now. No fair the Famers get to go in and we have to stay out here with the Rookies like a bunch of babies!"

"The sooner y'all do as I say, the sooner we have lunch, the sooner we go inside," says Big Lou. "You don't wanna eat, don't eat."

Cookie gives me a smug look and then finally snatches that sandwich out of my hand. "Counselors, let's motivate!"

She tosses it back into the box, picks it up, and starts walking toward the meeting point. "If you do want lunch, follow me." She says to Sara, "Could you get the other box, please?"

"Sure."

And, of course, Nike picks up the third box and follows her.

To hell with all these freakin' Ricans.

"**S**trike two, Willie," Barbara says before throwing me out of her office. If they want me to do a good job, why they give me the worst kid in the camp? Shorty Rock makes Dennis the Menace seem like Opie Taylor, I swear.

"Barb, just assign me another kid," I beg. "How hard can that be?"

"You need Stevie as much as he needs you."

"What's that s'posed to mean?"

"Think about it."

They don't pay me minimum wage to think. At the rate I'm going, they won't be paying me at all. I'll be working for free.

After some more blasé, blasé, I storm out of Barbara's office and run into Sara. She's changed out of her bathing suit and shorts back into her long-sleeved blouse and ankle-length skirt. She seems embarrassed that I caught her in her Pentecostal clothes.

"Hi, Sara."

"Hey."

"That's a nice top." I give her a big grin to let her know her secret's safe with me. I like my biddies a little sneaky.

"Thanks." Sara drops her eyes for a second and then starts to smile.

"You clocked out yet?"

"Yeah."

"Me too. I'll walk you." *Please say OK.*

"OK."

We walk out of the church and head down 138th Street. I figure Cookie's going to tell her anyway, so I give Sara my side of what happened in Barb's office. I prepare to defend myself, but Sara just listens without a hint of judgment on her pretty face. I keep venting, feeling better just to get it off my chest. "I feel set up," I say. "Like Barb, Lou, and everybody want me to mess up so they can just fire me."

"What's the point of that?"

"I don't know. To torture me, I guess." Sara laughs. "You tell me why, then, 'cause I ain't got no idea."

"I don't know how you do it," Sara says, shaking her head. "Stevie *is* a handful."

"He's a pain, right?" Barb, Big Lou, and Smiles, too, be actin' like I'm the problem, but Sara's a sweetheart, and even she can see Shorty Rock's demon ways. "That kid could drive Mister Rogers to drink."

Sara laughs. We pause at the corner to wait for the light, and she looks directly at me with those caramel eyes.

"Maybe Stevie's such a tough kid because he needs a male role model who can handle him."

"Word." It crosses my mind that maybe Sara's just saying all this to be nice, but I don't care. She wants to make me feel better. After the day I had, that's exactly what I need. We reach her building. "So you're just going to go upstairs and . . . stay there?"

"As you've probably figured out, my parents are kind of strict. You wouldn't believe what I had to go through in order for them to let me get this summer job. Except to go to work and run errands . . ." Then Sara's face glows. "I have to do some grocery shopping tomorrow. What was the store that you said that might have the ingredients I need?"

"The A&P."

She looks back in the direction of 138th Street, where the supermarket is located. "One o'clock?" Then Sara smiles at me.

"Most definitely."

"Take care." Sara opens the door and steps into the foyer. She disappears inside, and while I'm bummed to see her go, at least I don't have to wait until Monday to see her again.

SMILES

"I got it, Q!" I wave the encyclopedia and yell so he can hear me over his drill. Once Qusay told me that schools were named after Islamic holy cities, I figured there had to be a good name for the Bronx that wasn't already used. I broke out his encyclopedia set and discovered a city where Abraham and his family are believed to be buried in a sacred cave. "So the school in Harlem's the Allah Youth Center in Mecca, right? And the Brooklyn one is called Medina. We can call this school"—I slap my hands against the book to make a drumroll—"Allah's Youth Academy of Hebron."

Qusay shuts off the drill, grinning from ear to ear. "That's brilliant, God."

I blow on my nails and rub them on my shirt. "Don't mind if I agree."

I continue browsing through the books I'm sorting. Of course, he has *The Autobiography of Malcolm X.*

"So does this mean you'll be joining us?"

"I don't know, Q," I say. "I'm not shopping for a new religion. No offense."

"None taken, because the Nation is not a religion. Nor are we an offshoot of the Nation of Islam. We don't even believe in some divine being who is out there somewhere," Qusay says as he pokes the air with his drill. "The Black man is God, Raymond. He has an innate divinity that he can cultivate and harness from within, instead of beseeching some mystery god outside of himself." Now Q points the drill at me. "Now you see why I'm driven to create this organization. The white devil has been very effective in concealing the truth and slandering those of us who wish to teach it." He steps away from the wall to examine the three shelves he just created.

"The first one is still crooked," I say. "There on the right." I debate whether I should say anything. I like hanging out with Qusay. He teaches me things I would never know. I want to be a part of the five percent. Although I never admit it to anyone, I've been questioning everything, especially after Mama died. God, America, everything. Nike's right. Going to Dawkins is changing me, just not in the way he dogs me about. And not in the way the people at Dawkins would like or how Mama had hoped.

In public school, I got good grades for memorizing things for tests. At Dawkins, they push us to learn the facts but to interpret them ourselves. That's great until the sense I'm making upsets my teachers and classmates. The brochure says Dawkins is committed to equal opportunity, but you can count the number of Black kids in each class on one hand, we only learn Black history one month during the year, and the only Black adult in the school building is the live-in custodian.

"You got me in hot water at school, Q."

"And how did I do that, G?"

"Last semester we were learning about the Kennedy assassination and got to talking about conspiracy theories. I remembered you telling the homies about the Tuskegee Experiment when you used to build at Pulaski Park." Damn, I forgot that might be a sore spot for Qusay. He would hold parliaments there all the time until Junior threatened to beat Q down if he didn't take his "preachin' ass" somewhere else. Booby and some other Barbarians were getting hyped about Q's teachings, and I guess Junior saw that as a threat to his business. When Qusay doesn't respond to my mention of his exile from the park, I continue. "I asked my teacher whether, if something like the Tuskegee experiment could happen, it is far-fetched to believe that the U.S. government didn't have a role in this crack explosion, like you said." Before I know it, I add, "Or AIDS."

Q gives me that look my mother used to when I brought home straight As.

"And what did that white devil say?" I imitate my teacher stuttering, and Q laughs. "And while he was at a loss for words, I explained to the class how the U.S. government told almost four hundred Black men it was treating them for syphilis when the true point of the study was to let them die. That this only ended ten years ago." I hold back the fact that I learned about the experiment when I was doing research on sickle cell anemia, trying to understand the threat against my mother. Searching for hope. Still believing that I was fighting the right enemy.

"I can't wait to have the money to hire you," says Q. "You've already given me so many good ideas. You're going to make an excellent assistant and teacher."

I like the sound of that a lot. But sometimes Q says something that punches me in the gut, and I wonder if I'm cut out to be a poor righteous teacher. Since that debate, things have changed between Eric, Sean, and me, but I still don't look at them and see white devils. They're nice guys who mean well. That's what I want to believe, anyway. I *have* to believe it. I can't keep my promise to Mama and make it through one more year at Dawkins if I can't believe it. Who knew that good intentions could be so blinding.

But if he's willing to build with Booby, Pooh, and other homeboys even when they're stealing and dealing for Junior, Qusay's not going to turn his back on me the way Eric, Sean, and even Nike did. I hold up X's autobiography. "But when Malcolm completed his pilgrimage to Mecca, he met white people who embraced him and treated him as an equal. Not only did that change his views about them, he concluded that Islam was the solution to racism."

Q lays his drill on the floor and motions for me to follow him outside. Without naming them, he points at particular things. The litter along the curb. The burned-out building across the street with the shattered windows and sooty graffiti. Cutter trudging up the block, singing along with the D Train song blaring out a Grand Prix stopped at the light: " 'Keep keepin' on, you gotta keep keepin' on. Keep keepin' on, you gotta keep keepin' on.' "

"But this is not Mecca," Qusay says. Then he places his hands on my shoulders. "God, the truth is the truth, and it is available to anyone, regardless of race, creed, language, age, gender. . . . But the truth in this country is that everything here is for the white man and against all who are not white.

Any white man who wishes to be righteous must rebuke the very system that hands him everything based on the color of his skin."

"They exist, though." Still, I'm afraid he's right. Sean talks as if being Irish means he isn't white, and Eric won't even say the word *racism,* using *prejudice* and *discrimination* as if they mean the same thing. But if you had told me five years ago I would be going to a school like Dawkins and have white friends to bum about, I would have called you crazy.

"Yes, but they are rare." Cutter reaches us, now singing, "Mama Used to Say." Last year I was the only person in the world who couldn't stand that song. Funny how now it doesn't bother me in the least.

Qusay squeezes my shoulders and then extends a hand to Cutter. "God, how are you this fine day?"

Cutter says, "Brother, can you spare some change?"

"For you to buy that poison and inject it into your veins? No, I do not have any change to spare you, my brother," says Q. He puts his arm around Cutter's shoulder and steers him toward the door of the storefront. "But I do have something to eat if you're hungry."

"I am," says Cutter. "I'm so very, very hungry." I follow Qusay and Cutter inside the academy.

NIKE

"What's next?" I ask, resting my chin on Sara's shoulder.

"Willie . . ." I love when she sings my name like that. "Stop." Sara wiggles away from me.

"What? I was just trying to look at your list." I sway my head with El DeBarge as he sings, *All this love is waiting for you, my baby, my sugar.* I'm hoping to finish soon so maybe Sara'll have time to chill somewhere with me instead of rushing home.

Sara reads from the loose-leaf-paper she tore out of a notebook. "Some tomatoes, cucumbers, and scallions, and we'll be done."

I give Sara's cart a push, but the back wheel sticks. "You need a new cart, yo." I kick the wheel, and the cart juts forward. "Y'all making sofrito?"

"What?"

"I figured that, since Ricans don't use tomatoes in our recaito." I don't tell her about the Dominican girl I used to

106

mess with who told me that. Whassername said that Puerto Ricans are the only people in the world who don't put tomatoes in recaito, like we're a race of morons. I quit her for that. "That's how we're unique," I say, motioning between Sara and me. "Am I right? You making sofrito tonight?"

Sara studies her list. "Something like that." She takes a jar off the shelf and places it in the cart. "So you were saying about Smiles . . ."

"He waited until the last minute to tell me he was transferring to Dawkins." I follow Sara as she turns the corner and heads toward the fruits and vegetables. "I mean, I ain't no honor student, OK, but I know you got to go through a lot to get into a school like that. Applications, tests, interviews . . ."

"Geez, that was two years ago, Willie. And he's your best friend. Why are you still holding a grudge?"

"I could've transferred to another school myself if I had known he wasn't coming back to Port Morris with me." Once I say it, I worry that Sara'll ask what the big deal is. I don't want to admit how scared I was about going back there without Smiles. Without him on my side, I didn't know if the homeboys from the block would be my backup if any hoods at school started with me. I could've gone to DeWitt Clinton or someplace like that. Turns out I was worried for nothing because everybody pretty much acted like I ain't exist. That is, until I quit Vanessa at the end of this school year and landed on Junior's shit list.

Sara picks up a tomato and sniffs it. "Maybe Smiles waited until the last minute because he didn't know if he was going to go through with it. It's a big deal to go to a school where you don't know anyone and no one is like you." She adds it to the cart and looks me in the eye. "Take it from me. That's why I'd rather travel for an hour and a half than transfer somewhere closer to here."

That's exactly my point, but I don't say that. Somehow it's enough that Sara understands, even if she doesn't realize it. Her stare is pretty intense with those syrupy eyes, and I don't know what to do with myself. "Smiles still could've told me he was applying, though."

"He obviously was afraid of how you would react," Sara says. She grabs my baseball cap, puts it on her head, and looks for her reflection in a freezer door. "Can't say you proved him wrong, can you?" She pulls her ponytail through the hole in the back of my cap, lowers the brim down over her eyes, folds her arms across her chest, and pouts. "You left me flat, bro!" she says, her voice low. "That's wack."

"I don't be like that." Yes, I do, but pretending to argue is fun. And Sara looks cute imitating me.

She takes off my cap and swats me with it. "Yes, you do!"

"Do not." I reach for my cap back, but Sara pulls it away. "Do too."

She puts my cap back on, and we go on like this as I chase her with the cart to the register. Just my luck, Sara chooses the one handled by Blue Eyes. To make matters worse, Cutter is standing at the end of the conveyor belt, waiting to bag groceries. Blue Eyes and I been long done, but I still get nervous as those dots of ice bounce between Sara and me. Sara doesn't notice anything, placing groceries on the belt. I feel damned if I do and damned if I don't, but I'd rather do something than nothing.

"Hey, Blue Eyes, I heard you're an aunt now," I say all friendly. "Congratulations! What's the baby's name?"

She glares at me. "Matthew."

"That's a cool name."

"Excuse me," Sara says.

Blue Eyes snaps, "What?"

"I have a coupon for those chickpeas."

Blue Eyes sucks her teeth so hard it's a miracle Sara isn't drenched in spit. "You should've told me that before." She peers over the register and yells, "VOID!"

Sara says, "You know what? Forget it. It's no big deal."

I want to say something so bad, but it'll just make things worse. I already done tried to be cordial, but if Blue Eyes wants to cop an attitude, what am I supposed to do? I ease past Sara and grab a plastic bag so we can book ASAP.

"That's all right, youngblood," says Cutter. "Let me take care of that for you."

"No!" It comes out so loud that Sara and Blue Eyes stop staring at each other to look at Cutter and me. I motion for Cutter to step away from me, and he backs up. If I had my way, we'd just leave the groceries that dope fiend already started to bag.

Without another word, Sara pays. Blue Eyes gives her the receipt, her change, and a dirty look. I grab Sara's groceries while Cutter just stands there looking pathetic. Sara drops her change into the makeshift cup Cutter has made by cutting a milk carton in half. As she does it, she makes eye contact and says, "Thank you."

"At your service, young lady."

We walk out of the A&P and don't speak for a block. I finally say, "You shouldn't have done that." Why is it so easy for Sara to look that druggie in the eye but not me?

"Done what?"

"Give him money. He's just going to shoot it up."

"That's none of my business."

I have to laugh at that. "How's that none of your business? It's your money!"

"If someone needs help and I'm in a position to, I give it. That's between my God and me. Now what Cutter does with that money is between his God and him. Like my mother always says, *Do good and throw it into the sea.*"

"But you're *not* helping him, Sara," I argue. "The dude's got an addiction, which means he can't even help himself. By giving him money, you just—what they call it?—enabling him."

Sara mulls it over. Then she says, "Who doesn't have an addiction? Or at least an obsession. Everyone has something they struggle to resist even though they know it's not good for them."

"Uh-uh, not me!"

"Uh-huh, yes, you." Sara's dead serious. "You're addicted to clothes. Not just any clothes either. Brand-name clothes."

"Clothes ain't bad for you," I laugh. "The opposite. How you going to compare that to being addicted to crack or heroin?"

"Don't you spend almost all your money on them? Doesn't it give you a rush to buy them? Doesn't the high wear off fast?"

"Not the same."

"So the same." Sara snatches the Cutter bag from me, and we walk the rest of the way to her building in tense silence. When we reach her door, Sara avoids my eyes as she searches for her keys. "You know, Willie, sometimes you have to look past a person's surface."

Even though I feel defensive, I keep my tone in check. Let Sara be mad, so long as she keeps talking to me. "And people also got to be for real."

"It'd be a lot easier for people to do so if we weren't so judgmental." Sara finally faces me. "When you assume and judge, you never find out what they are. Or who they are. And if we're not going to know people for who they really are, then what's the point of having relationships?"

She motions for me to give her the other grocery bag. I hold open the door for her as she makes her way inside the building. "So if everyone has an addiction, what's yours?" I wait for her to say mythology or reading the newspaper. No matter what it is, I'll have a thousand more questions because I don't want her to go.

Sara smiles. "Like you don't already know." She runs her fingers through my frizzy curls. "I like your hair like this. It's nice and soft." Then pulls off my cap and lays it on my head. "I'll see you at camp Monday."

"Word."

As I walk home, I think about what Sara said. What she's saying about judgment is nice in theory, but it's just not like that. People judged me all the time, especially when I first moved here. They looked at my clothes, saw the food stamps, knew where I lived, and made all kinds of assumptions about me. OK, some of them were true, but they didn't know the whole story.

The reality is we *have* to judge. It's human nature. If everyone else is doing it, you can't be the sucker singing "Kumbaya." If you don't judge in a judgmental world, you won't survive. Not if you want to make something of yourself. If

111

you don't make judgments, you make the wrong friends. You walk down the wrong street and, yes, wear the wrong clothes.

No disrespect, but that thing Sara's mother says about doing good and throwing it in the sea is a nice idea, but that's not for real. One bad judgment can ruin your life. If there's only one thing my mother taught me, it's that.

Even though the door to her office is wide open, I knock. Lost in the printouts across her desk, Barb doesn't hear me. I knock again, louder, and she jumps. "Hey, you." She pulls off her glasses, rubs her temples, and forces a smile. "Long time no see."

I say, "You see me every day."

"You know what I mean, Smiles."

Yeah, I knew what she meant. And I want to know what has Barb so worried. She'd probably tell me if I asked. Instead, I say, "Can I have the key to the storage room?"

Barb reaches for the large key ring hanging from her belt loop. "Sure. What are you looking for?" She rifles through the keys, then hands me the entire set dangling from the key I need. "It's the one with the burgundy nail polish on it."

I remembered. Burgundy for the storage room, pink for the utility closet, red for the office. Mama did the same thing. Gold for the building door, silver for the police lock to our apartment.

"I'm helping Pedro learn English, and I figured I could borrow one of the textbooks we keep in there for Homework Help."

"That's a great idea, Smiles." Barb's face lights up, and my heart aches. "I'm not supposed to do this, but why don't you let Pedro borrow it for the summer. You just have to promise me that you'll get it back from him before camp ends, OK?"

"Sure thing, Barb." I have to get out of here. "Thanks."

The storage room is a cage off the stairwell leading to the emergency exit. Although it's clear no one's allowed back here, there's always some frisky kids making out. Sure enough, I find two Famers pawing at each other. "Busted and disgusted!" I yell. As they spring apart and hightail it back to the gym, I laugh at them. "Can't be trusted." I'm going to lord it over them all day, make them think I'm going to call home, but I wouldn't do that.

I undo the padlock to the storage room and let myself in. It doesn't take me long to find the books I'm looking for, because not only was it my idea to organize the place, I'm the one who created the system. Last fall Barb and I made a list of every title we had here, and then we numbered every copy. From three to six every day for an entire week, I took inventory by myself. Then one night Barb came in to get her keys. "Quitting time, Smiley."

I dried my eyes and wiped my nose with the sleeve of my sweater. "You go ahead. I'll lock up here. Just need to make sure the door's closed all the way behind me, right?" My nose was still running, and I had to sniffle a few more times.

"The dust in here," said Barb. "It can really flare up the allergies." I nodded, squinting back more tears. We both knew allergies weren't the cause of my suffering. "Smiles, even though I trust you, I can't leave you here by yourself. If something happened to you, I'd never forgive myself."

I nodded but couldn't move. I had a stack of phonics workbooks in my hands, the top one opened to the page with words and pictures for *th. Moth. Thread. Tooth.* The *Mother* in the picture was colored in with brown crayon and given an Afro.

Barb walked toward me. "How far have you gotten?"

"Not far."

"Looks like you've made lots of headway to me."

"Nah, I got a long way to go."

Barb took the phonics workbook out of my hand, smiling at the page. "How cute!"

"Not supposed to mark up the books, though," I said. "Supposed to write your answers into the composition notebook so that the next class can use the workbook."

"Yeah, that saves the school money, but it wouldn't kill these publishers to make textbooks that kids could relate to." Barb held up the workbook. "The kid who did this had the right idea." Then she flipped to the front cover and saw my name printed in my mother's soft print. "Did you get in trouble for doing this?"

I shook my head as I remembered when and why I did it, even though it was over ten years ago. Father Davis had called Mama to complain that I talked too much in class. *Raymond is a model student, except he's a distraction to the other children.* Mama politely uh-huhed him, but she hung up the phone livid. That night I overheard her say to my dad, *Ray-Ray isn't chatting up the other kids during quiet time to* be a "distraction." *He finishes his own work quickly and gets bored, that's all.* So Mama gave me permission to go ahead in my workbooks. *You don't have to stop learning for no one. Teach yourself if you have to. Keep going.* And that's when I turned the blond phonics mom into mine. Father Davis had a fit and called home again. Mama promised to give me a good talking-to. When she hung up, she asked me to show her, and when I did, she just laughed and laughed and laughed. Told me to tell Father Davis that she had done punished me good, and then bought me my own subscription to *Dynamite* so I could get it in the mail instead of waiting on the library.

But I didn't say any of this to Barb. I couldn't. Nor did I have to. I started to cry again. That was the first time since the funeral. Everyone kept telling me to be strong, to be a man about it. When I broke down in the storage room that night, I expected Barb to say the same thing. Instead she pulled my head into her shoulder and wouldn't let me go until I was done. At least done for that night.

And for the next week, Barb and me, we took inventory together from six to seven. I didn't cry every night, nor did I shed all the tears. One night I asked Barb why didn't Big Lou and she have kids. *I don't know.* I couldn't understand that, but I knew better than to ask when I saw her eyes well up. Instead I made a joke. *I mean, not like you need any more. You've got, like, dozens, with a new batch every year. We're like sea monkeys.* Barb laughed and wiped her eyes. *I guess that's true.* And we both understood that what I really meant was that she had me.

Once I find an English textbook with the matching workbook for Pedro and the teacher's edition for myself, I lock the cage and leave. When I return to Barb's office to give back her keys, the door's closed. I knock and open it, but no one's there. As I cross the room toward her desk, I hear Barb's voice on the other side of the cafeteria. I lay her keys across the printout and take a peek. I was right. She was poring over the budget.

After a quick glance toward the door, I lean in for a closer look. Having helped Barb prepare funding proposals and reports, I understand a few things. Before copying and mailing them, she asked me to look them over for any typos, and over time, weird things like *in-kind contributions* and *indirect costs* began to make sense. Before our falling-out, I had hoped to learn more. I grab a pen and quickly write down a number on the palm of my hand.

That's when I get the idea, and I know exactly where to look.

I rush over to the door and peek outside. Barb and Cookie are sitting at a cafeteria table. Cookie points out something on her dumb clipboard, and Barb goes into a long explanation. I close the door and race over to the filing cabinet.

The bottom drawer is where we file the old proposals and reports. I dive into the back of it, to the last folder in the batch labeled FUNDED. I flip through it quickly and find the proposal I want. The original that got Barb the money from the city to start the after-school program and summer camp. I lift my T-shirt and stuff it into the front of my shorts.

I hustle into the boys' room and lock myself into a stall. My eyes zoom onto the PERSONNEL line like metal to a magnet, and I compare that number to the one I scribbled across my palm from the current budget. Not only did Barb tell the truth about the funding cuts, her own salary took a deep hit. So did Big Lou's.

Now I feel guilty for taking the proposal, and I don't know why. If I had asked Barb if I could borrow it and told her why, she would've said no without any good reason. It's not like Qusay's academy is competition for the day camp or after-school program. I saw to that when we were brainstorming ideas. Q was intent on trying to be all things to all people, but I convinced him to focus on his strengths—*turning Kevins into Qusays* is how I sold him on it. Now he and Barb will be offering different kinds of services, helping different types of kids. He just needs an example to follow as he creates his own proposal. When Q's done copying it, I'll bring it back, even though I doubt anyone will miss it.

NIKE

Smiles is happy as a pig in slop that we brought the Champs to the Skatin' Palace. You'll never catch him dancing unless he's on those All American whites, and the Palace is his favorite rink because the DJ booth is in the middle of the floor. It's like the center ring at a circus, where all the best skaters put on a show. Easy Erv just put on "I'll Do Anything for You," and Smiles went berserk. *My jam!* he yelled as he raced to the booth. He started doing the crazy legs, and a crowd formed around him. I guess I'm happy for him. Can't always be me in the spotlight.

Big Lou said it was time to break up the pool trips, but I'd rather we'd gone to the park instead. I mean, I'm a fresh skater and bought my own pair, just like Smiles. I couldn't ruin my fly outfits with those fugly rentals with the fat orange wheels and matching toe stop. I'd just rather master my hollow back.

A slew of girls watches me rehearse my routine for the

competition, but out the corner of my eye, I'm scoping Sara and Cookie knee-deep in girl talk. I can tell they're checking out guys from another camp by the way they lean toward each other, giggle uncontrollably, and occasionally point across the floor. When Easy Erv mixes into "I.O.U.," Cookie jumps to her wheels. She tries to pull Sara into the rink with her, but my girl stays put. Cookie finally gives up and leaves her flat, heading straight for the DJ booth. Smiles'll love that.

Sara eyes the skaters circling the rink, her foot tapping along with the beat in those hideous rentals. I guess they do that so no one will want to steal 'em. Just when she picks up the newspaper sitting beside her, I slip on my All Americans and glide over to her. "Hey, Sara."

"Hi, Willie." Sara folds the newspaper. Maybe this means that she's no longer mad at me over the Cutter thing.

"How come you never call me Nike like everybody else does?"

"Why do you want to be named after a sneaker?"

"But I'm not," I say. "I'm named after a god, remember?" I bet Cookie busted me, telling her I wouldn't know diddly-squat about no Greek mythology. Why can't I name myself after a fly brand if Cookie can go around sounding like junk food?

"A goddess." I got a feeling that Sara might be a little bit into women's lib. Not on that all-men-are-chauvinist-pigs extreme that Cookie's into. Just enough that I shouldn't cringe at the idea that like an idiot I nicknamed myself after a female. "Tell the truth. You were thinking of the sneakers."

Sara has the best smile. Any other *Fraggle Rock*–looking chick, I would've told her to step off. "You telling me you've

120

never had a nickname?" I point to the shorts she'll take off and replace with an ankle-length skirt at three o'clock. "You obviously do things to make your outside match the picture of yourself in your mind." Uh-oh. She's getting tense. I wasn't trying to snap on her or anything, just show her how much we have in common. "What does the name Sara mean?"

Her grin returns. "Guess." Better than winning Zingo, yo!

"It means beautiful."

"No!" But Sara's giggling, and that's all that matters.

"It means perfect."

"Willie, stop!"

"It means queen."

"Close!"

"For real? Princess?" Sara jabs me in the arm, and you know what that means. "Ah, Sara means princess."

"You knew it all along."

"No, I didn't, I swear! Why would I know that?"

"Because it's in the Bible, maybe?"

"I guess something stuck from that one year at Saint Aloysius."

"Why would your parents send you to a school for just one year?"

Here's one thing that igs me about girls. To get close to them, you have to answer questions you don't like. Deep questions that only a dog would think of lying to in an effort to go all the way with them. Despite what they say about me, I'm not *that* much of a Casanova, and I'm not trying to be one either. Besides, a girl who doesn't ask these kinds of questions is the kind who be singing, *No romance without finance.* I don't want a girlfriend like that. That's the catch-22 with girls who ask ill questions. They're really into you, and nine times out of ten, you want to keep it that way.

"In '78 we had just moved to this neighborhood from Williamsburg. That's in Brooklyn." Easy Erv is now playing "I Like What You're Doing to Me." I laugh to myself at his timing. "Anyways, we moved here in the middle of the seventh grade, and let's just say I wasn't fitting in at IS 139. So my mother put me in Aloysius for eighth grade. When I graduated, I went on to Port Morris High School."

"You fought a lot when you first moved here?"

"Yeah, you know how kids like to test the new one on the block."

"Tell me about it. When I first moved here, I got teased so much," says Sara. "They used to—" She stops herself, and I don't push. I understand wanting to leave things like that in the past. What you can, at least. She says, "I didn't fight, though. I hate fighting. Too much fighting in the world."

"I only fought because I had to. It's different for us guys. That's why I started dancing. To avoid fighting." Time to change the subject. "So where do you go to school, anyways?"

"Saint Demetrios."

She might as well have said her school is on Mars. "Where's that?" Just when I think I've gone out with at least one girl from every high school in the Bronx, I discover I missed one. Good thing I'm persistent.

"Astoria. Of all places, right?"

"Queens?" She has Smiles beat by a long shot. "Like, near the pool?"

"No," she laughs. "The other way."

"Damn, girl, you're full of surprises." Then I realize something. "If your mother can let you go to school all the way in

122

Queens, then she can give you permission to go to a movie or concert with me sometimes."

"That's different."

"No, not really. Diana Ross is doing a free show in Central Park next week. Go with me."

"Maybe she'll let me go if my brothers come along."

"How old are your brothers? And how many we're talking about? And are they big like Conan the Barbarian?"

Sara laughs hard at my questions until I catch it. One topic leads to another, and the conversation flows easily between us. That's nothing new for me. My rap is always smooth with the ladies.

But talking to Sara *is* different. With other girls, I don't have to say much. They do most of the talking, and I just have to throw in an occasional *Word!* or *For real?* and I'm in like Flynn. Sara asks me questions, and I have to think before I answer, not because she's testing me and I'm trying to be fly, but more like we're both digging into each other for treasure. Other girls ask me which rappers I like, but Sara asks me why I like the Sugarhill Gang and the Treacherous Three, and I have to give that some thought. The more she tries to get to know me, the more I learn about myself.

Then Easy Erv dims the lights for the slow jams. The first song he plays is "Fire and Desire" by Teena Marie and Rick James. Now that's *my* slow jam. Everybody goes berserk over "Always and Forever," but that song's too damn long, if you ask me. I stand up and offer Sara my hand. "Skate with me, Princess."

"No, I can't."

"C'mon, you didn't rent those skates to sit there all afternoon."

"I'm so afraid of falling."

"I won't let you fall. I promise. I never fall." I look over my shoulder. Most of the little kids have cleared the floor and have made a mad dash to the arcade, leaving behind the teenage couples and the skate guards. "We can stay close to the wall if you want."

Sara pushes herself up to her feet, and skating backward, I lead her off the carpet and onto the hardwood. "See, you're way better at this than you think." I take her hands and place them on my shoulders and then put my hands on her waist.

Although she doesn't pull away, Sara looks nervously around the rink at the other couples. Most of them are skating forward while holding hands. "You're going to keep going backward?" she asks.

"Yeah, that's kiddie style," I say. "It's better this way." Plus, if Sara does trip, I can catch her. Or break her fall. Either way, I'm not going to say that and jinx us.

Sara drops her eyes. "Willie . . ."

I take that as permission to pull her a little closer to me. When I feel her breath on my cheek, I say into her ear, "No different than if we were dancing at a prom or something."

Sara and I are almost around the rink for the first time when we hear a girl's piercing voice, and it ain't Teena Marie hitting that high note. "I'm not playing with you, Smiles!" A red blur races past, and Sara clings closer to me out of fear of falling. There's Smiles weaving in and out of the couples and doing 360s to taunt Cookie with the rabbit's foot that she clips to her skates. And here comes Cookie, rushing toward us like she's Wayne Gretzky in braids.

The low static of the DJ's mic scratches the air. "This is

the couples' slow skate, people," says Erv. "Couples only. If you're not a couple, get off the floor."

Sara and I laugh. "Why do guys do that?"

"Aw, he's just playin' with her."

"Smiles teases Cookie because he likes her."

"If you don't want to fall, Sara, you can't be sayin' crazy stuff like that, 'cause I'll die laughing right here!"

Sara doesn't think it's anywhere near as funny as I do. "It's like you're still in elementary school, pulling our pigtails and knocking our books to the floor. If you like us, why don't you just come out and say so? And if you don't like us, fine. Just leave us alone."

In her frustration, Sara's holding on tighter and closer, and I'm down with that. "All I know is, one, Smiles can't stand Cookie. Two, Cookie may or may not like Smiles too tough either." I look Sara in the eyes and say, "Three, I like you. There. I said it."

And the second I say it, heat flashes throughout my body from head to toe. Just like the song says, I'm burned up within her flame. Fire and desire. It throws me. I stay rapping to biddies, but I never have just told a girl *I like you* before. I traded pulling pigtails and knocking books to the ground for delivering lines. Judging by the fever that just took me over, that's another kiddie way. I thought I was all slick and grown, but I was just playing keep-away with words.

"Willie . . ." Sara waits until she catches my eye. "You're blushing."

"No, I'm not."

"Yes, you are."

"Boricuas don't blush."

"Then why are your cheeks all red?"

"Because of the strobe light."

"The light's blue."

Before I can ask Sara if she likes me, too, someone slams into her back and sends us crashing to the floor. Breaking Sara's fall as promised, I wind up with hardwood under my ass, a head into my chin, and an elbow in my side. The first thing I think: *Shorty Rock*. But I hear him laughing somewhere off the floor and far out of yoking distance.

"What you gonna do?"

Sara rolls off me, and there stands Vanessa. She's not even wearing skates. The crazy girl just ran onto the rink in her jellies to knock us down. She lunges for Sara, but I block her. "Get off me!" yells Vanessa.

"Are you crazy?" Vanessa goes off, a spiral of arms and insults, as I fend her off and try to get up. With the advantage she has, she could hurt me if she really wanted to, but the sting of her slaps barely registers. "Yo, you better—" Now she swings at my face, and thanks to my reflexes, I dodge that one. "Vanessa, stop!"

Two skate guards come over and grab Vanessa, and I finally get to my feet. Now that I got myself together, the embarrassment sets in. If we were in the street, I'd break on her so bad. I can't believe she took this drama off the block and brought it to my job.

Smiles appears, screeching to a hockey stop. "What the hell, man?"

"The same ol' same ol' BS with this stupid chick!" Now the security guard is here, and the crowd stops skating to watch the commotion. As he hauls away Vanessa, thrashing and cursing the entire way, I look for Sara and see her scampering in tears toward Cookie. "Sara, wait!" She doesn't respond, but Cookie gives me a dirty look. I start to skate toward them when someone grabs my arm.

Big Lou says, "You're not going anywhere, Vega."

Oh, man. As mad as he gets, Big Lou never calls me by my last name. I can forget about getting docked. Vanessa done got me fired.

SMILES

When we get back from the Skatin' Palace, Barb calls me into her office. I walk the five-yard trip as if through quicksand, panicking for a good story to explain why I borrowed the proposal. When I reach her door, however, Barb says, "Smiles, go straight home. Your grandmother called. It sounds urgent."

I spin on my Pro-Keds and race out of the church basement all the way home, the memory of the last time Nana called me at work fueling me. I was in the gym refereeing a basketball game when Barb called me to her office over the PA system. She handed me the phone, her eyes bubbling with tears. *Raymond, come home now,* Nana said, her voice hoarse with sorrow. *It's time.* My feet grew wings and I made it in time to say good-bye to my mother and promise her that I would graduate from Dawkins and continue on to college. Every marking period Mama would rave over my Bs and tell me how proud of me she was, but I could never tell her that I feel like an outsider at Dawkins. A fraud. That I walk down

128

the marble halls waiting for invisible booms to lower. That I have a bad case of double consciousness like Du Bois talks about in *The Souls of Black Folk*. I swallowed down all of this as I clung to her hand. *You've got to promise me something, too, Mama,* I wanted to say. *Promise you'll watch over me, because I don't think I'm going to make it through without you.* But before I could get out the words, her hand went still and she was gone.

"Nana!" When I rush into the living room, my grandmother is sitting on the couch watching her "stories" like any other day. "What's wrong?"

I hear the bathroom door creak open, and in steps my uncle. "Naim!" I run over to him and give him a bear hug.

"Damn, Ray, last I saw you, you barely reached my shoulder."

"At this rate, next time you see me, I'ma be like this." I hunch over and hobble around the living room. "Nana'll still be kicking, though."

My uncle laughs, then says, "How 'bout you and I go take in that Eddie Murphy movie at the drive-in before they close it down?"

"Bet!"

I race Uncle Naim to his burgundy Grand Prix. Only when I hop into the passenger seat and spot some kids in Saint Aloysius T-shirts does it occur to me. "Uncle Neem, mind if we take my homeboy Nike?" I figure Barb's probably done dissing and dismissing him, and we can pick him up on the way to the theater. "He's having a bad day."

"Aw, Ray, you're a good friend, but I was hoping to have my favorite nephew all to myself."

"I'm your only nephew."

"Derrick wasn't kidding when he said you was a smart-ass." Uncle Naim climbs behind the wheel and sticks the key in the ignition. "Next time, OK?"

How can I argue with him? At least I tried. As we pull onto the Bruckner, I decide that having my uncle to myself is a good thing.

When we arrive at the drive-in theater, the cars are lined up almost to the highway. I didn't think there would be so many people at the movies in the middle of the week at four in the afternoon. Then again, it's *Trading Places*. "How many spots does this place have, do you know?"

Uncle Naim says, "About twelve hundred. They only added the second screen about five years ago." He inches the Grand Prix forward. "So many good memories, man. I can't believe they're tearing it down."

I get now why my uncle suggested we come here instead of the Dover. He only got out of prison and off drugs a few years ago, but the Bronx took a nosedive while he was gone. Before I met Nike and he told me why he moved from Williamsburg to Mott Haven, I would walk by the burned-out buildings in my neighborhood and just cringe at the eyesores. Now my heart aches for the people who used to call them home. I don't ever want to know how it feels to lose a place. Bad enough we have to lose people.

We get inside and find a decent spot. While my uncle heads to the concession stand to get us some sodas and popcorn, I pull the speaker off the post and attach it to the car window. Uncle Naim makes it back as soon as the previews end and *Trading Places* starts.

Man, that movie is hysterical. I almost die laughing, especially when Billy Ray Valentine says, *When I was a kid, if we wanted bubbles, we had to fart in the tub.* Although he laughs a few times, Uncle Naim isn't down with the movie. That whole opening scene with the Vietnam jokes turned him off. But we both snort at one line that wasn't even a joke—the one about the best way to hurt rich people is by making them poor.

On the way home, we drive through White Castle for some burgers, shakes, and onion rings. We decide to park there and eat in case we want to order more. I sink my teeth into my first murder burger like Jaws on a surfer. I'll be up all night with the runs, but they're worth it.

Uncle Naim says, "So, Ray, I hear you've taken an interest in Islam."

I almost choke. "What?" Then it clicks. Nana summoned my poor uncle from Neptune, New Jersey, to give me a talking-to about Qusay. "No offense, Uncle Neem, but religion is the furthest thing from my mind these days."

"Your grandmother says you've been spending a lot of time with the Five Percenters."

I brace myself for the lecture. Uncle Naim pulls the lid off his shake and drinks from the cup. "Look, I get it, Ray. I really do. You're a young Black man—a smart Black man—who lives in a neighborhood where addicts roam the streets, gangs run the block, the policeman isn't your friend if he's even around, and some of the hardest-working people don't have two dimes to rub together. Then you go to that tony school and see a whole different way of life, and that life is of a different color. You've got questions about that. A whole lot of questions. Then a guy like Q comes along and seems to

131

have the answers." My uncle reaches into the bag for an onion ring and pops it into his mouth. "Here's the thing, Ray. Having answers isn't the same thing as having solutions. Some answers are anything but solutions. You catch my drift?"

I nod even though I don't. My stomach is rumbling, and I don't think it's the murder burgers.

Uncle Naim says, "If you ever do want to know more about Islam, you call me anytime. In fact, you should come visit me in Neptune. I'll take you to my mosque, and we'll spend the day at Asbury Park."

"OK." The acid in my stomach is bubbling, and for the life of me, I don't know why I'm so angry. This is my uncle. He loves me and only wants the best for me. I like the idea of making a trip to the Jersey Shore to spend the weekend with him. Just not for that reason. When I go to Neptune, it'll be as his favorite and only nephew. Not as a project.

"Uncle Naim, I think you'd better take me home."

"You OK?" I belch, and he laughs. "Boy, stink up my Grand Prix, and you'll be hitchhiking home."

NIKE

Barbara let this one slide since everyone vouched for my innocence, but she still subjects me to *You should have more respect for girls,* blasé, blasé. I tear out of Saint Aloysius like a bat out of hell, taking the roundabout way toward my building so I can see anyone on the stoop without them spotting me. No one's there, so I dash up the stairs. The apartment's empty. My sister's probably consoling Vanessa. Who knows where my mother is. Probably at the Mill Brook Houses bochinchando.

For once I've got the apartment to myself, but I don't want to be here. I want to be chillin' with Sara, but she stayed clear of me on the subway ride. She disappeared as soon as we got back to the church, instead of waiting outside with the twins until their mother picked them up. I don't blame her for being upset, but how is what Vanessa did my fault? I think about going to the roof to practice my routine, but I already know I won't be able to concentrate.

I look out the window. No Barbarians in sight, so I bolt. Before I know it, I'm in front of Sara's building. Only when I'm at the intercom with no clue which apartment number is Sara's do I realize how much I'm trippin' over this girl. I don't have a phone number. All I know is which window is hers. If I had any sense, I'd just say forget her, head over to Saint Mary's Park, and find some other girl to mess with me this summer.

Instead I back down the stairs and cup my hands over my mouth.

"Sara!" I've hollered for some girl under her window plenty of times before, but this is the first time I feel like a head case. "YO, SARA!"

A few seconds later, another window opens. This girl about my sister's age pokes her head out. "Who you?" Her hair is too damn frizzy to be rocking that Farrah cut. "What you want?"

"Not you, Sasquatch, that's for sure."

"So what you calling me for?"

"I wasn't calling *you*. What you think? You the only Sara on the whole block?"

"Later for you!"

"Ciao, Chewbacca!" The girl sticks her ugly face back inside and slams her window shut. Sara probably doesn't like me doing this, but if I no longer have a chance with her, I don't want to wait until tomorrow to find out. "SARA!" I don't even know what her last name is.

Her window flies open. "Willie, what on earth are you doing?"

"Yo, Sara, I need to talk to you. Can you come down here for a minute?"

"No."

"Well, can I come upstairs?"

"No!"

"You don't even have to let me inside. I'll stay in the hall-way."

"What part of *no* don't you understand?"

"Sara, please," I plead. "Pretty please with sugar on top. Five minutes on your stoop, that's all. Then I'll go away and keep to myself if you want."

Sara fumes at me for a few seconds. "Wait." She closes her window, and I wait. And wait and wait and wait. I wait because if Sara had no intention of coming downstairs, she would've told me point-blank, and I could holler her name until someone called the cops or Bellevue to get me.

A half hour later I'm set to ring every buzzer on her floor and ask for her when she finally comes. "Willie, you're still here?" And maybe it's just wishful thinking, but Sara sounds happy. She opens the door and motions for me to come into the building.

The lobby is nice and cool. Sara leans against the mail-boxes and folds her arms across her chest.

"And what does that tell you?" I sit on the radiator.

"That you're crazier than I thought."

"Crazy about you."

"Don't start with the lines, OK? You're wasting your time. I don't want a boyfriend."

"Ok, bet," I say. "Just let me explain what happened today."

"I know what happened today. I was there, remember?"

"But you don't know why it happened."

"What's to explain, Willie? Your crazy girlfriend has been

following you around until she finally caught you with another girl. Then she jumps me because she thinks I knew you had a girlfriend and couldn't have cared less."

Vanessa would've jumped her irregardless, but that's neither here or there. "Who told you that was my girlfriend?" I don't wait for the answer I already have. "Look, Sara, do me a favor. If you want to know anything about me, don't go to Cookie. Come ask me." Sara scoffs. "No, for real!" Then I tread carefully around dissing her homegirl. "Cookie may tell you things because she thinks she knows the truth, but if you want to be sure, come to me. I'll tell you straight up for real."

"Fine, Willie. Is that girl . . . who jumped me today . . . your girlfriend or not?"

I knew it! Sara does care if I'm free. "No, Vanessa is not my girlfriend."

"Uh-huh."

"Seriously! She's my ex-girlfriend. I quit her right after school ended, and she's not taking it too tough. Vanessa thinks that if she jumps bad with any girl I'm with, eventually I'll give up trying to be with anyone else and go back to her, but for real? I'd become a monk first, and you know I can't dance in no robe."

Sara cracks a smile so small I might not have caught it had I not been staring at her so hard. Then it's gone. "Is she pregnant?"

That rumor again. I haven't heard it in a while, so I thought I was scot-free. "Who told you that?"

"Everyone is talking about it. I hear about it everywhere I go—the Laundromat, the bodega, everywhere. For someone who cares so much about his image, Willie, you're really oblivious to how people talk about you."

Truth is I don't want to know if Vanessa's pregnant. Still, with my sister and her being two peas in a pod, I figured there's no way I wouldn't know if she was. Plus, if she was, and the baby was mine, she would've used that to try to get me back, right? "Yo, Sara, I swear I don't know nothing about Vanessa being pregnant."

"Maybe you should find out if you're going to be a daddy before finding a new girlfriend." Sara turns her back on me to head toward the stairs. "I have to go. I'm supposed to be checking the mail, and it doesn't take this long."

"Well, aren't you going to check it?" I know I sound desperate, but I can't help myself. Anything to make her stay a little longer.

"I already did when I came home from work," Sara says. She sounds disappointed, and my stomach tightens. Sara's probably got a boyfriend in her old neighborhood or that school in Astoria, where she goes. They write letters to each other trying to hold on to whatever they have, and Sara's upset because she hasn't heard from him yet.

I hate that sucker's mere existence.

As Sara starts up the staircase, I say, "Just tell me one thing, Sara." She stops, resting her foot on the first step. "Do you like me at all? Even a tiny bit? One thing."

"There are lots of things I like about you, Willie, but there are some things that scare me, too." Sara takes a few more steps, then stops again. "Why do you like me, anyway? And don't tell me because I'm pretty. Lots of girls are pretty." Sara smirks at me. "Vanessa's *very* pretty."

"I also like you 'cause . . ." I shrug. "I don't know. Geez, you make it sound like a crime. Why can't I just like you?"

"I think you like me because I'm not throwing myself at you."

"Is that Cookie's cockamamie theory?" That girl be thinking she's Ann Landers, except Ann Landers waits for people to ask for her advice. Cookie be butting into other people's business uninvited.

"I can think for myself, Willie, thank you."

I throw up my hands. "Maybe it's because I first saw you during an eclipse." Sara laughs. "For real, it's supposed to make people bug out."

Sara's arms are across her chest again, but at least she's stopped climbing the stairs.

"Did you know Columbus used a lunar eclipse to pull a fast one on the Indians when he landed in Jamaica?"

"I did," says Sara, but she seems impressed. "Do you know the myth of Horus?"

"No." I'm learning not to play the role with this girl. I walk over to the staircase and stand at the foot of it. I want to sit down and ask her to join me, but I'm afraid that might scare her off. "Who's Horus?"

"Horus was a sky god. One of his eyes was the sun, the other the moon. He had a brother named Seth, and they were the sons of Osiris, who ruled over Egypt. Seth killed Osiris for the throne, and when Horus battled his brother to avenge his father and gain the throne, Seth tore out his eye. According to Egyptian mythology, that's why we have a lunar eclipse."

"Wow, Sara, that school you go to in Queens is worth the trip."

Just as I'm about to ask her if she ever watches *Shazam!*, a door upstairs opens. "SARA!" The woman sounds pretty pissed.

And she's gone. No good-bye, no *See you tomorrow*, nothing. I hear her speaking to her mother in rushed whispers and wait for the apartment door to slam before I leave.

I hope I didn't get her in any trouble. That'd be another first, because usually girls are the ones giving me headaches. Do they get a kick out of it? I sure don't feel too good. Maybe it's because I've never been able to not be with someone I like who likes me back. And still, I know that as long as I have a chance to win over Sara, I'm going to take it no matter how hard it is and how much it hurts. So this is what Romeo felt like. Or Tony in *West Side Story*.

When I walk out of Sara's building, I peek up at her window. The curtains flutter, and even though I don't see her, I want to believe that Sara is sneaking one last look at me. Just in case she is, I smile and wave before heading home.

SMILES

"Tu no puedes usar esa palabra," I say, doing my best not to raise my voice. One, I don't want anyone to hear what we're talking about. Two, it's not Pedro's fault he's confused, so I don't want him to think that I'm upset with him. Damn, everyone does say it, but the second that word comes out of Pedro's mouth in front of the wrong people, it'll be open season on the poor kid. And three, if I overreact, he'll want to say it even more. "Es una mala palabra."

Pedro pouts. "¡Pero todo mundo lo dice!"

"No todo el mundo." I search for words to explain. "Eso es una palabra solamente por la gente negra." No matter my debate chops, this is a hard case to make in English to someone my own age, never mind to a ten-year-old who only understands Spanish.

At the storefront, Qusay put a price on the word. If you say it, you have to put a quarter in the jar on his desk. If you actually call another person it instead of referring to him as

God or G, it's fifty cents. Once Booby said, *C'mon, Q, niggas don't mean nothing by it. 'Sides, I've heard other Five Percenters use it. Even Malcolm said it once in a while. Nigga, nigga, nigga . . . ain't no big deal.* Q held out the jar and said, *That'll be a dollar, G.*

Pedro shakes his head so hard you'd think it'd pop off and roll across the floor. "Stevie siempre lo usa. Y Nike a veces también."

"¡Porque ellos están estúpidos!"

"Son estúpidos," Pedro corrects me. At least the kid's laughing.

Me, I'm frustrated as all get-out, and not because I screwed up my verbs again. "Damn. I mean, son estúpidos." I look across the cafeteria toward Barb's office. The door's open, and Cookie is sitting at Barb's desk, calling kids who haven't been to camp in a while. She punches the keypad with her middle finger as if she doesn't want to smudge her nail polish. Once in a while, Barb crosses the doorway, reading a file and blocking my view. Each time, she glances outside the door to survey the cafeteria. At one point Barb and I catch eyes, and I look away from her and turn my attention back to Pedro.

I should ask for help on this one. My first resort—Nike—is useless. Plus I don't trust homeboy not to tell Pedro a whole bunch of stuff that I don't understand and would never ask him to say. Just like Nike to say something like *Do as I say, not as I do* and then stick me with a rebellious kid while he goes and chases after Sara.

Cookie finally gets up from Barb's desk. Just as she reaches the door, she stops, turns around, and smiles. Barb must have said something to her. I could ask Cookie. As much as she never misses a chance to show me up, she's not going to say anything to Pedro that might get him into trouble just to mess with me.

I decide on another tactic. "Por favor no dice esa palabra," I say. I finally remember a phrase that's useful, although inaccurate. "Porque me duele."

Pedro's smile melts, and it makes me feel good that he cares about my feelings. I hate being a hypocrite. The other day I found my dad's Redd Foxx album on my bed. Had to dig out my old Mickey Mouse record player to listen to it. Richard Pryor, Eddie Murphy, Redd Foxx—they all say the word. Come to think of it, I remember Pop using it, too, so long as Mama wasn't in earshot. She hated the word, and he would avoid it out of respect for her. Then Nana came to live with us to help care for Mama and stayed after she passed, and that word became null and void in my house. Only now do I realize how little I say it, even when I'm chillin' with the guys on the block. Maybe it's Dawkins, maybe it's Qusay, maybe it's Mama, but I have no use for it, nor do I miss it. If Pedro says it again, it *would* hurt me. "Me duele mucho."

Pedro pouts. "Stoooooop beggin'!" He throws his arms across his chest, b-boy style. Before I can react, he rushes to add, "Psych!"

I laugh. "You're a trip." He already knows what that means, so I don't have to explain it. "Give me five." Pedro slaps my hand, and I flip it over. "On the Black hand side." He slides the back of his hand across the back of mine.

Cookie pops up in front of us. "Smiles, Barb wants to speak with you."

My heart pounds. I have to return that damn proposal. " 'Bout what?"

"I don't know. Go find out."

I turn back to Pedro. "Get out my face." The translation comes in a heartbeat, given all the times I've heard Nike use it with Gloria. "Salte de mi cara."

"Don't talk to him like that!"

"I'm only messin' with him, and he knows it, so shut up." I point to Pedro's jack-o'-lantern grin. "See? Mind your business."

As I walk toward Barb's office, Cookie shouts, "Forget you, forgot you, never thought about you!"

"Nice comeback for a third grader." I peek through the doorway of Barb's office and find her sitting at her desk. "You wanted to see me?"

"Have a seat and give me a sec," she says. Before I sit, I glance at the green-and-white-lined computer printout on Barb's desk. I jiggle my knee, and my eyes flit across her desk for other clues as to what this conversation is about. To think that two months ago I would've been chomping at the bit to brag that I was in the House That Ruth Built when Rags pitched the no-hitter, and Barb would've hung on my every word.

Barb finally exhales and puts aside the printout. She twists her wedding band, a surefire sign that something is weighing on her mind. It hits me that maybe between the budget cuts and my feud with Cookie, she has decided to fire me. On the one hand, I don't want to get fired. That'd be crazy humiliating, and I don't deserve it. On the other hand, I'm tired of it all. Camp used to be fun, even when there was work to do.

Nike and I would bug out, flirt with the girl counselors, and teach the kids who were afraid of the water how to swim.

But besides suffering Nike's moods, taking orders from Cookie, and getting reprimanded by Barb, why am I here? Nike'll keep fighting with Stevie, chasing Sara, and getting docked. Cookie'll keep ordering people around as if the camp were called Saint Carolina's. I keep coming because I need the money for Dawkins, and I like the kids, and mine's the best. I'd like to think Pedro would miss me, but now that Stevie and he are as thick as thieves, who knows?

"So, Smiles, how've you been?"

She called me Smiles. Maybe this isn't that serious after all. I just shrug. "What's up?"

"This bickering between Cookie and you. It's gotta stop. Now."

"Talk to her then."

"I have talked to her. Know what Cookie said?" She actually waits for me to answer.

"I don't know." She probably kissed her behind. "*Yes, ma'am?*"

"She said, *OK, Barb. You're right.*"

Same thing. "Figures."

"The point is Cookie didn't say, *Talk to Smiles.* She took responsibility for her part in whatever problem you two are having and agreed to put the kibosh on it." Barb pauses to let that sink into my head. "If you're still wondering why I chose her for senior counselor, that's one reason right there."

Before I can even think about it, I snap. "You made Cookie senior counselor 'cause she's Puerto Rican!" It jets from my gut out of my mouth, bypassing my brain like a blocked exit.

Saying it made me feel strong and scared at the same time. I wait for Barb to deny it and fire me, and for a moment, I don't care. The next second I start to worry and wish I could take it back.

"Let's talk hypothetically here, Smiles," says Barb. "You yourself told me that you could just leave the church and work for Qusay. You know why that's an option for you? Because he's a Black man who cares about Black boys. If there's one thing I'll give that man, for all the mistakes he's made in his life, Q always cared about the young men in this community. He didn't learn that in jail, and no Five Percenter taught him that. Even when Qusay was Kevin, that's the kind of man he was." Something in Barb's voice tells me she misses Kevin even if he was a Pretty Boy Floyd who hot-wired cars and broke her heart.

Barb rolls her chair toward the file cabinet, and when she opens the bottom drawer, a nervous sweat bubbles up on the back of my neck. She pulls out a manila folder and hands it to me across her desk. In her blocky print, the tab says LET-TERS OF SUPPORT. I swallow down a sigh of relief as I open it, finding a stack of letters, each on different letterhead and filled with paragraphs saying that we needed an after-school program and summer camp in Mott Haven and that Barbara Cuevas was the right person to create one.

"There are ten letters of support in there that I asked different community leaders to give me so I could raise money for these programs seven years ago. I must've solicited about thirty. Do you want to know how many of them came from Black organizations? Only two, including the one from Father Davis here at the church, which obviously gets the rent it otherwise wouldn't if I had the programs somewhere else." You would think that Barbara would be telling me this with crazy attitude, but her eyes are on her hands folded in front of her on the desk as if she were a kid in detention. "It had crossed my mind to create a program just for Hispanic kids, you know. I mean, it's ridiculous that Black History Month is the shortest month of the year, but at least you get those twenty-eight days of recognition. We only get a week, and it's not even official."

My mixed feelings grow tighter in my stomach like a knot. On the one hand, I understand what Barb's saying. If I were in her shoes, I might feel the same way. On the other hand, I want to grab the I LOVE NEW YORK apple-shaped pencil holder on her desk and smash it on the floor, because if I were in her shoes, I wouldn't take it out on me or any other Black person. We're not the problem. The white devil is.

"But I said, *No, I'm not going to do that,*" Barb continues. "Black, Puerto Rican, white—any kid who lives in this neighborhood needs all the services she can get." Barb laughs. "The year we opened, my husband and I went door to door with flyers. I'm stuffing one in this mailbox labeled PINE, and he says, *Honey, what're you doing? Those folks are Jewish. We don't have that many flyers, so that's a waste.* I say, *I don't want them to think that because we're at Aloysius, their kids can't register. This isn't a Catholic camp. It's not even a Christian camp. It's a neighborhood camp.* Lou says, *They're not going to send their kids to us. They have their own programs.* He even takes the flyer out the mailbox, but I stuff another one right back in. I say, *These folks didn't run out of here the second the Blacks and*

146

Puerto Ricans moved in. If they don't have a problem being our neighbors, I've got no problem looking after their kids. And you should know by now, Smiles, not to argue with a Puerto Rican woman."

I just stare at Barb as she laughs at her own joke. This isn't *The Magic Garden,* and I didn't come in here for story time. I say, "So I'm supposed to just suck it up and take shit from Cookie, that what you're telling me?"

Barb stops midlaugh and clears her throat. "Raymond, I know one of these days you want to have a program of your own. You're old enough now to understand some of the politics that are involved in making that happen. No matter how you feel about me, I still want to mentor you, and that means making you hip to how these things go down. I wish I could tell you that as long as you want to do something positive, people will line up to support you, but that's not true. When push comes to shove, everyone has an agenda. Some of the people who didn't come through for me I'd known for years. I gave time and money to their causes, treated their kids like they were my own, and otherwise gave them my support, never thinking, *I should look out for my own.* But when I needed their support—even when what I was trying to create benefited them, too—they didn't give it to me, for no other reason than I wasn't Black. When the recent budget cuts came down, it was Black folks on the community board who voted to cut this program to have seed money to give to Qusay, who has no experience creating and running an organization."

"But he does have experience in getting through to certain people," I say. Nike's the worst counselor in the history of

Saint Aloysius, but he's not Pooh. And as much as Pooh is my least favorite of the homies who come to Q's storefront, spending time with him there has reminded me that Pooh isn't just Pooh either. "The people everyone complains about and no one wants to help." *But Mama used to. Unlike you.*

Barb ignores that. She has to. "That's why I could afford to hire only one senior counselor," she says. "And Cookie actually applied for the job. You didn't."

"I didn't think I had to!" I yell. "You already knew I wanted it and made me believe I had it in the bag. First day of camp, I came here expecting to fill out whatever paper-work to make it official." I stand up. "So you admit it? You promoted Cookie over me because she's Puerto Rican. You discriminated against me because I'm Black."

"Smiles, lower your voice," Barb warns me. "I'm saying no such thing. What I'm telling you is Cookie wanted the job bad enough to follow the protocols, and that said something to me about her leadership and initiative."

"This is bullshit."

"You're being disrespectful when you could not have a job at all."

"You want my respect?" I bum-rush the door. "I would've had more respect if you had just fired me."

"Raymond . . ."

I storm out of her office and into the cafeteria. I make my way through the tide of kids and counselors, their bodies blurry and voices muffled as if I were swimming underwater. Only when I finally get to the exit that leads to the alley be-tween the church basement and the avenue can I breathe.

And there's Cookie playing double Dutch with a group

of girls from the Famers. Those girls turn for her while she spins around, crisscrossing her legs, touching the ground, and showing off as usual. She has them all impressed. Instead of letting them play, Cookie has taken over their game, but she's Barb's choice for senior counselor. Puerto Ricans looking out for each other.

"Promise not to laugh?" I dig into my back pocket for the Polaroid I found, and I hand her the picture.

Sara clamps her hand over her mouth. "You guys are so adorable! Was this for Halloween? How old are you?"

"Yeah, we had to be about twelve, thirteen."

Sara reads the caption that Cookie scripted across the white border in red Magic Marker. "'Smiley Smiles, Cookie Cee, and Willy Will'?" She almost keels over in a fit of giggles.

It *is* funny, corny even. It feels like far more than four years ago, though. "I wanted to be Chill Will, but some other dude beat me to it," I say. "Can you guess who we're supposed to be?"

Sara points at Smiles's huge 'Fro, bow tie, and white shirt. "He's obviously Michael Jackson." Her brown finger travels across to me and my fluffy hair and satin shirt. "No wonder Big Lou is always calling you Deney Terrio."

"Not him!" My mother bugged out when I told her I

150

wanted that shirt for my birthday. She lit candles at Saint Aloysius for a week, praying that I wasn't some fairy. No way am I telling Sara that. "I'm John Travolta from *Saturday Night Fever.*"

"OK, I see that. And Cookie . . ." Sara squints at Cookie's long, loose hair and big hoop earrings. "The *Flashdance* girl? No, that just came out."

"She's Donna Summer. We're all dressed up like our favorite album covers." Then I laugh at another memory. "Ask Cookie to tell you about her 'Bad Girls' rap. You see this?" I point to the tiny bald spot in my left eyebrow where Cookie scarred me for life. "Your homegirl gave me an oops upside my head when I told her that 'Bad Girls' was about hookers." I crack up now, but back then I acted like I was dying. Not because it hurt so much, but because I was getting blood all over my fly new shirt. "I'm like, *Why you hit me?* Cooks says, *You should've told me that before I wrote it.*"

Sara leans in so close that I can smell the Violets I brought on her breath. I should've shown her my scar weeks ago. I'm just about to steal a kiss when the buzzer goes off on the washing machine. Sara jumps up and rushes over to add fabric softener to the last cycle and check on the progress of her whites.

I remember how it all began, how it used to be, and how sometimes I wish it still was. I always was a well-dressed kid, even if I couldn't afford the brand names. Problem was my flyest gear was destroyed in the fire in Williamsburg. All I had left were a few old things at my grandmother's apartment at the Mill Brook Houses, where we were staying until we found another place. None of the clothes at Mamá's fit, but they were all I had, and no way was I going to spend my entire summer hiding out in her stuffy project apartment.

I'd see the guys sitting on the stoop of Smiles's tenement, and I wanted so bad to just hang out with them. I stood to the side, keeping to myself except to laugh at everyone's jokes, even though only Smiles's were funny. One night when the streetlights came on and Pooh had to go home, I made a mad dash for his spot on the stoop next to Smiles, accidentally stepping on Booby's dogs. I would've said sorry had I been given half a chance, but Booby started dissin' me, snappin' on my clothes. He shoved me and pointed at the hems of my corduroys. "Watch where you going," he said. "You and your high-waters!"

And then Pooh doubled back just to put his two cents in it. "And who the hell wears corduroys in the middle of July?"

"This wack nigga, that's who." Booby seemed satisfied with that, but Pooh egged him on instead of making himself scarce before he got the belt. I guess dissing me was worth the powpow waiting for him at home for missing curfew.

Pooh said, "And look at his shirt." He flicked my collar. "What are you, homeslice? One of 'em belly dancers?"

"All right, leave him alone," Smiles said. I remember how he always had a smile on his face and dressed pretty cool himself. Everybody liked him—guys, girls, kids, parents, everybody. Although we weren't really homies yet, when Smiles walked past me with the rest of the fellas, he'd give me a single nod while the others saw right through me. I thought, *If he became my friend, then living here could be cool.*

But I hadn't dared try to make friends with Smiles. What if he was cool so long as I kept my distance? What if I said,

What's up? and Smiles dissed me in front of everyone? What if he really wasn't as nice as he seemed?

But then Javi jumped on the bandwagon. "Yo, Willie, where's your pops at?" Kids whiffed static and dropped their games of box ball and colors to gather around us. Javi elbowed Booby and then said, "Do you even know who he is?"

"Why you breakin' on him for?" asked Smiles. "He ain't do nothing to you. Leave 'im alone already."

"Shut up, Smiles." Then Javi cackled at me. "I know who Willie's father is 'cause he's named after him. El Wilfredo!"

That's when I snapped. I jetted off the stoop and landed on Javi's throat. In my mind's eye, his head bounces when it hits the curb like it happened yesterday, and I thank my lucky stars that I didn't kill him. Then Booby jumped in for Javi, giving me a rabbit punch, and that's when Smiles jumped in for me. I didn't even realize it until Cutter—he was Mr. Cutter then and not no alky dope fiend—broke us up. Booby's nose was bleeding down his shirt, and for a moment I thought, *Wow, when did I hit him?* But I hadn't hit him. Smiles had. Mr. Cutter was holding on to Smiles by his shirt because he was still gunning for Booby.

Mr. Cutter was sending us all home to cool off when he realized that I lived in the same direction as Javi. "No way, José," he said, grabbing me by the arm and spinning me in the opposite direction. "You take a walk around the block first. The long way."

I didn't want to, and Smiles immediately understood why. What was to stop Javi, Booby, and them from going around the block and jumping me on sight? Then I would be even farther away from the Mill Brook Houses, where we were staying four to a room with my grandmother to avoid the homeless shelter. "He's supposed to stay with me until his mother comes home," Smiles told Mr. C. Then he motioned for me to follow him upstairs.

Before he opened the door to his apartment, Smiles said, "You got to be quiet because my mom's not feeling well and might be asleep." When he let us into the apartment, I was surprised at how modest but colorful it was. For some reason I had it in my head that Smiles was kind of rich. Not like his pop was a millionaire or anything, because if that was the case, why live in the South Bronx? But Smiles was just so happy all the time that it never occurred to me he ever wanted for anything. His apartment reminded me of the one time I visited my father in Puerto Rico. Although I was real little, I never forgot it. I'd catch fragments of the island in Williamsburg and even the Bronx, but nothing like the peace I felt that week. Smiles's apartment was the closest I'd come to the same colors and rhythm, and I immediately felt like I belonged there.

I even asked Smiles, "Yo, you Puerto Rican?" I mean, I had a great-uncle who was darker than he was. It was totally possible.

But Smiles looked at me like I asked if he was from Mars. "I'm Black, homeboy!" he said proudly. Then, in patois, he added, *"Jamaican on mi mudda's side, memba me tell you."* He knocked gently on his mother's door and went in to check on her. I waited in the hallway for a few minutes before Smiles called, "Willie, come here." I stopped at the doorway, but he motioned for me to come into the bedroom. "My mother wants to meet you."

Smiles was the spitting image of his mom, from the high

cheekbones to the single dimple in her chin. Her small Afro smelled of coconut, and she wore gold hoops and lip gloss even while sick in bed. She put aside the book she was reading—something about colored girls and rainbows—and offered me her hand. I took it and just held it, afraid to hurt her. "Nice to meet you, Willie."

"'Lo, Mrs. . . ." I didn't know Smiles's last name.

"Mrs. King." Then she inhaled deeply and closed her eyes. Her head rolled as slow as the moon until she was facing Smiles again. Mrs. King opened her eyes and said to Smiles, "I hate to break it to you, son, but you're no longer the most handsome boy on the block."

"This clown?" Smiles thumbed at me. "He could never take my crown."

"My son the poet," she said. "And he doesn't even know it."

And they laughed as if nothing were wrong. Even though she was sick, I wished Mrs. King was my mom from the moment I met her. I knew from jump street that the fire was my mother's fault, so in my daydreams I killed her off and got adopted by the Kings without any guilt. When we were getting along, I'd include Gloria in my fantasy, but most times, I shipped her skinny behind off to Puerto Rico to live with those relatives so I could become a King all by myself.

I don't know if the idea was Smiles's or Mrs. King's, but when we got to his room, he immediately opened a drawer and started pulling out clothes. "These should fit you." He gave me four pairs of pants and twice as many shirts. When my grandmother asked my cousins to give me some clothes, they whined as if I were taking their best gear off their backs instead of relieving them of last year's hand-me-downs. Not once did Smiles pass off to me anything he wouldn't have been caught dead wearing. I tested him, grabbing for his Wrangler jeans even though they were still stiff and tagged. Smiles shrugged. "OK, take 'em."

"Nah, man, I was only messin' with you," I said. "I hate bell-bottoms."

"Maybe your brother can use 'em."

"I ain't got no brothers. I wish! All I got is a bratty little sister."

"How old is she?" Smiles grinned. "She cute?"

"Whoria? Hell no." I laughed at my own joke. "My sister's Gloria. Get it? Whoria!"

Smiles laughed a little, but then he said, "That's wrong, man. She's older or younger?"

"She's ten going on twenty."

"Damn, that's even more foul than I thought."

"You must not got no sisters."

"Nope, I'm an only child, but when I have a sister, even if she were the biggest brat in the world, I wouldn't call her no ho."

I remember feeling relieved when Smiles finally shook off the seriousness. "I mean, after my mother slapped me into next week, my father would snatch me back to today." He cracked me up. Then Smiles said, " 'Sides, how're you going to call your sister out her name and then expect not to be fighting with dudes out here when they try the same mess? You got enough problems fightin' your own battles." He tossed a jacket at me. "Here, try on this."

"It's too hot for no jacket."

"For when school starts, genius."

As the clothes piled up on the bed, it already felt like Christmas. I pulled my arms into the sleeves relieved to finally be wearing something that covered my wrists. "I guess your mom doesn't work."

"Sure she does. Whenever she's healthy. She works, swims, and everything." The question must have scrawled across my forehead like subtitles in a movie. "You ever heard of sickle cell anemia?" Smiles asked. "They teach y'all about red blood cells in your country?"

I smirked at his wisecrack. "In Brooklyn we got the same wack public schools you do here. The red ones fight infections, right?"

"No, those are the white ones. The red ones carry oxygen throughout the body. When a person has sickle cell, those blood cells aren't shaped right. Instead of full circles, they're more like quarter moons. Because of that, they jam up the flow of blood." It sounded like it hurt, but I fought the urge to cringe so as not to offend Smiles. "We never know when Mama is going to get sick," he continued. "All we can count on is that she *will* get sick from time to time, and when she does, she has to take it real easy 'cause her immune system's fragile."

"Do people know?" It sounded to me like just a bad luck of the draw and nothing to be ashamed of. Still, people look for excuses to be nasty, so I had to know if mum was the word.

"Oh, yeah," said Smiles. "No big secret." I remember being disappointed. I really wanted to be buddies, and that meant keeping each other's secrets. "Everybody pitches in whenever Mama has a crisis. The last time she needed a transfusion, some people came to Bronx-Lebanon to donate blood, like Mr. Cutter and even Booby's mom." And maybe because he was tired of talking, Smiles said, "My mother's a social worker and has helped a lot of people around here. My dad works for the train system. What do your parents do?"

I wasn't the only kid on the block whose father didn't live with him, but most of the kids at least knew where "their fathers" could be found. That's why I appreciated that Smiles didn't assume the gossip was true, even though it was, so I told him the deal. "Back in Brooklyn my mom used to sew in a factory. I'm not really sure where the hell my father is. Somewhere in PR. Ask me if I care."

"Is that why you went berserk when Javi said you were named Wilfredo after your father?"

"That ain't what he meant, though," I said. "He dissed me and my whole family." Smiles stopped rummaging through his drawer, waiting for me to explain. For a moment there, I wondered if I could trust him after all. What if he was really in cahoots with Booby and them, and the next time Smiles saw me in the street wearing one of his shirts, he made a point to tell everyone where I got it? All these questions crossed my mind, but for some reason, I decided to trust him. "Puerto Ricans call welfare *el wilfredo*. When the husband books, the wife gets Wilfredo to pay the rent, feed the kids, or whatever."

Smiles took that in. "That's messed up! No wonder you housed him. I would've kicked his ass, too."

That's when his doorbell rang, and it was Cookie with piononos from her father's lechonera for the Kings. I could never say this to Sara, obviously, but I remember seeing

Cooks playing dodgeball with the guys and thinking she was too cute for a tomboy. Cookie joined Smiles and me in the kitchen for some Fig Newtons and Nehis, leaving the piononos for the grown-ups. For a while we were a trio, the Mod Squad: Bronx Division, homies 4 eva. The next day Booby, Pooh, and the other guys acted as if the brawl never happened, everyone on the block was cool, and we all lived happily ever after.

Yeah, right.

Things changed.

Like dynamite.

Junior came out of juvie, started the Barbarians, and recruited Booby and 'em.

Cookie let Javi go all the way and got herself a bad reputation.

And Smiles dissed me for Dawkins.

Sara's voice pushes me off memory lane. "Willie, help me load the dryer." This is how it's been for the past few days. Sara wouldn't give me her number, but she took mine. After work I walk Sara to her building, race home, and wait for her to call me. Then we talk until she hears a key in the door. Twice Sara has snuck a call to me later to let me know that she was being sent on some errand, and I rush out so by the time she comes downstairs, I'm waiting on her corner. I've never felt so lucky to spend three hours doing laundry.

"Sure thing, Princess."

"And turn up that song!" We're listening to BLS, and Frankie Crocker's playing "I Wanna Thank You." It turns out that Sara and I have the same taste in love songs.

SMILES

The proposal I lent Qusay helped. Following it to write his own, and including some of my ideas, he convinced Mama's old social service agency to give him a small grant to start a pilot program. If he can recruit and retain a certain number of kids from the neighborhood over the summer in a series of workshops—that's what I said he should call the parliaments instead—they might give him more money. Q offered me a little stipend from his seed money to canvass the neighborhood. *The more participants I enroll, the more money I get, the sooner I can hire you to assist me,* he said. I walk into Silvio's game room to pass out flyers for Q's initiative and find Flex and the Don going at it.

"I don't want you with those guys, Flex," Don Silvio yells. "They're hoodlums. Every last one of 'em." He sprays the glass counter with Windex and wipes it in a fury. He has all kinds of knickknacks for sale—name buckles, fake gold chains, rabbits' feet, hair feathers, whatever's in style. Don Silvio still sells some albums on vinyl and cassettes and even a few 45s if the joint is hot. Except for some candy, however, I've never seen anyone buy anything from him. Don Silvio stays in business running the game room and the numbers. Every other business in the neighborhood is a front for another kind of hustle. JD sells all the latest fashions in his window, but in the back room he has knockoff Ray-Ban sunglasses and Gucci handbags for half the price. If you want to get HBO but not pay for it, look no further than Ms. Rhi at the Laundromat, who'll sell you a black box to descramble the signal. Sometimes Elsie at the bodega "cashes" the WIC check for a mom who needs the money more than the baby formula, taking a cut for herself and submitting the vouchers to Uncle Sam for full reimbursement. And I can't even count all the half empty hardware stores, pharmacies, and five-and-dimes that are really weed spots. Like Melle Mel says in "Message II," *It's called survival.* But Don Silvio is the only one who has yet to be raided or busted.

In the back some guys yell, *Oh!* I walk past Flex and peek into the back room, where the games are. Just a bunch of kids in a heated round of Mario Bros.

Flex hooks his fingers into his belt loops, swaying back and forth while staring at his Converse. "Man, Silvio, you can't be telling me who I can be down with, yo." He's a soft-spoken dude who holds the block record for solving the Rubik's Cube—one minute and thirty-eight seconds. The Professor doesn't even come close, and he's the indisputable neighborhood genius.

"Every day I have to chase one of 'em sonsabitches outta here," says Don Silvio. "They have no shame, trying to sell that garbage to kids. Vergognoso!"

"How many times I gotta tell you? I ain't involved in none of that. We just be chillin'." When I give Flex a sympathetic nod, he says to me, "Dude want I should be turnin' my nose up at niggas, and you know that won't fly."

"Word 'em up."

Don Silvio notices me. "Smiley!" Then he does what a lot of adults in this neighborhood do that I wish they wouldn't. "This is who you should be trying to be down with," he says, mimicking Flex's slang in a sarcastic tone. "È così onorevole. He goes to school, church, work. Smiley's a good boy, and you should be more like him."

Flex looks at me like, *You believe this shit?* "Yo, Smiley be maxin' with Booby and 'em, too."

Don Silvio shoots me a look. I sneer at Flex as if to say, *For real, B?* I turn back to the Don and explain, "It's not the way it sounds." I hand Flex and him a flyer. "Flex and I are part of a new program that Qusay is creating—"

"Koosay!" Don Silvio begins to rant in Italian. He crumples the flyer.

"Yo, Silv, what're you doing?"

Flex says, "He be goin' off like that over nothin', B."

"That Koosay's no better than Junior and his gang of pushers. You gonna see. Different scheme, same mentality."

Now it's my turn to give Flex the *You believe this?* face. Flex snickers. I've known Don Silvio all my life, and except for the occasional scolding when the guys and me would get a little too raucous or bang on his machine if it ate a quarter, I've never had a problem with the man. I mumble to Flex, "I know this white dude isn't standing here judging the homies when he runnin' numbers."

162

"What was that?" says Don Silvio. "Speak up!" Then he turns toward the game room. "Hey, hey, hey, take it easy back there!"

Flex throws his hands up. "Yo, my name ain't Bennett, and I'm not in it." Then he books, leaving me with a fuming Don Silvio. I get it, though. Flex can only talk back just so much to the only man who will hire him. This is why the brothers need Qusay's program to break free of vultures like him, preying on our people.

Don Silvio points his finger at me and says, "Your father know about this business you have with Koosay?"

"Look, Silvio," I say, "I didn't come in here looking for trouble. I just wanted to pass out some flyers about a great opportunity for the kids in the neighborhood. You're the one started poppin' shit about hoodlums and schemes. I mean, they don't call running numbers the policy racket for nothing."

"You. Get out! Out my game room now!"

He spews another few choice words in Italian. Some kids rush out the game room to follow the commotion. I put my hand behind my ear. "What's that you said? You called me a what? I'm a moulinyan?"

Don Silvio's face gets red. "I called you no such thing! Get out already. Before I call the police."

He doesn't have to tell me a third time. Some of the kids follow me outside, where Flex is sitting on a hydrant and smoking a loosie. I explain what happened, give them some flyers, and build with them until I see Don Silvio making his way out from behind the counter and toward the door. Before he can chase me from his storefront, I say to Flex, "See you at Q's, G?"

"Most def."

Then I hit the parks, the corners, the pool hall, everywhere the homeboys congregate, passing out flyers. I even swing by Pulaski Park. Surrounded by his usual minions and a couple of girls, Junior holds court at a concrete checkerboard table and eyes me. We were never friends, but I also never had any beef with him either. Before I know it, he summons me over. It takes the fifty-foot walk to summon the courage I need to play the role.

"Junior Junior," I say, offering him my free hand.

He gives it a quick clasp. "Smiley Smiles. What's up?" Junior gestures toward the flyers in my other hand.

"Yo, Qusay's starting this fresh new program for the brothers around the way. It's called the Bridge." I hand him a flyer. It's a long shot, but I can't help but imagine what it would be like if someone like Junior got down with the Bridge. A lot of the homeboys would follow suit, and the neighborhood would be a completely different place. Even if there'll always be some cats who want to sidle up to the devil for a quick buck, what if the uplifted minds outnumbered them? "Come check it out, B, 'cause it's gonna be all the way live."

Junior takes the flyer and skims it. He snorts and hands it to one of his associates. By the way his eyes dart across the page and with the quickness he hands it off to the next dude, I deduce that homeboy can't read. Then, in Spanish, Junior says something to the effect that he needs to do something about ese conden'ao Qusay before he becomes the bane of his existence. My spine grows cold, but I pretend to not understand a word he said. Junior says, "Very nice, Smiles, but I'm a busy man. And so are my homeboys." He motions across the park to where Booby and the others are slinging. "But thank you for the invitation."

I speak thug better than Spanish. Translation: *Make like a tree and leave before I drop-kick you into the East River.* I salute Junior and scram—my second eviction of the day. If this is how Q felt, no wonder he never tried to build here again. I'm halfway across the park when Junior calls, "Oh, Smiley, do me a favor and tell your homeboy Nike that I'm looking forward to catching up with him real soon." I turn around to give him a nod and a plastic grin, and he adds, "And if he doesn't catch my drift, do me the favor and spell it out for him. I know he ain't the sharpest knife in the drawer."

I figure I've done enough canvassing for the day and take my Black ass home. When I walk into the apartment, Nana asks, "Where have you been?" But before I can even answer, she says, "A friend of yours from school called."

I almost say, *I don't have friends at school anymore.* "Who?"

Nana points toward the credenza, where we keep our mail and telephone messages. "Said his name was Sean. Call him back now, don't wait until it's late."

Why Nana's so keen? She's never this chipper when Nike calls. As upset as I get with him at times, that's just not right. She's never even met Sean, and he's no saint. He's the guy who's convinced that Kennedy was taken out by the Mob— *No way, man, would anyone kill the president over civil rights*—and said he didn't have time to read *Bad Blood* even though all the proof he needed about the Tuskegee experiment was in it.

I pick up the message and debate calling him back. Funny,

at the end of the school year, we traded numbers, and I secretly hoped he would call me. Sean's different when Eric's not around. Now that he has, though, I'm suspicious about what he really wants.

I grab the phone, go into my room, and dial his number. He answers. "Sean, it's Raymond. King. From school."

"Yeah, man, what's up? How ya doin'?"

"I'm cool. Chillin'." I remember how he didn't put Eric in check when he started poppin' all that mess about the judges giving me the debate that I won fair and square. For a moment, I have the urge to confront him, but I hold back. "What's up with you?"

"One of the other kids hooked me up with an internship at his dad's law firm, and yo . . ." The slang cuts into me like it never has before. After all, Sean's one of those Irish kids from Hell's Kitchen, where the *word*s and *B*s roll off their tongues like a first language. The second day of school, Sean was standing behind me on the lunch line when I snapped on Dawkins's elaborate spread. I mean, at Saint Aloysius you only had two choices for lunch: whatever the meal of the day was or a cheeseburger in a tinfoil sack. Sean overheard my wisecrack and snickered, so I panicked, thinking, *Damn, one of these trust-fund kids done busted my scholarship behind dissing the gourmet cuisine like an ingrate.* Then he said, *They can keep the Grey Poupon, B, where the ketchup at?* Sean sounded like home to me, and we became friends like that. At least, I thought we were friends. ". . . I'm dying here, B. Why call 'em briefs when they're a gazillion pages long? Answer me that. And the jargon?" He snorts into his receiver. "If it weren't already dead, B, I would've killed Latin by now, I swear!" I choke on my laugh. That sounds like something Nike would say, and under different circumstances, I would have cracked up and come back with something funnier. Instead I just hold back and make Sean fill the dead air. "You workin'?"

"Yeah. Day camp. Counselor."

"One of those Summer Youth Employment Program joints?"

"Uh-huh." To this day Sean still takes me off guard whenever he knows something about my life. I keep forgetting all the ways we're two satellites in the same orbit. He's probably had a job through SYEP at one point. Mama pressed me to go to Dawkins, saying that it would open doors for me, but none of them led to an internship at a law firm. They hoard those opportunities for their own kind. "Been doing a little volunteering in the neighborhood, too."

"That's fresh," says Sean. "Where?"

"Helping this brother open a school."

"Ah, droppin' science. Word. What kind of school?"

The way I square my shoulders and jut out my chin, you'd think Sean were standing right in front of me instead of on the other end of the line. "Allah Youth Academy of Hebron."

"The Ali what? Is it some kind of boxing program?" I repeat the name, hitting every word like a slap across the face. Sean laughs, "Yo, Ray, don't tell me you gonna come back to school rockin' a dashiki and shit. 'Cause you know that's against the dress code." It takes Sean a minute to realize that he's laughing at his own joke by his lonesome. "No, seriously, what kind of school is it?"

I'm done with him, though. Just like Q warned me, Sean isn't the exception that proves the rule. "I have to book."

First, silence. "All right," Sean sputters. "So let me call you later in the week."

"Yeah, let you."

"Maybe we can catch a flick."

"Maybe." Sean and I both know what time it is. He's not calling me, and I'm not calling him. It's like that, and that's the way it is.

"Later, Ray."

"Bye." I hang up the phone and stare at it, shaking my head. Sorry, Run, we're not all written down on the same list. That's OK, though. No loss. Seriously. It isn't.

NIKE

"No more laundry today?" Not only do I want to see Sara again, this heat wave is killing me, and Miss Rhi has AC at the Laundromat. Somebody downstairs is blasting "Just Be Good to Me," so I shut the window since there's no cool breeze to save me anyways.

"We just did three loads two days ago," Sara laughs. "Can you give us a week?"

"What about groceries?" She laughs again, but I'm serious as a heart attack. "The refrigerator's full?"

"Yes, Willie."

I crawl back into my bed and switch the phone to my other ear. "Guess I have to wait until tomorrow to see you." I pick at the tape I used to put up the Roxy flyer on my wall. "So, like, what do you do when you come home from camp and are done with your chores?"

Sara scoffs. "There's *always* chores. Don't you have any to do? Your mother spoils you."

"Ha! I wish." I almost ask Sara how am I spoiled when

169

every little thing I want I have to buy myself. "I take out the garbage."

"That's it? You grab a Hefty bag and bring it to the alley. Someone call the Bureau of Child Welfare."

Damn, she makes me sound like a bum. "Ain't my fault I'm a guy. I'd rather wash dishes any day." No, that's not true, but it creates an opening. "Let's swap. You come take out my garbage, and I'll wash your dishes."

"Yeah, right."

"Ah, see, you know the deal. Taking out the trash is treacherous. Ain't no telling what you going to find in those alleys. Crackheads . . ."

". . . rapists . . ."

". . . drug dealers . . ."

". . . child molesters . . ."

". . . rats . . ."

"Did you say rats?"

Now I'm stupid embarrassed for making us sound like a bunch of cochinos over here. "Look, we can't help that. Critters don't discriminate, so if your neighbors are pigs . . . Mr. Clean would have rats and roaches, too."

"It's not that people are pigs, Willie. It's that the city lets the garbage pile up for days before they come get it. By the time the sanitation truck comes, the rats have gotten into the bags and dragged the trash all over the street."

"And on them days when it's really hot?" I gag. "Oh, my God, it smells so nasty."

"And let me tell you something. It's not a citywide thing either. I can tell you from experience that they don't let every neighborhood get as dirty as this one." Sara exhales. "I hate living here."

I don't know what to say to that. This neighborhood is awful, with all the drugs and gangs and pollution. The teachers think you're stupid, and the cops think you're criminals. But the truth is that ain't no different than where I used to live in Williamsburg. Same shit, different zip code. And while there are some wack people around ruining it for everybody— Junior, Cutter, Dee Dee, and them—there are also really cool folks. Whatever beef I got with Smiles, the Kings are good people. Cookie's family, too, for that matter. And my mom might be a welfare queen, but I got a job. That's what's really bothering me. As bad as it is, I still want Sara to like this neighborhood because *I'm* here. "I guess your old neighborhood in Queens was really different, huh?"

Sara hesitates. "Yeah, except . . ."

"What?"

"Forget it."

"Nah, tell me."

"We had to move because of, you know, prejudice."

"For real?"

"My parents would kill me if they knew I told anyone. . . ."

"Why? Y'all were the victims. What they do to you?"

"We used to live on the first floor of a two-family private house. Somebody made, like, a firebomb and tossed it through our window."

"Damn, that's messed up!"

"The worst part is my parents swear the couple who owned the house and lived upstairs had something to do with it. We had been there for almost a year with no problem. Then suddenly their daughter stopped inviting me over. They complained about the smell of our food, went through our mail, and took a year and a day to make the simplest repairs.

If we played the radio or TV, no matter how low, they'd bang on our ceiling with a broomstick."

"Assholes. Didn't they know you were Puerto Rican when y'all moved in? Not that it should matter, but you know what I'm sayin'." Sara doesn't say anything. "I guess that's one good thing about moving here, huh? You're with your own kind, and no one's going to mess with you on account of that."

She still doesn't say anything, but I get it. Even though her family was done wrong, stuff like that is hard to admit. It hurts to hold it inside when you know you're innocent, but by the same token, it makes you all sensitive to reveal it. Like, why, of all people, you the one it done happened to? What's wrong with you that you couldn't put yourself in a better situation to avoid that crap? You think maybe whatever happened, you deserve it.

Then it hits me. "Were you home when they threw that bomb in your window?"

"Yeah. We were dead asleep and just heard this loud crash, then a boom in our living room. The bomb landed on a chair, which caught on fire. My dad was able to snuff it out with his pajama top, so that was the only thing that was damaged, but . . . yeah. We wasted no time getting out of there. My parents just knew it would happen again, so we packed up and moved in with friends in another part of Queens until we found this place." Sara sucks in a deep breath, then says, "Willie, please . . . don't tell anyone."

That just makes my chest swell. Proof positive that Sara truly likes me. That it ain't just about my looks, my clothes, my moves, or anything like that. You can like someone in that way but not really trust 'em. Trust is a whole other level of like—it's halfway to love.

"Man, Sara, we got so much in common," I say. "We kind of moved for the same reason."

"Really?"

"You not going to believe it, though." For a second, my skin rings thin, and I wish I had not said anything. There's a big difference between being chased out of your home by racist neighbors and getting burned out by the person that's supposed to protect you. "We got burned out of our apartment in Williamsburg, too."

"I've been reading about that in the paper a lot. It looks like the crack addicts are accidently setting fires while getting high, but landlords are actually paying them to set fires on purpose. I'll show you the article tomorrow."

"What a stupid thing to do!"

"Not really. Think about it. They'll get more money from the insurance than rent." We're quiet for a while. Then Sara says, "Willie, if you want to see how far people will go to drive someone out of their homes, just look at what's happening in the Middle East."

I half listen to Sara while she's on her tangent about Beirut and refugees and whatever. I get that she's into international affairs, and it's kind of cute, but I'm about local events. You know, my own life. Ask me if I don't wish it was our landlord who done sent some crackhead to burn up our apartment. I wanted to trade secrets with Sara, but this makes my skin feel like it wants to crawl off my bones.

Then Sara mentions Puerto Rico, and my head comes back from Brooklyn to the Bronx. "Say that again—Puerto Rico."

"I said that on some level, the situations in Puerto Rico and Palestine are similar, right?"

"Right." What situation in Puerto Rico? I didn't know Puerto Rico had a situation.

"They're both colonies in a way. There are even Palestinians in Puerto Rico. Willie, are you listening to me?"

"Yeah, bring me that article, and let me ask you something."

She hesitates. "Sure. Anything. What do you want to know?"

"About you?" I lower my voice and pause for maximum rap appeal. "Everything."

The long silence at the end of the phone makes me smile. I imagine Sara as if she's right in front of me, her eyelashes fluttering while she giggles behind her hand. "Willie . . ." Finally, she says, "My mom's home, so I gotta go."

My heart sinks. "OK. See you tomorrow at work."

"Bye."

"Bye."

I hang up the telephone. I change out of my cutoffs into my track pants, grab the roll of linoleum and my boom box from my closet, and head up to the roof to practice my routine for the competition at the Roxy.

Sometimes my dreams are so vivid I believe they're real, only to wake up to my disappointing life. Other times I think I'm dreaming to awaken to Sara stroking my hair while I nap with my head in her lap by the pool. I finally finished this routine and have been practicing it for the past three days. Each time I do it, I feel like I'm waking into my dreams of dancing around the world as a member of the Rock Steady

Crew. That dream no longer seems somewhere out there but at my fingertips.

I used to think about all the girls who would be screaming my name, imagining that my crush of the moment—Kelly from *Charlie's Angels* or Phoebe Cates—was there and I'd choose her to become my girlfriend. That movie in my mind has changed, too. Now I only imagine Sara there, cheering me on and proudly telling all the girls that I'm her boyfriend. That dream feels within reach, too. By the time my birthday comes, it'll be official, and Sara will be by my side when I rock that competition.

But first things first. I have to nail this swipe-to-windmill transition. It's the one combination that I know Hazardiss can never do.

SMILES

The weather said a high chance of rain, so Barbara made us stay in. Nike, Cookie, and I teach Sara how to play spades. Of course, Nike sticks me with Cookie as a partner. "Don't get your hopes up, mami," he tells Sara, " 'cause we ain't ever going to beat these two."

"What you tryin' to say?" I ask. "You calling us cheaters?"

"Stop diggin' your bony-ass elbows in my side, yo." Nike slides to the edge of the bench. "I meant it as a compliment, geez! Everybody knows Black people throw down when it comes to spades."

Qusay warned us to question all stereotypes, but especially those presented as flattery. "That's stupid," I say. "And Cookie's not Black."

"How you figure?" says Cookie. "Puerto Ricans come from three races—"

"And one of 'em is African," says Nike, interrupting her. He eyeballs me, and knowing Nike, he's more worried about looking ignorant in front of Sara than considering that maybe what he had said was racist.

Then Cookie plays him. "Africa is a continent, Willie. That's like saying North Americans or Antarcticans."

"You know what I mean, and for the record, we *do* say North Americans."

"Not as a race, doofus."

"Who you calling a doofus, acheface?"

"Will you both please stop?" says Sara as she turns up the volume on Nike's boom box. "I can't hear the news."

Secretary of State Shultz continues to urge the Israeli government to withdraw its troops from Beirut in an effort to compel Syria to agree to the peace agreement brokered in May.

"Yo, we should just blow all those A-rabs off the map already," Nike says. Then he asks Sara, "How many books you've got, Princess?"

Sara says, "What are you talking about?"

"There are thirteen possible books, four cards apiece—"

"No, not that. What you just said about Arabs. Why would you say something like that?"

"'Cause it's true." Nike shrugs. "The U.S. should just bomb all our enemies and be done with 'em. The Communists, the Muslims—"

"Not all Arabs are Muslim, ignorant!" yells Cookie.

"And not all Muslim are Arabs, never mind the enemy," I say. "You know my uncle Naim is Muslim."

Sara's eyes open wide. "Really, Smiles?"

Nike's face betrays his thoughts. *First time he agrees with Cookie the Crab and it's against me and in front of Sara.* "First of all, your uncle's name is Nathan."

"Not anymore." Nike knows this, too, so I don't know why he's playing the role. "He legally changed it."

Nike slams his cards on the table. "Which brings me to number two. He only changed his name because he converted to that stupid religion. Number three—"

I slap down my cards. "I don't know a whole lot about Islam or what's going on over there in the Middle East, but let me tell you something." I stand up. "My uncle fought in Vietnam. He put his life on the line to spread democracy for a country that doesn't practice what it preaches. When he came back all strung out after doing the white devil's handiwork, the government turned its back on him. Muslims saved my uncle's life. They helped him survive prison, got him off the dope, and found him a job and an apartment when he got out of Sing Sing." I'm one wrong word away from housing Nike, homeboy or no homeboy.

"Yo, take a chill pill, B. The Muslims in Iran and Libya and Lebanon or wherever aren't the same, OK?" Nike says. "Those Nation of Islam cats are some Malcolm X Muslims. I mean, they're way out, too, but at least they're trying to help people."

"So long they're not Caucasian," says Cookie.

"Shut up, Cookie," I say. "You don't know what you're talking about."

"Don't tell me to shut up!"

"Look, Smiles, no disrespect. Your uncle's a patriot. And Muslim or not, he's an American who served his country. But that lunatic who drove the truck into the U.S. embassy a few months ago and killed sixty-three people? Those crazy Muslims are Arabs, and they're our enemies, and we should just get rid of 'em, no ifs, ands, or buts about it."

"Half the people killed in that suicide bombing were actually Lebanese employees of the embassy," Sara says. "Do you actually know any Arabs, Willie?"

Nike sucks his teeth. "Hell no! Don't want to neither. The lot of 'em can kiss my American ass. We should nuke the Russians, too."

"That's stupid." Cookie says, "How would you like it if people judged all Catholics because of the Crusades? Or because of the part we played in slavery?"

"*We* didn't do squat," says Nike. "And that was back in the Middle Ages, when people still thought the world was flat. If Arabs think it's copacetic to blow up things in 1983 over some beef that happened a thousand years ago, then let them kill themselves and each other." Nike plays a card as if to signal that he's done with this conversation. I throw in my card, too. He asks Sara, "What you got, Princess?"

Sara lays down all her cards and shoves them toward the middle of the table. Then she stands up. "I don't feel so well." And then Sara runs out the cafeteria.

"Sara!" Nike jumps up to chase after her.

Cookie grabs his arm. "Nike, don't. Just . . ." Then she calls to Sara and runs after her herself.

"You don't want to get involved in that," I say. "That sounds like girl trouble, if you catch my drift."

Nike still looks concerned, but he eases back into his seat. "I'll buy her a Charleston Chew and catch up with her later. That's what Gloria likes to eat whenever her 'friend' comes."

"Can we not talk about this, please?" I sweep up all the cards into a stack and start to shuffle. "How 'bout I whoop you in a game of spit."

We play a few games, but neither Cookie nor Sara comes back. I actually wish one of them would. The silence between Nike and me is awkward. No trash-talking, no rhyming along with the radio, not even any arguing over who's finer—Daisy from *The Dukes of Hazzard* or Thelma from *Good Times*. Not that he could ever win that one. Even Stevie Wonder could see that Thelma is the finest girl on TV.

The tension between us puts me back on my feet. "I need to take a whiz. Then I'm going to see if there are any sandwiches left. Want one?"

"Bet."

Before I can step into the boys' room, Cookie grabs my arm. "Smiles!"

I shake her off. "Step off already!" When I walk into the bathroom, I catch three Rookies giggling over a *Mad* magazine with that Howdy Doody look-alike dressed like Tootsie on the cover. "Busted!" I yell, and hold out my hand for it. "Fork it over."

"Aw, Smiles, don't be like that."

"Y'all too young for *Mad,* and you know it. Whose magazine is it?"

"He's a Famer," one kid says.

Another says, "And he'll murder us if we don't give it back to him."

"Don't worry about that. *I'll* give it back to him." That and a talking-to about corrupting the Rookies. After I read it myself.

Then crazy-ass Cookie busts into the boys' room. Of course, the Rookies start with the oohing and pointing. One finally starts singing, "Cookie and Smiles sitting in a tree . . ."

"What are you doing?" The kids take advantage and run out of the bathroom, still singing that dumb song. "You're a trip, Cookie. You pull stunts like this, then wonder why people talk about you behind your back."

Cookie's face drops, and for a second I wish I could take back my words. Does she really have no clue what they say about her? Then Cookie juts out her chin and says, "They can talk behind my back all they want, 'cause that means I'm ahead of them. Let 'em gossip about me. I can take it. So long as everyone leaves Sara alone."

"She your girlfriend now? Is that why you're jumping on Nike's case? He stole her from you." I laugh, but my joke doesn't seem funny, even to me. Instead I feel these pangs of guilt. What's going on here?

Cookie bends down to look under the stalls. The girl's certifiable, and I'm calling Bellevue. Once she's sure we're alone, she says, "Can you keep a secret?"

"No. The second you finish, I'ma run out of here and announce it over the PA." Of course, I wouldn't do that, and Cookie knows it.

"Why you gotta be so sarcastic?"

"Why you gotta be so annoying?"

"Nike needs to lay off the prejudice."

"What prejudice?"

"All the bomb-the-Arabs talk."

"What do you care?"

Cookie runs to the bathroom door to make sure no one is coming and then returns. "Sara is Palestinian, and she doesn't want anyone to know." The second it comes out her mouth, the guilt spreads across Cookie's face like a rash. "Smiles, you have to swear not to tell anyone. The only reason I even told you is because Sara really likes Nike."

"He likes her, too," I say, still confused by what she just told me.

"But the doofus just assumed that Sara's Puerto Rican. She's afraid that if he finds out she's not—let alone Arab— he's not going to like her anymore."

That's bogus, but it dawns on me that for someone who prides himself on being such a playboy, Nike has never even gone out with a Black girl. And all his celebrity crushes are white. "So she lied when she said she goes to some Catholic school in Queens."

"No!" Cookie sounds as if I just called *her* a liar. "She never said Saint Demetrios was a Catholic school. Again, y'all be assuming. It's a Greek Orthodox school."

Now I'm more confused than ever. "Why's an Arab going to a Greek school?" I'm behind on my homework.

"Shhh!" Cookie checks over her shoulder. She wants to close the bathroom door, but Barb doesn't allow it. "Why you have to be so loud?"

"That's the pot calling the kettle black."

"Think of it like this. Sara is a minority within a minority within a minority, OK? And she never meant to lie about anything." Cookie puts her fists on her hips. "People make assumptions and say ignorant comments like *somebody* I know."

"Hey, he didn't know." Why am I defending him? Nike's always saying dumb stuff, and usually I get the brunt of it.

"So what, Smiles? That's no excuse. He wouldn't like it if somebody said all Puerto Ricans are on welfare or in gangs."

No, he wouldn't. Especially that welfare thing. Nike'd fly someone's head over that one. "What do you expect, Cookie? Nike's just being Nike."

"Nike is not Nike." Here she goes with the finger wagging and neck rolling. "Nike is Willie. Willie is pretending to be Nike—"

"OK, OK, OK! Damn, Cookie, why you gotta run everything into the ground?" I throw my hands up. "What you expect me to do? How am I supposed to make Nike chill out without warning him that he's blowing it with Sara?"

Cookie's mouth drops open. "For serious, Smiles? Nike is such a dog, he makes a Rottweiler look like a Chihuahua! Honest guys don't two-time every girl they meet."

"Hey, Nike has never told any girl that she's the only one he's rapping to. You girls be assuming, too. Until he asks someone out, she shouldn't believe that they're going steady."

Cookie flaps her hands against her thighs in despair. "What's the big deal, Smiles? I'm not asking you to hide it forever. Believe me, I've been getting on Sara's case to tell Nike the truth. If you're really his friend, you'll keep him from making a complete ass of himself, 'cause you know he really likes her."

"He does go too far sometimes," I admit. And be impossible to talk to. I was dreading going to Port Morris High, our zoned school. I was supposed to go to Cardinal Hayes or Fordham Prep, but Mama's illness ruled that out. Her social worker's salary covered my tuition at Saint Aloysius, but not only was high school far more expensive, sickle cell saw to it that she worked less yet paid more in medical bills. I had taken the test for the specialized high schools like the Bronx

High School of Science and Stuyvesant in Battery Park City but missed getting into one by a handful of points. Having already graduated from the eighth grade, I was too late for programs like A Better Chance and Prep for Prep.

Nike swore Port Morris would be OK so long as we stuck together and backed each other up. *It'll just be like on the block. We manage, right?* He made me make a pact. *You can't make me go there alone, B.*

Nike was right that Port Morris wasn't that bad. The problem was that it wasn't good either. Even though I was in the honors program and he was in regular classes, we stuck close and avoided the chaos, but it wasn't enough. I knew that every day I entered that building, I did so at my own risk because no place was safe. If a drug gang didn't catch me with a knife in the stairwell, a prejudiced teacher with an outdated textbook would get me in the classroom. Nike and I had some laughs during lunch or in gym, but it did nothing to shake the feeling that I was just choosing my poison.

Then one day I ran into Cookie in the train station, and I realized that I never saw her at Port Morris. She told me that she was using a play cousin's address so she could commute to Kennedy High School in Riverdale instead. Over the winter recess, I worked up the courage to ask my parents' permission to do the same, except I wanted to transfer to De-Witt Clinton. That sparked a big discussion because neither liked the idea of lying about my address to get out of going to my neighborhood school. I finally confessed how bad things were at Port Morris—gangs, drugs, worse—and that I was afraid to keep going there. That heated conversation in my living room with my own parents might have been my first hand at debate. *It's all boys, and James Baldwin, Ralph Lauren, Stan Lee, and a whole bunch of other famous people have graduated from there.* The only question I didn't answer is when Mama asked me why I didn't tell them sooner.

And I had an answer, which was that I could never figure out when is the best time to break your parents' hearts. Do I wake up Pop when he needs to sleep so he can work the twelve-to-eight running a subway train that's dirtier and more dangerous than my school? Do I tell Mama when she's healthy and make her worry away her gratefulness, or do I lay it on her in the midst of another crisis since she's already suffering? When is the right time to make your parents feel like no matter how hard they work, no matter how much they care, no matter how much you understand that they're doing the best they can, it's not enough? Instead, I said nothing.

Mama still responded. She contacted my principal and demanded a meeting. The principal talked to my teachers. My teachers gave me additional tests that nobody else had to take. People from schools I'd never heard of—some as far away as Vermont—were calling and visiting the apartment, and Mama had me writing essays, getting recommendations, and going on interviews as if I were applying to college instead of transferring between high schools. Pop hated the idea of boarding school from jump street. Said I'll *be damned if I send my only son hundreds of miles away to be raised to be saditty!* Mama pushed back. *Keep an open mind, Derrick.* Despite Pop's attempt to draw that line, getting me into a prestigious high school was Mama's project. *Let's see all the options we have and then decide what's best for Ray-Ray.* Before the recruiter from Dawkins visited, Mama was fixed on Loyola, it being a Catholic school and all. Then came Russell. He souped up Mama for real. Told her he grew up in University Heights, which makes our neighborhood look like the Magic Garden. Once he graduated from Dawkins, he went on to Princeton, and that was all Mama needed to hear. No other school existed after that. The fact that Dawkins was an all-boys day school in Manhattan—no girls, no dorm, no trek to Massachusetts or New Hampshire—was the icing on the cake. Both my parents were sold.

I was glad, too. Even though I didn't admit it, the thought of attending a school out of state scared me more than staying at my zoned high school. Maybe dealers and addicts surrounded the school, but at least I knew how to handle them. If there were hoods in the school, I had Nike and other guys for backup. Booby, Flex, Javi, and Pooh aren't my ace coom booms, but push come to shove, I could count on them, too. I could make friends and avoid trouble here, but what if none of those rich white kids at Andover or Exeter wanted to make friends with me? Or what if they did, and I couldn't afford to do the things they do for fun? Could I even have fun, or would I have to miss out on everything to study 24-7 to keep my scholarship? What if there were no Black or even Hispanic girls? What if none of the white girls liked me? Or worse . . . what if they did? Then Dawkins came through with a full scholarship. I thought I had the best of both worlds. A great school where I was Raymond by day, and a hip neighborhood where I was Smiley Smiles by night.

But I didn't tell Nike until Labor Day of sophomore year that I was transferring out of Port Morris. Between my adjusting to the commute and workload and his holding a grudge because I broke our pact, we barely spoke my first year at Dawkins. Nike came back around when Mama passed, but things have never been the same between us. He ran out of her funeral, and I've never told him what her hematologist now believes really killed her. Those few rounds of spit today are the closest we've been.

"Earth to Raymond," Cookie yells, waving her hand across my face. "Come in, Raymond."

I finally say, "Sara has a week to tell Nike the truth. And you can't tell her I know. You're pressuring me to keep a secret from my homie? You have to keep a secret from yours."

Cookie is excited. "Bet! She begged me not to say anything to you. I'm totally down to let her think I didn't say squat!" She starts to jump up and down, and before I know it, Cookie is throwing her arms around me. "Thank you, Smiles—I owe you!" Then before I can tell her to step off, she kisses me on the cheek and runs out of the bathroom.

I wait a few seconds, praying that no one saw her leave the boys' room. I peek my head outside the door, and when I think the coast is clear, I dash out and back into the cafeteria. Nike is right where I left him, arranging his cards in his hand.

"What'd you do? Fall in? I was about to have Barb call the fire department."

"Hardy har har." I pick up my half of the deck and start to lay out my cards. "Prepare to get dusted."

"I'm so scared." Then he asks, "No more sandwiches?"

I completely forgot. "Yeah, we're out."

Nike shrugs and switches back to BLS on his boom box just as the prerecorded station ID gives way to "The Message."

The second we hear the opening beat, Nike and I bob our heads and yell, *Hooo!* and give each other five. We play cards for the rest of the afternoon, the only words between us the rhymes we trade as they flow from Nike's radio. Funny how the music emphasizes everything that brings us together even as it drowns out all the things that push us apart. If we were listening to an album, after every three minutes of rhythm and truth, we would have to suffer ten seconds of silence and secrets.

Thank God for the mastermix.

NIKE

Girls can be so moody, especially when it's that time of the month. Sara's gotten all grouchy like I did something to her. She barely says two words to me at a time and wriggles away when I try to put an arm around her. I asked if she wanted me to run to the bodega for some aspirin—not Tylenol since some kook is out there poisoning people—or get the hot-water bottle Barb keeps with the first-aid kid. She just told me to leave her alone and slunk off with Cookie somewhere.

"Give her a few days," Smiles said. "When you're not feeling well, you want someone in your face?"

Actually, I *do*. OK, maybe not in my face, but trying to make me feel better. Checking on me from time to time. I let Sara be for the rest of the day but still walk her home from work, 'cause I'm a gentleman, you know. I do all the talking, though, mostly how I think Smiles is getting carried away with all that Black Power talk. When I say, "Talk to you in a

189

bit," Sara doesn't say that she's not going to call me, so I rush home and wait like I always do.

An hour passes—nothing. What am I supposed to do? I can't come within two feet of my sister when she's on the rag if I want to keep my teeth, but Blue Eyes would get really pissed when I tiptoed around her during her period. *Stop acting like I'm a leper!* she'd yell. *It's not some contagious disease.* If I act like it's no big thing, I'm insensitive. If I acknowledge it, I'm invading her privacy and embarrassing her. A dude can't win!

I'd call Sara and tell her I'm sorry for whatever, except I still don't have her number. She says her parents are crazy strict and wouldn't like it if a boy called for her. Maybe one of them is home and she can't call me. Or maybe Sara's taking a nap since she ain't feeling too tough. I'd like to think she'd keep our routine and call me before crashing, even if only for a few minutes. And then I hear my sister laughing on the other side of my door.

Not much else I can do but dance. It's still raining, so I'll have to practice in the hallway outside my apartment. I tell Ma and Glo that I'm expecting a very important phone call, so to come get me.

I'm not out there a half hour when I smell that rancid odor of burned plastic and ancient vomit coming from the stairwell. Frustrated and sweaty, I run back into the apartment before it can overwhelm me. These crackheads are getting bolder and bolder every day, yo.

Gloria's on the floor in front of the TV, yapping on the phone and tying up the line. "Yo, get off the phone! I done told you already. I'm expecting a call."

"Ay, but he's so conceited, especially around his friends," she says while twirling the cord around her finger. "When they're not around, he's all in my face, but let them be there, and he acts like he don't know me."

"Gloria, I said get off the phone!"

"Yeah, that was the bowlegged doofus!" Gloria rolls her eyes as if the other person can see her. "Good thing Sara's not knock-kneed. Otherwise, they'd walk down the street spelling the word OK!"

I storm over to Gloria and snatch the phone out of her hand. Before I can break, I recognize the giggle. "Cookie?"

"You *are* a bowlegged doofus."

"Yo, is Sara mad at me or something?"

"Why don't you ask her yourself?"

"I would if you and my sister weren't monopolizing the line." But Cookie doesn't hear me, because she's whispering to someone. "Cookie!"

"Hi, Willie."

"Sara?" I pick up the phone off the floor and carry it to my room.

Gloria yells, "Don't you stay on there forever, 'cause you ain't the only one who lives here."

"You're not the heir to New York Telephone either," Ma calls through the bathroom door.

I'd tell them both to shut up, but I don't want Sara to hear me go off like that. I slam my door and let that say it all. "Hi."

"Hi."

"Are you at Cookie's?" Cookie lives in the building next to Smiles's. I could be there in five minutes. Three if I run.

191

"No, she's at mine."

"Guess your parents aren't *that* strict."

"They really like Cookie. It took her some time, but she won them over. If not for her, I wouldn't be working at the camp."

"I could win them over, too, if I had a chance." With Cookie there, this phone call is going to be as short as it is late, so I don't have time to mess around. "Sara, why you mad at me?" She doesn't answer. "I'm sorry if you feel I wasn't paying enough attention to you. Sometimes people want to be left alone when they're not feeling well. I hope you're feeling better."

She doesn't say anything. Damn, isn't this hard enough without Cookie sitting there hanging on every word? "Listen, August fifth's my birthday, and I've got something special planned. There's going to be this b-boy battle at the Roxy. You've heard of the Roxy, right?"

"The nightclub . . ." Her words come slowly over some rustling in the background. Cookie's probably pantomiming. ". . . in Manhattan."

"Yeah. Well, on my birthday, I'm going there to celebrate by crushing that battle, and you have to be there, Sara, 'cause you're my good-luck charm." Since Sara doesn't repeat that, I'm positive Cookie has her ear stuck to the other side of the receiver with Krazy Glue. "Think about it. Ever since we started, you know, chilling with each other, I haven't gotten docked, not once." Come to think of it, me and Smiles aren't fighting as much. Vanessa and Junior aren't bothering me anymore. On our last payday, I went back to JD's and got my Sergio Valentes out of layaway. I even saw Booby and Pooh in front of the bodega on my way back home, and one gave me a nod and the other said, *What's up?* With Cookie being nosy, I don't say this to Sara, but it's true. The more time I spend with her, the better my life goes.

Sara says, "I'd like to go, but there's no way I can go out at night, never mind downtown."

I was afraid she was going to say that. "Do you really want to go?" In the past, that would have been the first stop on a guilt trip. I would've told the girl, *Oh, you don't really want to be with me.* But I don't want to play games with Sara. I just need to believe that she means it when she says that she wants to celebrate my birthday.

"More than anything."

"Maybe they'll let you go if you tell them that Cookie's going, too."

"Willie, I don't know. . . ." Her voice trails into some girl-ish whispering. "Hold on. Cookie wants to speak to you."

"Nike Fresh." She never calls me that. Cookie genuinely seems to be on my side.

"Cookie Cee in the place to be."

"My parents aren't gonna let me go downtown either, but bust this. They probably wouldn't mind if I spent the night at Sara's house. If she can convince her parents to let her stay at *my* place . . ."

"Word!" I'm getting excited. If Smiles came, too, it'd be like old times. He won't be too keen about Cookie tagging along, but he'll understand and be down with the plan. Ain't like Sara and I are trying to match them up or anything.

Sara gets back on the phone. "I can't promise you anything, Willie. My parents still might say no to the sleepover, but I'm going to try."

That's all I want, I start to tell her, but Sara's whispering with Cookie again, so I have to wait. I'm forever waiting for this girl, but she's worth it. They start fussing at each other. "Hello! What's going on over there?"

"Cookie told me that I shouldn't agree to risk getting into trouble unless . . ." I see where this is going, and I'm down with it. ". . . unless we're . . . you know . . . going out together."

"You been my girlfriend, Sara." I hope she can hear me grinning. "That's why I invited you."

Cookie feeds her another question. Sara asks, "But am I the only one? Are we just messin' around or going out for real?" She's repeating after Cookie word for word. So cute, because even though Sara's a fly girl, she doesn't talk like one. I like how she's going to the trouble of putting me in check. It shows that she cares as much as I do.

"There's nobody else but you, Princess." Then I rush to add, "G'head and ask Cookie if I would take you to the Roxy if I was interested in rapping to other girls." I wait for her to ask my question. Cookie better tell the truth.

"OK."

"Yeah?"

"Yes."

We hang up, and I look at the flyer for the b-boy competition at the Roxy on my wall. The movie in my mind starts again. I walk in rocking my new Sergios and holding Sara's hand. She looks fly in my Nike Fresh sweatshirt, miniskirt, and belt buckle. All the guys check out my fly girl, but she can't see anybody but me. Hazardiss tries to talk to her, and I'm like, *Step off, B!* He pops shit, I call him out, and when Grand Wizzard Theodore plays "Looking for the Perfect

Beat," we battle. I rock Haz's world, and then the entire Rock Steady Crew wants to try me. I take them all on, burning each and every one of them toys—Crazy Legs, Bam-Bam, Easy J, C-Money, all the way down the line until the whole crowd at the Roxy is cheering me. *Nike, Nike, Nike!* Paco from KTU hands me a giant check for a thousand dollars. Sara runs into my arms and tells me that she loves me, and we kiss like Adrian and Rocky.

I can't wait for my birthday.

SMILES

After work I drop by the storefront and find Qusay, Flex, and this guy named Dougie taping dingy bedsheets to the floor with masking tape. Their presence surprises me. I would've bet that everyone was still headed to the free Diana Ross concert, despite the ugly weather forecast. There are stacks of paint cans, brushes, and rollers in the corner. "Y'all need a hand?" This looks like fun and I'm glad the homies are here instead of Central Park.

"Always," says Qusay. He points to my Saint Aloysius T-shirt. "You may want to change out of that first."

"This?" Barbara would rather everyone wear the T-shirt every day—especially the kids—but she knows better than to make that mandatory. I usually do because I own three now, and it makes getting ready a breeze. "Ain't no big thing." I reach for a roller.

After mixing the off-white paint, Qusay assigns each of us a wall and covers the storefront window with another sheet.

196

As we work, he plays a speech of Clarence 13X's on the boom box. I push the roller to the rhythm of his voice. Glancing around the room, I see we're all in a trance, absorbing his teaching as the walls soak in the paint. We're like a machine, and 13X is our engine.

Fifteen minutes into this flow, Pooh busts through the door carrying a bag from the hardware store. "Why y'all niggas send me to the store if you wasn't gonna wait till I got back?" he asks.

Qusay gives him a stern look. "A quarter in the jar, Parris." The homeboys made a deal with Q. He was stressing us to shed our "slave names" for Arabic ones, but most of the homeboys weren't down with that. I suggested that we call each other by our given names instead of our tags when we were at the school, if nowhere else. Qusay liked that compromise, saying that if we weren't ready to give up our government names, we could at least address each other with the names of men instead of children. The homeboys liked the sound of that, and we all shook on it. Some of us had to relearn each other's names, but the practice is spilling onto the street. The other day I bumped into Booby as I was coming out the corner bodega. He said, *What's up, Raymond?* I was like, *Peace, Mark.* Junior looked at him like, *Who the hell is Mark?* Back at the storefront, we cracked up over it.

"Sorry," says Pooh. He digs into his pocket for a coin and drops it into the jar. Knowing Pooh, he paid the fine with Q's own change and kept the rest.

Flex holds out a hand already splattered in paint. "Give those here," he says, motioning for Pooh's bag. "I can use 'em."

Pooh reaches into the bag and pulls out a pair of gloves. "Word, put those on now, B," he teases as he tosses them to Flex. "You know ain't no white boys allowed in here." We all laugh as he tosses another pair of gloves to Dougie. Then he looks at me and gets hyped. "What you doing here?"

"Same thing you are," I say, holding out my hand for my gloves.

"Thought you worked for that white woman at the camp." On no planet is Barb white, but I'm not getting into this with Pooh. He's just mad because she never gave him a job. Barb favored Cookie over me when it came to the promotion, but she still hires plenty of Black kids. Truth is I wouldn't hire Pooh either. Pooh turns to Qusay. "For real, Q? I thought you said this place was for the *real* homeboys."

Here comes that BS again about my not being down because I don't run the streets robbing and stealing. I look to Q for backup. He says, "This place is for all Gods, and the universal parliaments are for everyone, Gods and Earths alike." I sigh inside. But then he says, "We should appreciate Brother Raymond for his support. It's not like he has to volunteer his time here."

"Volunteer?" Pooh and Dougie burst out laughing while Flex looks down at his tattered Pro-Keds. He must've dragged them out the closet to come paint. "What's so funny?"

Qusay says, "Join me outside, brother."

Pooh snatches the paint roller out of my hand. "Sayonara, sucka."

"Parris!" Qusay opens the front door and motions for me to follow him. "Raymond . . ."

As I step outside, Flex mumbles to Pooh to chill out. Qusay

waits for the door to close, and déjà vu kicks me in the gut. "Raymond, I'm humbled that a young man such as yourself wants to be a part of the academy. But this first initiative isn't for a brother like you."

"What do you mean, a brother like me?" I ask. This I got to hear. "What's wrong with a brother like me?"

"Nothing." Qusay flashes me a smile. At least Barb didn't grin at me like a jack-o'-lantern when she dissed me. "The Bridge is for young Black men who need opportunities because they lack what you have." Qusay recites them as he counts them off on his paint-speckled fingers. "You already have a job . . ."

"I can quit." For this I would. There is more for me to do here than at Saint Aloysius.

"You attend a very good school . . ."

I laugh and say, "You mean that white man's institution?" How can Qusay preach that the Five Percenters are obligated to enlighten the masses and then fault me for getting the best education I can? You'd think that my going to Dawkins but still wanting to be down with the program literally in my own neighborhood would be a good thing.

"You have a father at home," says Qusay. "And Derrick is a good man at that."

Out of respect for my father, I won't argue with the truth, but I'm getting heated. So I can't work for the Bridge because my father isn't in jail and doesn't abuse drugs or liquor or have a bunch of his-and-her kids all over the place that he can't afford? Pop himself would snap all over Qusay if he could hear this. Nothing sets him off quicker than a Black man who expects a pat on his back for doing what he should.

My silence has Qusay thinking he's making headway with me. "I'm sorry, Raymond. Of course there's always a place for you here at the academy. But according to the conditions of my grant, I can't enroll you in the Bridge."

"That I knew, but—"

"And if I'm going to stay on mission, my first employee has to be one of them." Qusay motions toward the homeboys and stops to take a deep breath. "I've decided to hire Mark first."

I throw open the door and head back into the storefront. Dougie, Flex, and Pooh stop painting to watch me march to Q's desk. I grab the flyer that I've been posting all over the neighborhood since he got that grant for the Bridge using the proposal I done vicked Barb for him. "All it says here is that you have to be Black and between the ages of fourteen and twenty-one and live within one of these three zip codes to be in the program." I hit the mimeograph of Qusay's own handwriting harder with every tap. "But in order for you to pay me for what I've been doing all this time for free, you're telling me I have to be unemployed, go to a wack school, and have a no-account for a daddy?" Outside, a boom of thunder emphasizes my disbelief.

Qusay raises his palms. "Raymond, please lower your voice. Let's speak brotherly to each other, God to God."

"But you're the only one playing God, Q!" I say. "I helped you create this program." It didn't end with the proposal or the name of the school. I came up with the name of the program, too. Q wanted to cast a wide net while recruiting and enroll fifty cats in the pilot, but using what Barb taught me, I convinced him to start small and go deep.

But I don't repeat what Qusay already knows. Instead I

ask, "Q, if it's a skill-building program, how are you going to hold it against me that I work?"

"We work too, nigga!" yells Pooh.

Qusay barks at him, "Please!" He turns back to me. "This isn't an employment project. It's an entrepreneurship program, one specifically for young brothers in the underground economy, G. Its mission is to take young Black men who are involved in any kind of organized criminal activity and show them how the skills they use on the street can be transferred into a legitimate business. Take Pooh."

"Nah, you keep Pooh." Flex and Dougie laugh. Pooh flips me the bird and then goes back to painting.

"We're all family here, so let's not mince words." Qusay points to Pooh. "He's Junior's biggest seller. He'll use that same salesmanship to sell something that actually benefits the community. All he needs is a structured, guided way to figure out what that something is. Flex? He's Don Silvio's best numbers runner. Keeping all those figures straight without writing them down is a gift. There's no reason why Flex couldn't go into business for himself as an accountant or bookkeeper and make himself an honest living. He'd have to get his GED, at least, but that's one of the requirements since—"

"And Dougie?" I interrupt. Homeboy's just a petty thief who does it for the thrill. When he's not chain-snatching, he boosts penny candy from Woolworth's even when he has the money to pay.

"You heard he got arrested last week for taking a joyride in another man's Coupe de Ville?" says Qusay. "Well, that's another criterion of the program. All those brothers here have been involved in the criminal justice system in the past year. Raymond, you've never seen the inside of the precinct."

"No," I bark. "Am I supposed to be embarrassed by that?"

"Not at all! You should be quite proud of all you have and do," says Qusay. "But that just goes to show you, Raymond, that you don't need the Bridge. You're well on your way to making something of yourself. The program is geared toward your brothers like Doug, Parris, and Frederick, for whom this could be the difference between a life behind bars or death on these streets and being a law-abiding contributor to this community."

And crazy as it sounds, this just makes me want to work here even more. You'd think Qusay would want me around to be a role model. A poor righteous teacher. Part of the program is to help these guys get their diplomas or GEDs, and I could tutor them. I had to ace an interview as the last step to get into Dawkins, so I could show Pooh and the fellas how to handle a job interview or impress someone at a bank to get a business loan. In exchange for sharing what I already know about how to make something of myself, I could learn how to start my own business or organization. I stop myself, though, from giving Q any more ideas that I won't benefit from.

And I already know what Qusay'll say. He's going to blame the conditions of his grant, just like Barb blamed the cuts to her budget. He'll say that if he doesn't stick to what he promised to deliver in his proposal, they won't fund the Bridge. That I'm taking a job away from Booby when I already have one. That it would be my fault if Pooh ended up in Sing Sing or, worse, dead.

Isn't that some bullshit? First time something positive is

going down in the neighborhood, and I'm *too good for it.* Doing everything that I'm supposed to only to get dissed and dismissed. The resources, the experiences, the opportunities, they're never there for someone like me. Only the damn rules and expectations from both sides of the color line.

And here I go, getting all misty-eyed like some punk. I wipe my hands across my face and make for the door. Qusay puts his hand on my shoulder, trying to stop me. "Raymond, don't leave this way," he says. Then he mutters under his breath, "First that girl, now this."

"What?" That stops me in my tracks. "What girl?"

At first Qusay chuckles as if he's embarrassed. "Never mind. I just had to explain to a young Earth why the program was only for boys. Let's just say her reaction was less than ladylike."

"You ain't know, Q?" says Pooh. "That Puerto Rican girl with the mouth on her is Smiles's girlfriend. Surprise, surprise."

"Your homegirl came in here talking a mile a minute about an idea she had about teaching these hoes out here about self-respect, women's empowerment, and all that jazz," says Flex. "Q was real nice. You know how he is. *Oh, sister, I'm sorry, but we first have to address the Black man's crisis, and then we'll reach out to the young Earths in the community.*" The homeboys and even Qusay laugh at Flex's dead-on imitation. "Man, ya girl was livid, screaming about sexism, discrimination, the whole nine. And when Q tried to break down how the young Black male was endangered, she told him to step off."

Flex, the fellas, and even Q just crack on up, and that's

when I break out with no good-byes. I'm halfway home when thunderclouds overcome the sky, rip open and drench the street, bringing the heat wave to an end. People who live close race for cover while other run and wait under store awnings. I storm alone through the downpour, but I can't cool down. Knowing that Qusay also dissed Cookie is no consolation. In fact, it makes it all that much worse. Like Nana would say, *Sorry fi mawga daag, dem tun roun bite you.*

NIKE

"Willie, get off the phone, dammit!"

Heat rages across my face. "I'm sorry, Sara, can you hold on a minute?" Before she can answer, I drop the receiver on my bed, throw open my door, and barge into the living room. "Why you got to be screamin' at me like that when I'm talking to somebody on the phone?" Outside, thunder claps like it has my side.

My mother grabs a handful of Chee-tos from the bowl on her lap and stuffs her face. "You don't want to look bad in front of your girlfriend of the month, get off the phone. It's been an hour, and you don't pay the bill. I'm not telling you anymore."

I storm back into my room, and it takes my all to not slam the door. If Sara weren't still on the line, I'd tear it off its hinges like the Incredible Hulk. I take a few breaths and then pick up the receiver. "Look, Princess, I got to go."

"Yeah, I do, too. I'll see you tomorrow. Bye."

205

"Remember to save the overtime for me."

"Willie." I wait until I hear the dial tone and then crash the receiver into the base. I fling open my door and charge into the living room, but my mother's not there. The water in the kitchen runs as she washes the dishes as the rain beats against the windows.

I change the channel on the TV and throw myself on the couch. I swing my feet onto the coffee table for good measure. Two can play this game. *Neither heat wave, thunder showers, nor winds stopped pop legend Diana Ross from performing a free concert for almost half a million fans in Central Park.*

When my mother comes back into the living room, she scoffs and knots her arms across her chest. "Oh, really?" she cracks. Then Ma walks in front of the TV to block my view.

"Move."

She doesn't budge. "You don't own the TV, Willie." She sounds pathetic.

"Neither do you." I could have stopped right there, but she started it. "Wilfredo does."

Her face turns red. She comes toward me until she is hovering like one of those thunderclouds outside. Wagging her finger at me, she says, "No te ponga fresco conmigo, Guillermo . . ."

"How am I being fresh when I'm just telling the truth?" I tilt my head so I can see the TV screen. "It's called AFDC. Aid to Families with Dependent Children. Wilfredo bought the TV for Gloria and me, and now's my turn to watch it." My mother stands there, breathing hard over me. I sense the dramatics coming on, but why should I sit through this performance again? "As the only man in this house—and the only one with a damn job—I deserve a night in peace, so move."

Ma's heaves grow stronger. I scoot across the sofa, pretending to be into *Magnum, P.I.,* and watch her clenched fist from the corner of my eye. My mother finally says in a low, even voice, "You think because you buy a carton of milk here and a box of cereal there you're the man of the house? If you're such a man, Willie, why don't you move out on your own?"

I've heard that shit before. "Trust me, I will when I'm good and ready," I say, avoiding her angry stare. " 'Sides, my being here gets you a bigger check."

"Not more than what you eat," my mother cracks. "You're not doing Gloria and me any favors."

"I shouldn't have to do diddly-squat 'cause I'm your kid."

"So now you're a kid. . . ."

"You know what I'm sayin'. You the mother!" I jump to my feet, the coffee table scraping across the floor. "You're supposed to get a job and take care of us."

Gloria walks into the living room. "I heard my name."

"I do take care of you! I've been taking care of you." My mother claps on *been* so close to my face that my ears ring. "I got a job!" The thunder outside mimics her and I almost want to fight Mother Nature, too.

"Doing what?"

"Being your mother!"

Gloria whispers, "Guys, stop. C'mon. Please."

My mother turns to her and says, "Bring the Monopoly game." Gloria wrinkles her nose in confusion as she heads for the bedroom. "How much you make at your summer job, Willie?"

"Not enough, but at least I'm working." With minimum wage now three thirty-five an hour, I make two hundred thirty-five dollars every two weeks, but I only take home a hundred and fifty-five. I mean, when they're not docking me for some wack reason. Plus the feds nab almost fifty-four dollars, and the state snatches up sixteen more. And I'm a minor, so why do I have to cough up another ten damn bucks in Social Security?

Gloria returns with Monopoly and hands the tattered box to my mother. Ma slaps the box against the plastic on the sofa, rips open the cover, and flings it aside. She grabs the play money and counts off a stack of tens, twenties, and fifties. "Again with this?"

"You afraid to know the truth?"

"No." I swipe the money and count it. Six hundred and seventy dollars. "Welfare gives you almost seven hundred dollars a month?" Man, I actually thought it was a lot more. Even so, she still gets way more than I do, and I have a full-time job.

"You think this covers everything we need? First thing we have to do is pay rent. Give me two hundred dollars."

She reaches for the stack in my hand, but I yank it out of reach. "You don't pay no two hundred dollars in rent," I say. "Section 8 pays most of it." Busted and disgusted, can't be trusted. Just because I hate welfare doesn't mean I don't understand how the damn thing works.

Through her teeth, Ma says, "The program only pays seventy percent of the rent. I have to pay the remaining thirty. Give me sixty dollars."

I'm no math whiz, but I know that fifty percent means half, and half of two hundred is one hundred. Since she didn't try to be slick and say she had to pay more than that, I peel off three twenties and toss it on the coffee table instead of handing it to her.

Gloria raises her hand like she's Horshack in class. "I'll be the bank!" I roll my eyes as my sister scampers to kneel by the coffee table and straightens out the twenties.

"That doesn't cover utilities. Gas and electric are another ninety-two dollars." My mother motions for me to subtract the money. I count out another four twenties and a ten. "And thanks to the both of you, the telephone bill is another fifty dollars."

I give my sister a dirty look. "I ain't going to argue with you about that one." Gloria sucks her teeth at me as she snatches the bills and lays them across the table. "You still have almost five hundred dollars."

"No one's eaten yet, and nobody eats more than you."

"So break out the cupones then." I don't have to ask her how much she gets, because I know this by heart, too. "Every month you get three hundred and forty dollars in food stamps, so don't try it."

"How far do you think that money goes? For three almost-grown people, not far. Unless you want to eat bony chicken and fatty meat."

"Ew," says Who Else.

"Look me in the eye, Willie, and tell me that I buy that cheap meat for you." I'm not stupid. If I say that, she'll buy that nasty stuff to spite me. When I don't answer, Ma adds, "And all that canned and packaged food that you like so much. Campbell's soup, Chef Boyardee, Hungry-Man dinners . . . The way you eat that stuff is the way that stuff eats through the cupones. To buy you those things, I have to take another two hundred dollars out of the money we get under ADFC." Ma slides four fifties out my fist and hands them to Gloria. "And you know what else? I can't use food stamps to buy all the other things we need to get from the supermarket."

"Like what?"

"Toothpaste, soap, shampoo and conditioner . . ."

Gloria puts her two cents in. "Toilet paper!"

"Paper towels, batteries, lightbulbs, your shaving cream . . ."

"Kotex . . ."

"Gloria, shut up."

Ma reaches for two more fifties, but I yell, "Hold up! Another hundred dollars? Just for toilet paper?"

"Yes! This is for everything I need to keep this place clean. Palmolive to wash the dishes, Brillo pads to scrub the pots and pans, Mop & Glo to clean the floor . . ." Ma returns the fifties to the Gloria's "bank," so the welfare stack is down to one hundred seventy bucks. "Now let's talk about clothes."

Now she's really trying it. "I buy my own clothes."

"You spend all your money on your trendy jeans and sneakers, but who buys your socks and underwear?" She takes me off guard with that one and snatches a fifty out of my hand. "If it weren't for me, you'd be running around with dingy calzoncillos under all those brand-name clothes."

"¡Ay, fo!" Gloria says while pinching her nose. "And perpetrating a fraud."

"Yo. Shut. Up."

"And fifty dollars per month for the both of you is conservative, especially during the winter. You of all people know good shoes aren't cheap. And let's not forget the cost of doing the laundry each month."

Gloria pops up and yanks money out my hand. "That's another fifty."

I only have three green twenties and a yellow ten left. I make a fan out of them and wave them in front of my mother's face. "You still got seventy dollars."

"That's gone before the month is halfway over," she says.

"How you figure?"

Ma snatches one of the twenties. *"Mami, I need supplies for a school project."* She grabs another. *"Mami, I want McDonald's tonight."* She snatches another. *"Ma, can you lend me five dollars so I can go to the movies with Smiles? I'll pay you back.* Which you never do. *Ma, I neeeeed to have that tape, but I'm short two bucks."* She grabs the ten. *"I need, I want, I want, I need . . .* It's endless. But let me ask you to buy a few loosies while you're at the bodega, and you humiliate me in front of the entire neighborhood. You want to talk about embarrassment."

"I'm supposed to pay you back for little things here and there?" I say. "And what's wrong with wanting to eat lean steaks and wear nice clothes? You don't like bony chicken and welfare cheese either." I really wanted to go all the way off and tell her that only girls can buy cheap clothes and still look good. When we first moved to this block, my mother wasn't the one getting made fun of for wearing Woolworth sneakers and Korvette jeans. "Ever since you told me that if I wanted to wear Lee jeans and Nike sneakers, I had to buy them for myself, that's exactly what I've been doing. I do legit work when I could be robbin', stealin', slingin'. . . ."

211

"So what you're telling me, Willie, is you want to be paid better for doing the right thing. Guess what? We all do." My mother's voice breaks. "I can't win. If I let someone out there pay me to do what I do here for nothing—not even appreciation or respect—I'm a bad mother for leaving my kids alone or letting someone else watch them. But if I take care of my own home and raise my own kids, I'm a bad mother because I collect welfare and food stamps. Bad enough I'm judged by strangers who have no clue how much more month there is than money, but I have to take this shit from my own son!" Ma tosses the bills in her hand in the air and runs out of the living room.

After a moment of stunned silence, outside our window lightning crackles and thunder booms. Gloria and I drop to the floor to scoop up the scattered bills. At one point, though, I say, "This is stupid. It's not like it's real." I throw the bills I'm clutching back into the game box on the sofa. I wait for Gloria to say that I'm the one who's stupid for making Ma cry like that. Instead she stands up, walks into the kitchen, and finishes doing the dishes. I go back to watching *Magnum, P.I.,* but I have no idea what's going on.

SMILES

We take the Champs to the pool at Crotona Park, only to find out that it's closed for emergency maintenance. This budget crisis is bogus. How does the city let the biggest pool in the Bronx fall apart? I bet the ones on Twenty-Third or Seventy-Seventh Streets never have problems.

"Let's just wait a little," I suggest to Big Lou. "Maybe they'll fix it fast, and we won't have come all the way here for nothing."

"That's a good idea," says Cookie. "I mean, it's a nice day, and this is a huge park. Not like the kids can't play until we know if they're letting anybody in today." So we stay in the park for about an hour, and the kids are having a blast.

Then things get dicey. Another day camp from a nearby community center is having a field day, and we challenge them to some friendly competition. It's all harmless fun until the Champs lose to them at tug-of-war and Stevie starts popping mess. A little trash-talking is no big deal, but now he's cracking welfare jokes, which, of course, POs Nike.

213

"How you know they's on welfare?" he says, flicking Stevie's ear. "They're wearing camp shirts and cutoff jeans just like you, dummy!"

Stevie grabs his ear and backs out of Nike's reach. " 'Cause they go to public school, moron! If they had money, they'd go to Catholic school and camp like us. That's how you know their parents don't work."

"Stevie, you're so ignorant!" yells Cookie. "How you're going to assume they go to public school or their parents didn't work? Just because their camp isn't run by a church? Stop it." She apologizes to the counselors of the other camp, and we whisk away the Champs back to the oak tree we've designated as home base. Those campers just dusted us in tug-of-war. The last thing we want is to go mano a mano with them.

"We need to burn off some of their energy," says Nike. "Let's march their butts over to the lake."

"For what?" Cookie and I say in unison.

"Because."

Cookie says, "Have you been to the lake lately, Nike? It's full of reeds up to here." She flings her hand over her head. "God knows what else is in there."

"Not to go *in* the lake, dummy. On that side of the park there's a playground with sprinklers."

"OK, true, but . . ." Cookie surveys the park. Thugs to the left, addicts to the right. Walking these kids to the lake would be a live game of Mined-Out. "If the pool isn't open by now, I'm going to tell Big Lou we should just take them back to the church."

And that's what we do. Big Lou tells us to hand out lunch in the school yard and let the kids play until dismissal. They get over their disappointment quickly and dive right into their usual games of ringolevio, hopscotch, and box ball.

"Who wants to play red light, green light?" I say, walking toward the wall. About a dozen kids, including Pedro and Stevie, run behind me. "This crack right here's the starting line." After Stevie explains to Pedro in Spanish how to play, I turn to face the wall. "Red light, green light, one, two, three." I spin around, and all the kids freeze, trying hard to not bust a gut. Most folks would just turn around again, but that's not how I play. I run up to Stevie until we're nose to nose and laugh like Scooby-Doo. He snorts, then keels over cackling. That cracks up Pedro and half the other kids. "Moving violation! All of you, back to the line!"

Pop!

I look around for the knucklehead setting off fireworks in the school yard. This is one thing about this neighborhood that works my last nerve. The Fourth of July starts on July 1 and continues for the entire month.

Pop! Pop!

Another counselor yells, "Yo, those are gunshots!" Everyone screams and runs for cover that doesn't exist.

"Get the kids inside!" I say, running toward the church.

Cookie shouts, "No time! Get everybody down." Sara is hysterical, diving to the ground and screaming as if we were being invaded. The twins are crying, and Cookie yanks them to the concrete and throws herself over them. "Everybody, down now!"

I tackle Pedro and Stevie to the ground, then shield my own head with my arms. My mother's face flashes behind my closed eyes.

Pop! Pop!

Kids and counselors sob as we lie across the hot pavement. I can smell the old bubble gum wedged between the slabs of concrete and feel the sweat on Pedro's back seep through my shirt into my chest.

When I think the gunshots have stopped, I lift my head and peek across my forearm. I catch Nike's feet as he climbs off the ground and runs into the street. I pull myself up to my knees. Pedro and Stevie cling to either side of me, whimpering. "It's over, it's OK, everyone's all right." But I really don't know this. I look around the school yard, praying to see each and every kid and counselor rise off the pavement.

I'm in the middle of a frantic head count when Nike races back into the school yard. "Smiley!" He has blood on his shirt, and his voice trembles. "They shot up Qusay's storefront."

NIKE

They came for Qusay but killed Cutter.

Those savages just opened fire in the street in the middle of the day with kids running through the water gushing from the fire pump, mothers chilling on the stoop with their babies, and the viejos sitting on milk crates and playing capicu in front of the bodega. The Barbarians could've killed so many innocent people.

Word is that Qusay and Cutter were unlocking and raising the security gate to the storefront when Junior's Mustang convertible came tearing around the corner. Booby hopped out the passenger side and fired one shot from a Colt .45 before Qusay ran for cover. The second shot caught Q in the shoulder as he fled into the school, and Junior ordered Booby to go after him. Cutter got in his way. They exchanged words because Cutter wouldn't move so Booby could get to Q. Booby pumped three bullets into Cutter's stomach, fired another shot through the storefront window, jumped back

217

into Junior's Mustang, and fired a few more shots just for the hell of it as they sped off.

That's what everyone's saying, anyways. Just none of it to the cops, lest Junior does another drive-by and opens fire on *their* stoop. They brought Junior to the precinct but couldn't keep him. No one has seen Booby since the whole thing went down. Some folks say he's booked. I'm sure he's dead.

I sit out here on the curb watching an endless stream of folks enter the funeral home. Every time I think it's over, another crowd turns the corner or piles out of a car. Elsie, JD, Moncho, Don Silvio. Black, Rican, Irish, Jewish—everyone shows up to say good-bye to Cutter.

Smiles comes out of the funeral home and lowers himself next to me. "You coming in?"

I shake my head. I've already tried, and say no go. Took one look at that giant poster full of pictures of the old Cutter in the foyer and couldn't stay. Tossing his cap in the air after graduating from Baruch College, feeding his bride wedding cake, helping his son rip off the wrapping of a Big Wheel one Christmas. Then there's the one of our Little League team the year he coached us to the Bronx World Series. Cutter stands right next to me, his hand on my shoulder. After that I can't bring myself to go inside and see him lying pale and stiff in a silk-lined box. "Smiles, what's he wearing?"

I wait for Smiles to read me for asking such a dumb question. Instead he smiles. "They dressed homeboy in a fly burgundy Brooks Brothers suit with gold cuff links and a matching tie clip. And your rosary beads are in his hand."

"Fresh."

A pair of mules wobbles next to me and down plops Cookie.

"I hate these things." She pulls them off her feet and smooths her sailor skirt between her mosquito-bit legs. Cookie gives me the once-over. "Nice suit, Nike. Don't think I've ever seen you in one before."

"Yeah, you have," says Smiles. "Mama's funeral, 'member?"

"I think he booked before I got there."

"Oh, yeah." That old suit is still hanging in my closet. I didn't realize it was the only one I owned until I went looking for something to wear today. I had to ask Ma for the money to buy a new one because it didn't fit. As she went into her purse for the cash, I waited for the lecture. *You remember this the next time you want to mouth off to me about money.* But she didn't do that. Instead, Ma stuffed the bills into my palm and kissed the back of my hand. She and Glo are holding a seat for me inside, with no idea I'm never coming in. Almost nobody's going to see me in this suit either.

"Is Sara coming?" I ask Cookie. I already know the answer. After the shooting, Sara freaked out. She was crying so hard and trembling so bad that walking her home was impossible. I had to hail a gypsy cab for us, and the whole way Sara clung to me in the backseat, sobbing into my chest and gripping my bloody shirt.

Cutter's blood on my shirt.

When I broke from the school yard after the shooting, I saw his body lying on the street. People who weren't running for their own lives were shielding their children and seniors. I didn't know who it was until I was kneeling beside him. Cutter was clutching his stomach, his blood seeping between his fingers.

He reached out for me with his bloody hand. "Willie." Cutter remembered my name, but I wouldn't take his hand.

Instead I said, "Cutter, hold on. We getting help." I yelled over my shoulder, "Somebody call 911!"

"Willie."

"I'm here, Cutter." But I wouldn't take his hand. "I ain't going nowhere till the ambulance comes." But I wouldn't take his hand. "You're going to be OK, Cutter."

"Willie, how you like my threads?"

His suit was a polyester catastrophe. It was cheap but new and clean and even tailored. Booby had torn a huge wet maroon stain in its gut. Cutter was dying in a sports jacket and slacks I wouldn't be caught dead in. "Real fly, Cutter. Straight out of *GQ*."

My crucifix was dangling above his face from the rosary I wear around my neck. Cutter reached for it, and I leaned forward so he could wrap his bloody fingers around it. Then I pulled it over my head, allowing him to clutch it to his chest. But I wouldn't take his hand.

Cookie shakes her head. "She's traumatized by all this."

I nod. "We're used to this madness, but I guess she's never seen anything like this before." Cookie bites her lip and scratches at one of her mosquito bites. "Maybe this is all for the best," I say. "Cutter was going down a bad path. Now he's out of his misery."

"What are you saying?" Smiles says with an edge in his voice. "Cutter was making a comeback. Q was turning him around."

"Who in this fuckin' place—"

"C'mon now, Willie," says Cookie. "Have some respect." She motions to the funeral home as if it were a church.

"My point is nobody here turns around. You don't turn around and stay in this hellhole. You turn when you leave. If you grown and still here, it's because you can't do no better." I turn to Smiles. "That's why you going to Dawkins, right? And that's why you lie about where you live to go to Kennedy, right, Cookie? That's why Sara still trekking all the way to Astoria for school." No one answers, so I continue. "Q might've helped Cutter out, giving him a little money to help around the school and getting him on methadone and all that. But in time something would've caught up to him." The more I talk, the more I believe what I'm saying. "Cutter was bound to relapse or land in jail or get AIDS if he ain't have it already. Booby did him a favor."

"Sometimes, Willie," says Cookie, her eyes brimming with tears, "you're a real asshole."

Smiles says, "Word."

Barb comes out of the funeral home. "Kids, come on inside. The service is about to start." She waits for Cookie and Smiles to get to their feet and cross the sidewalk. When Smiles walks past Barb and into the home, they briefly grasp hands. Then Cookie walks into Barb's arms and breaks down. As Barb holds Cookie, she looks at me, her eyes asking, *Are you OK?*

I turn away. I'm not OK. I'm worried about Sara. I get why she couldn't bring herself to come—God knows I do—but I still wish she had. Maybe if she was here, I could find the strength to go inside and volunteer to be a pallbearer like the other old Little Leaguers. I might have even had the guts to walk up to Cutter's casket and tell him how he looks flyer than ever, thanks for teaching me how to pitch a slider and helping me dodge the Barbarians when they were fixing to jump me at the park, that I hope to become a good-enough man to catch him in heaven seventy years from now, and that I'm so sorry for being an asshole to the very end.

Instead I just stay out here during the service and book the second they open the doors to take Cutter to Saint Raymond's Cemetery.

SMILES

When Cutter's burial ends and everyone else starts to file out of the cemetery, I walk in the opposite direction. "We'll wait for you, Smiles," says Barb, knowing where I'm headed. "And we'll give you a ride."

"Nah, go on. I might be a while." Her grave's probably going to need some freshening up.

Cookie says, "You want me to go with you?"

"No, thanks."

They know not to push, yet I feel their eyes on my back as I make my way across the cemetery.

When I reach my mother's resting place, I find a bundle of fresh pink carnations next to the dried bouquet I left on her birthday. "Hey, Mama." I kiss her tombstone and kneel. "Who brought you these? Pop or Nana?" I lean in for a whiff of the slight aroma of cinnamon.

"So you already know that Pop's union avoided the strike. With the Con Ed workers still out of work, neither side

223

wanted to risk getting the people riled up. Has Mr. Cutter come to see you yet? I'm sure he's making the rounds of his own relatives first and will catch up with you soon. And let him know that I meant what I said at his service. The only memories of him I'll hold on to are the good ones, and I pity the fool who tries to bad-mouth him in front of me. Oh, and Mr. Cutter has probably already forgiven him, but Nike only pops that mess because he feels guilty. Not that it makes it OK, but you know how Nike is, Mama. He be trying it!

"He did get me thinking, though. It could've been someone like Mr. Cutter who gave you HIV. Mr. Cutter himself even. I know, Mama, I know . . . you don't want me thinking like that. I don't know if Mr. Cutter had HIV, and if he did—or any of the other donors, for that matter—it's not like they knew they had it or that they could pass it on through the transfusion. They were only trying to help you, and I shouldn't be angry at them. All this stuff is just coming out now.

"But what I'm mad about, Mama, is the fact that these diseases even exist. All of them. Sickle cell, AIDS, even drug addiction. See, you thought I wouldn't remember, didn't you? How was I going to forget, the way you tanned my hide that day you busted me making fun of Mr. Cutter, imitating the way he be nodding off in the middle of the street. And then a day or so later you sat down and explained to me that substance abuse was a mental illness and that alcoholics and addicts were sick people who needed help and deserved our sympathy, no different than someone like you.

"And then you took me to see *Richard Pryor: Live on the Sunset Strip*. Man, I bragged about it for weeks. *My mother let me see a rated-R movie!* And you know how Cookie is.

She was like, *For serious, Smiles? I wish my mother was cool like that.* And Nike just used that as an excuse to whine about how wack his mother is, that poor lady.

"And I almost performed the whole show for them, imitating Richard, repeating all his stories and telling his jokes. What I didn't tell them is how we went to White Castle afterward and talked real deep about what he was saying beyond the wisecracks. About racism and poverty and addiction.

"So, Mama, I kind of have the feeling that you wouldn't have been too keen on all that time I was spending with Qusay. Not because I was going to buy everything he was saying, hook, line, and sinker. You knew I'm smarter than that. More because Q was going to get me riled up about the way things are for us—even those of us who play by the rules—and you wouldn't want me to get caught up in raging and rebelling when I should be working hard and fitting in and all that.

"But, Mama, you started it. You were the first one that got me thinking about these things. And sometimes—like when things like this happen—it's really overwhelming. Like, real hard, Mama. Especially with Pop working the night shift, Nana being so old-school, and you being gone. Still, Mama, I'm glad you opened my eyes, even if I can't always make sense of what I see or don't know what I can do about it, if anything. But the way you were is why I want to try.

"And I know you don't want to hear this, but I think there's something to Qusay's theories about, you know, the government bringing drugs and disease into the Black community. Calm down, Mama. Let me explain before you start summoning angels to whoop my behind. Do I believe that Ronnie

Reagan's sitting in the White House twiddling his fingers and cackling like a wizard and going, *Bwah, ha, ha, drugs! Shower the inner cities with drugs. More drugs!* No. But I do think that if all these problems were affecting white folks, the government would be pulling out all the stops to help people. That suddenly the money would be there. The jobs, the clinics, the programs, they'd be there. C'mon, Mama, if God hasn't filled you in yet on the reason behind all this madness, you got to wonder.

"But don't worry. I'm not going back to Qusay's school. Not that I don't miss it, but it really isn't the place for me. And I'm going to get through Dawkins like I promised, even though I don't think that's the place for me either. I'll figure it out.

"I just wish you were here to help me. I mean, I know you're the reason I wasn't at the storefront the day Junior drove by and that he's not going to come after me. No matter how bad things get, I don't walk around scared anymore. I know you're with me, guiding me and protecting me. Your only child. The miracle baby the doctors said sickle cell would never let you carry to term.

"Your Ray-Ray of sunshine . . . really, really, really misses you."

I take a few minutes to arrange just right the carnations I brought with me around the ones that are already there.

"Look, Mama, I better go. Barb offered me a ride back, and I'm going to see if I can catch up to her. Otherwise it's going to take me an hour by bus, and I think you would want me to go to Mr. Cutter's wake and have some of Mr. Camacho's pernil for you."

I get back on my feet, kiss my mother's tombstone again, and run across the cemetery to the Balcom Avenue gate, hoping to spot Barb's red Chevette. I wait there, catching my breath, but when no more cars come, I finally leave. That's when I see Barb parked on the street. She spots me and reaches over to unlock the passenger door.

I get in and look around the empty car. Barb explains, "Everyone's already headed over to the restaurant. I told Lou I was waiting for you, so he packed as many people as he could into the station wagon." Barb motions for me to put on my seat belt. There's a fresh box of tissues sitting between us.

As she pulls out of the cemetery and toward the highway, I say, "Y'all still got that gas guzzler?"

Barb laughs. "I keep tellin' my husband to get rid of it, but he refuses." She becomes serious. "Says we'll be happy we kept it when we finally can afford to adopt." Then that sadness comes over her.

I nod. "Yeah, he's probably right." With the budget cuts, the Cuevases are going to have to wait longer.

Barb looks at me. "And I figured maybe you'd want to talk. You know, about whatever. Or not. It's up to you." She pulls onto the highway. As she checks her rearview mirror, Barb asks, "How's Netty?"

I smile. "Mama's good. She says thanks."

Barb hands me a few tissues, then takes one for herself.

The shooting shook her up so much that Sara skipped a few days of camp. "Maybe you should lay low, too," she said.

"You mean Junior? I ain't scared of him." Yes, I am a little, but he the one need to be laying low, right? I can go back to dodging him after my birthday.

You would think the shooting would have brought Sara and me closer, but I sensed her pulling away from me. We still spoke every day on the phone for at least an hour, but I got to worrying that maybe she remembered how I dissed Cutter and was holding it against me.

Then Sara finally came back to work on Wednesday, and gave me the best hug ever. I said, "Does this mean we're still on for my birthday?"

She said yes, of course. But I don't know. I got this sinking feeling. Like I'm going to do something to screw everything up.

"With all that bouncing around, you know who you remind me of?" Smiles asks as we cross the street to Sara's building. "Shorty Rock."

"Yo, I don't want to know nothing more about that kid today, B," I say. The brat kept singing "Happy Birthday" to me, Stevie Wonder–style, all day. I mean, *all* day. When I told him if he didn't knock it off, I would fly his head, Shorty started singing "Feliz Navidad" like he's José Feliciano. Then Sara called him over to play Uno with her and the twins. She saved Shorty Rock's life and my job, and hopefully that's just the beginning of the birthday presents she has for me.

"Is that Polo? Damn, B, what'd you do? Pour the whole bottle over your head?"

"Stop exaggerating. I only used that much." I use my fingers to show him a capful. I don't tell him that Ma gave it to me. She has to be on point at least one day in the year.

When we get to Sara's building, I lean against the door of a mustard-colored Mustang a few yards from her stoop and hit play on our signal song on the boom box. *I want to thank you, heavenly Father, for shining your light on me.* Smiles rolls his eyes, and I'm starting to wish he'd stayed his ass home. "What's your beef now, B? This song's crush."

"It is, but you do realize it's a gospel joint, right?"

"No, it's not."

"Listen to the lyrics, B. It's all *God* this, *heavenly Father* that."

"Because she's thanking God for sending her a good boyfriend."

Smiles cackles. "She's thanking God for sending her Jesus, and she don't mean homeboy who lives on Jackson Avenue above the pawnshop neither."

Ignoring him, I turn up the volume a bit to be sure that Sara can hear it and fix my eyes on her window. I love to catch her peeking through the curtains looking for me. She lives too high up for me to see her face from the street, but I feel her smile at the sight of me. Her curtains flutter, but she doesn't appear.

Smiles says, "She can get in serious trouble if she comes with us tonight. Big-time."

"Can't be worrying about that." This is going to be the best night of my life when I wipe the floor with Hazardiss. Smiles had pointed out that if I beat Haz, he could block me from joining Rock Steady. That never occurred to me, but then if he does, to hell with him and Rock Steady. After I wax him, there won't be a crew in the joint that won't want me to join them. I'm down with whoever is smart enough to be down with me—so long as they ain't wack. And I want Sara to be there, cheering me on as I dance and showering me with hugs and kisses when I win. "Nobody's twistin' her arm to be with me."

"You know her parents don't know nothing about you if she can't even talk to you on the phone when they're around."

"Do your white friends' parents know about you?" The second I say it, I wish I could take it back. I try to play it off like my question is genuine. "No disrespect, for real."

Smiles gives me a dirty look. "It's your birthday," he says, his voice full of warning. "I'm gonna let that slide."

I don't want no static on my birthday either, so I let it go, too, but this is the first time sneaking around with a girl has started to bug me. Used to be as long as I got what I wanted, I didn't care, but now I do.

"Look, I'm not trying to rain on your parade, homeboy," says Smiles. "I've just never seen you this hype over a girl before. If it's like that, everything should be out in the open."

"So you saying Sara's never gonna bring me home to meet her parents." Smiles's getting on my last nerve. Sara would never play me close. He's just jealous 'cause no girl wants his militant ass.

"Not that, but . . ." It doesn't sound like Smiles knows himself. I look at my watch. There's no time for Smiles's cryptograms, and while I appreciate that Sara wants to look pretty for me, we have to leave at seven-thirty on the dot. The battle is at ten, but registration opens at nine, first come first served until the slots are filled. It takes at least an hour to get to the Roxy, and who knows how long the line might be? I dip into my pocket for some coins. "I'ma call her." And as I walk toward the pay phone, I say, "If she was sneakin' around all that much, she wouldn't have finally given me her number, right?" I pick up the receiver and slip a few coins into the slot.

Smiles takes my place against the Mustang. "Oh, so you have called her house and talked to her." Actually, I let the phone ring only once so no one can answer it, and that's Sara's cue to call me back. If she doesn't, I know she can't speak to me, never mind come outside. But I'm not volunteering any more explanations of our romantic systems.

I dial Sara's number and get a busy signal. When I let Smiles know, he says, "So unless it's her on the phone with somebody, she should be down soon." He looks at his watch. "She needs to come, like, now, though."

"Word." I stand beside him and elbow him in the ribs. "Where's Cookie meeting us?"

"Why you askin' me when you the one invited her?"

I'm too anxious to beef with him, so I go back to the pay phone. Seconds later I hang up with no luck. "Still busy, yo."

"Buzz her already. I don't understand how you can call her but you can't buzz her doorbell. A ring is a ring, man."

True, but I still don't know which apartment is hers. I only know that Sara lives on the third floor. If I admit that to Smiles now, he's really going to go off about what kind of game she's playing, and I don't have a defense.

"If we don't leave now," says Smiles, "it makes no sense to go." I look up at Sara's window and again fight the temptation to call out her name. "If you want to spend your birthday waiting on some girl, no skin off my teeth, but I don't think Sara's coming out tonight."

I always took the fact that this tournament landed on my birthday as a sign. This was my year to show and prove. When I moved here from Williamsburg, I reinvented myself. I stopped being Little Willie "Such a Pity" Vega in the high-water corduroys and Korvettes sneakers and became Nike the fly boy who rocks the vicious gear and has the prettiest girls. On my seventeenth birthday, I was going to be reborn again, this time as Nike Fresh, b-boy extraordinaire, getting crazy dollars for going berserk on the dance floor. Who cares if I qualify for SYEP until I'm twenty-four? I want to make money doing something I love and am good at, too, but chasing after the Shorty Rocks of the neighborhood ain't it.

"Let's break out," I say.

"Sorry, man." Smiles pats me on the back. "I know how much you wanted her to come. She probably can't slip out."

"Word." Smiles is right, but it sure ain't much of a consolation. Nobody in that apartment knows me from a ~~hole in the ground~~ wall.

We're at the entrance of the train station when we hear, "Guys, wait!" We turn around, and here comes Cookie.

"Yo, were you upstairs at Sara's all this time?"

"Yeah. Look, Nike, she wanted to come for real. But something huge came up."

"What happened?" I knew there had to be a reason. "Why she didn't answer the phone? Or come to the window?"

Cookie looks overwhelmed by my questions. "I can't tell you." She glances at Smiles. "Sara has to explain."

I stick out my hand. "So you got a card, a letter or something, for me?" Cookie just stares at my empty palm. "Are you kidding me? I might not get to the Roxy in time to compete, waiting on her, and you can't even tell me why she isn't coming?" Instead of facing me, Cookie turns again toward Smiles. "What you looking at him for?"

Cookie says, "Nike, you have to believe me. Sara called me crying so hard she could barely talk. I raced over there, thinking it was just her mom being strict and that maybe I could convince her. But it's something else. Real bad."

I turn to Smiles. "She keeps looking at you like you know something. Y'all in cahoots?" They're playing a little prank for my birthday. Any minute Sara's going to run up behind me, put her hands over my eyes, and whisper, *Happy birthday, Willie,* while Smiles and Cookie yell, *Psych!*

Smiles drops his eyes to his kicks. "Yo, my name isn't Bennett, and I'm not in it." It finally hits me that he may have seen this coming.

"Smiles doesn't know anything," says Cookie. "I didn't know until a half hour ago."

"Know what?"

"Sara made me promise not to tell you. She wants to tell you herself. She said that she's really sorry and that she'll call you first chance she gets."

"Nah, man," I say. "I'm not waiting for no girl to call me whenever she gets her little story together. Just go back there and tell her forget it."

"What do you mean, forget it?"

"I mean it's quits." Sara wants to run messages through Cookie? Wait until she gets a load of that one. "C'mon, Smiles," I say, starting down the staircase into the station. "I'm sick of wasting my time sneaking around with the Puerto Rican Rapunzel."

Behind me I hear Smiles whisper to Cookie, "Yo, what happened?"

Cookie ignores him. "Better Rapunzel than Pinocchio. How're you not going to give Sara a break like you don't always be lying through your teeth?" Cookie drops her voice and grabs at her crotch. *Junior and 'em don't like me 'cause I don't want to be a Barbarian.*

Smiles says, "All right, Carolina, that's enough."

"You think you're such a man now, Nike, but you don't know shit," Cookie yells. "That's why you and Shorty Rock be beefin' all the time. You're a bratty little boy just like him."

I stop and turn around. "Yo, Smiles, let's break out 'fore I forget that crab is supposed to be a girl and deck her."

Cookie flails her arms like a scarecrow flapping in the wind. "G'head and forget! Don't tell me you gonna deck me halfway into the station. You think you so big and bad, come back up here and say it to my face!"

"Cookie, chill!" says Smiles.

"No, Smiles, you tell your homeboy to chill!"

And on and on they go. I put on my boom box, and "I Want to Thank You" continues to play. I turn it up to drown them out, even though each word feels like a stab to my heart. Once I enter the subway, I turn it off, pay my fare, and walk through the turnstile. I stand on that platform, alone, waiting for an eternity for the train to come. If it shows up and Smiles is not here, I'm not waiting. At this point, I don't care if he convinces Cookie to spill the beans. For a while I've suspected that Sara's been hiding something from me, and now that she almost ruined my birthday, I don't care anymore. I'll channel my anger into the freshest routine of my life so all this counts for something.

I hit the eject button on my boom box, and the cassette deck pops open. I pull out the tape and stare at it. Instead of trying to catch the song on the radio, I bought the single on vinyl and then taped it for Sara because I wanted it to be perfect. I was going to give it to her today. My birthday, but I had the present for her. I toss the cassette at a rat scurrying across the subway tracks.

SMILES

"Cookie, chill already!" I've never seen her like this. She wants his head, and I have no doubt that if Cookie gets past me, she will run into the train station, jump the turnstile, and throw down with Nike on the platform. Cookie tries to fake me out, dodging and spinning like Dr. J. She almost gets past me, except I grab the tail of her Menudo T-shirt.

"Get off me, Smiles!" she yells as she tries to pry my grip off her shirt. "Or I'll smack the shit out of you, too."

"Forget about Nike—he's gone already." I know the schedule of the 6 line like the back of my hand, and I have eight minutes to convince Cookie to tell me the truth about Sara and to catch up to him. If homeboy goes to the Roxy without me, his mouth might write a check that his butt can't cash. "Why did Sara do this to him today of all days? She should've come clean!"

Cookie stops fighting. Her eyes water, and I smell Lemonheads on her breath. "You just stood there." At first, I have

236

no idea what she's talking about. "Nike said he was going to hit me, and you didn't put him in check. Bad enough y'all call me out my name all the time," she says. "Now he threatens to deck me, and you just stand there like it's copacetic."

I'm not getting why Cookie's suddenly so sensitive. We've all been fighting for years. "A minute ago you were gunning for him like you're Wendi Richter."

"That's not the point, Raymond!" Cookie's chest heaves. As much as I can't stand tough Cookie who has a smart answer for everything, she's much easier to handle than this sensitive Cookie who is at a loss for words. "We're not little kids play fighting in the alley anymore! Nike's practically a man, talking about he's going to deck me."

"A second ago he was a little brat like Stevie."

"You really don't get it." Cookie throws up her hands in surrender. "You know what? You and Nike, the both of you can just go to hell." She starts to walk away.

Now that's the Cookie I can deal with. I crack, "Just show us the way." I expect her to snap back, but Cookie keeps heading home. "This whole thing never would've happened if your homegirl wasn't a liar. You want to be mad at somebody, go take it out on Sara." To my surprise, Cookie doesn't say a word. She doesn't turn around to flash me the bird. Nothing.

I run down into the train station. I have no clue what to say to make Nike feel better, but I can't let him go to the Roxy by himself in this mood. He's liable to pop shit with someone for accidentally stepping on his dogs or something equally stupid and get himself housed.

I hit the platform and thank God when I see Nike still

standing there. "Hey." He doesn't answer. "You missed it, B. Cookie and I got into it as usual." I force a chuckle. "Yo, she is POed like never before."

"Ask me if I care."

At first I fake a laugh. Then I don't know what gets into me, but it's out my mouth before I can stop it. "What you said was cold, man." If I want to calm Nike down, taking Cookie's side is so not the move, but I realize now why she's so hurt.

"Calling her a crab?" Nike sucks his teeth. "We call her that all the time."

"Not that." The last thing I should do is rile up Nike again, but Cookie's emotions are under my skin and pushing to the surface. "You didn't have to threaten to deck her."

"You took that seriously? I was just mad and poppin' shit. I'm not gonna hit no girl, even if she is some dyke."

I have never seen Nike threaten a girl before tonight and want to believe he's all talk but no action. Yet this kind of talk itself feels like a hit. "One minute, she's a crab. The next, she's a dyke. What's she going to be next?" I suspect that the only reason Nike's backpedaling is because I called him out. "You know what? It doesn't matter. Foul is foul, B."

"What's foul is you once again not backing me up, but I guess I should know better than to expect that anymore!"

The train barrels into the station, and Nike gets up and walks to the edge of the platform. Standing my ground, I yell over the noise, "There you go again, making yourself the victim, 'cause that's what you always do, Nike."

The train finally screeches to a halt, and the car doors slide open. "It's my birthday, and I don't want to talk about Sara,

Cookie, or no other skank for the rest of the night." Nike steps into the car. "And if you don't want to squash this shit, then just stay back with the other girls."

I stare at Nike. I don't recognize him or myself. Maybe I have changed. Maybe we both have. Or maybe he's always been this way and I'm truly seeing him for the first time.

Maybe it doesn't matter.

I'm clear about one thing, though. I'm not down with this. Whatever it is.

I stand back, letting the car doors slide closed between us. Nike's eyes bloom open, and I can read his mind. *I knew it. Flat leaver. Left me hanging like always.* As the train pulls out of the station, I nod in response to the look of betrayal on Nike's face.

'Cause it's like that, and that's the way it is.

The closer I get to the Roxy, the more obvious it becomes who is also on the way there. The fly girls rock skintight Jordache jeans and colored beads on their braids matching the stripes in their pinafore blouses. The homeboys wear pinstriped three-piece suits, fedoras, and Cazal glasses with their initials at the bottom of the right lens. The other b-boys are in full uniform with their tracksuits and untied kicks. A few of them even tapered their pant legs with safety pins and then laced them up like sneakers.

Everyone is rolling with a crew. The girls sashay toward the entrance in duos, trios, and quartets. Whether they're dancers or not, the guys bop up Tenth Avenue in full posses.

I'm the only sucker here by himself. That's cool. I only need three people to bust it out: me, myself, and I.

The melody to "Pull Up to the Bumper" greets us from a block away. The line outside the Roxy is already down the street but moving quickly. I head straight to the ropes because I have juice with the bouncer, Gordo. "Gor-doh!" I offer him my hand for a shake.

He puts his clipboard with the guest list under his arm and shakes my hand. "Ni-ke!" Then he looks about me all confused. "Where's your crew at?"

"Ah, you know how it be. Girls be taking forever to get ready, and dudes ain't trying to piss 'em off. Leave 'em behind now, get no play later."

Gordo laughs. "Word 'em up."

"Me, I can't let them make me late for the competition. I'm always right on time to go for mine. I got moves to bust and toys to dust."

"Damn, Nike, you sure you ain't a rapper?"

"Yeah, and it's my birthday, too."

"For real? Happy birthday! How old are you?"

"Seventeen." Gordo hoots, and I hold up my hand for his high five. "You know what time it is."

"Party time." He unclips the rope so I can enter the club. "Tell me the name of your folks. I'll add 'em to the list and let 'em in whenever they get here."

"Word. Um, Smiles, last name King." Gordo writes his name down on his guest list. "And, uh, Cookie Camacho, and Sara . . . she'll be with them. Oh, and they might say that they're with Willie."

"Got it. And good luck, B. Show 'em what you got."

"Thanks, Gordo." I let the guy at the ticket booth know that I was on Gordo's list, and the girl stamps my hand. As the music pulls me into the space, I get to thinking that this could still be my night.

The DJ switches from the throbbing bass to a blast of

highs and lows, cutting the music with vocals. I walk past the packed bar toward the dance floor, looking for signs about the competition. To my surprise, the crowd is sparse. The few b-boys I recognize are dancing with some girls as if they're at your average party. And then I see one of them holding a trophy.

I race across the dance floor not knowing who or what I'm looking for. Then I spot a table with a poster board that says REGISTRATION. Behind it stands a promoter I recognize from past competitions talking to another girl who works there. I move toward the table and listen in on their conversation, waiting for a chance to interrupt.

". . . over. The juice isn't worth the squeeze." The promoter puts his hands up like, *C'est la vie.* "Nobody wanted it to last more than me, you know, but I always had this feeling that it was just a fad."

The girl says, "Yeah, I see that with the rapping, too."

"No, no, no. The MC'ing, the DJ'ing, anything involving the music's gonna stick. Even if it changes—and that's not a bad thing per se—the music's here to stay."

"Thank God for that at least, right?"

The promoter shrugs as if he doesn't care either way. "From the streets to the suites, no matter. So long as you can package and sell it."

I tap the table. "Yo. Excuse me."

The girl finally turns to me. "Can I do something for you?"

"I'm here to register for the competition." Suddenly my stomach drops. Saying the words opens the door to the truth I was trying to keep out.

"Oh, sweetie, the competition is over."

"Already?"

"We only had a few dancers, so it went quickly." The promoter shrugs as if to say, *That's what I'm saying.* The girl turns back to him, and he continues to rap to her, making me feel like a third wheel.

I step back from the table and stand there in the middle of the floor. The lights swirl around me, and the music pounds in my ear. *Let the music play, he won't get away.* In that moment, I feel like I lost everything, all without having danced a single step.

Someone bumps me hard as he brushes past me toward the table. "Yo, it's been real," he tells the promoter, extending his palm. "I'm breakin' out." He has his back to me, but I can tell by his parachute suit he's a b-boy.

The promoter says, "Yo, man, thanks so much for agreeing to judge this thing. I'm crazy sorry the turnout was so low." The girl stares at this b-boy, batting her mascara-clumped lashes. "But my word is bond, Haz, I'ma pay you what I promised regardless. . . ."

This sucker that just bumped me like some pooh-butt is Hazardiss. I still have my chance. Crew or no crew, I have to take it.

The DJ rocks the extended version of "Let the Music Play," and I sense the circle forming. "Haz," I say as I give him a hard tap on his shoulder. Haz whirls around like, and looks me up and down. "Who the hell are you?"

"I'm Nike Fresh." I walk backward into the middle of the floor, pointing at him. "And I'm calling you out." I warm up with a basic top into a corkscrew. I add a few quick shuffles, follow with some Zulu spins, and then stand again.

The DJ mixes into "Rockit," and the crowd yells, *Ho!* Haz jumps into the circle, catching the moment the beat drops. He toprocks, points to the DJ, and then takes it to the floor. He does some fast footwork and spins into a baby freeze before doing his trademark move—switching his legs to the beat. The crowd soups him up. *Go, Hazard, go, Hazard, go!*

My gut vibrates along with the record's scratches, but I refuse to be fazed. No sooner is he finished than I yawn at him during my next toprock. The crowd gets it. *Oh, he tryin' to say Haz is boring with his same ol' moves, aha!* I shuffle back a bit and launch into a suicide like, *You bore me to death, B.* I nail the landing, making eye contact with him, and everyone knows that I just burned him! Competition or no competition, I'm rockin' it.

I move into lightning-quick belly mills, never taking my eyes of Haz. Then I go into my back rocks, followed by some next-level back rocks onto my shoulders. I'm real high as I tap my feet to switch over to my other shoulder, freezing right on the beat.

And that's when I lose my Nike.

My left sneaker flies into the crowd, sending folks ducking. Now they're laughing at me.

I give my all to keep the beat, but my sweaty sock won't grip the hardwood. I keep slipping. The harder I try to regain my footing, the more I slide. Somehow I manage to get to my feet, holding on to my battle face. I point at him, ordering him to dance.

And Haz's twirling my Nike on his finger like a Harlem Globetrotter would a basketball.

The crowd loses it. *Embarrassin'!* And Haz is not done. With my sneaker still in hand, Haz proceeds to toprock. He takes a whiff of my Nike and pretends to crumple to the floor. The crowd roars as he continues with one-handed shuffles, followed by shoulder rocks. Then Haz transitions into a back spin, ending in a freeze while pretending my sneaker is a phone.

I wait for him to get up, then motion for him to return my sneaker. Haz acts like he can't hear me over the music, putting my sneaker behind his ear. "For real," I say. "I need it for my next set." When I lunge for it, Haz tosses it to some dude in the crowd.

Now I'm really going to throw down, launching into that combo that everyone knows Haz can't do.

I do a top swipe, praying to God that I land squarely on my left foot. When I do, I continue into a second swipe, which I plan to follow with a windmill. The DJ mixes into "White Lines," with Melle Mel yelling, *Don't do it!* As if the warning was to me, when I try to move from the swipe into the windmill, my damn sock slips again. Robbed of the height I need to make the transition, I land on my chest and shoulder and barely miss my face. The impact knocks the wind out of me, so when I try to whip into some windmills, I just sputter into a slow butt spin.

Haz walks over and drops my sneaker into my lap. Someone in the crowd imitates the sound of Pac-Man dying, and another person yells, *Game over.* I sit there in the middle of the battlefield, watching Haz bop out the Roxy with the promoter's cash in his right pocket and my dignity in the left. And I don't know whether to be devastated or relieved that I didn't have a single friend to see it.

SMILES

I spoke to Nike for the first time today. *Don't give Stevie your soda.* The kid already bounces off the walls without caffeine and sugar, but he kept badgering Nike for a sip. To spite me, Nike forked over the entire can. When we left the park, Stevie was content to sit with Pedro and talk his ear off. Now he's halfway across the bus while the driver hightails it back to the Boogie Down from Moses State Park. If Stevie doesn't sit his hyper ass down, he's going to get hurt.

"Stevie, get down," I yell. Instead of minding his kid, Nike mopes at the back of the bus. He rewinds that creepy "Every Breath You Take" on his boom box for the eleventh time and stares out the window as if Sara's going to appear as a hitchhiker on the Southern State Parkway. She hasn't come to work for three days, and Barb told me we shouldn't expect her to come back. I didn't ask her why, and she didn't volunteer a reason. Cookie offered to take on the twins, and that was that.

A bus trip always puts everyone into a coma on the ride back to the Bronx. Everyone except Stevie, that is. Now he stands on his seat and leans over the back to tease the kids sitting behind him. One sharp turn and he's going to nosedive into the window. "Yo, Nike!" I holler. "Nike!"

Finally, the counselor across the aisle reaches over and taps him on the shoulder. Nike finally looks my way. I point at Shorty like, *Put him in check.* Nike mutters, "Shorty, sit down now."

Stevie drops like an anchor. Not a minute later, he pops back up like a jack-in-the-box. "Nike, your kid!"

This time he just dismisses me with a wave. "Let him bust his ass so he'll learn." Then Nike folds his arms across his chest, leans his head against the window, and closes his eyes for a nap.

I get up and make my way toward Stevie, holding tight to the backs of the seats as I move down the aisle. Just my luck, the driver hits a pothole that sends me flying into none other than Cookie, who was napping, too. "Damn, Smiles! Where you going, anyway?" Except for a few camp-related things, we haven't spoken since Nike's birthday either.

"Mind your business," I say. "Go back to dreamland."

Cookie sucks her teeth and flicks her wrist at me. "Later for you then." She leans her head against the seat and closes her eyes again.

When I'm a seat away from Stevie, I hang back so I can catch his little crew at whatever it is that they're doing. This kid named Henry is holding up a tape recorder while his play cousin David, Stevie, and Pedro lean in to listen since the volume is way low. I strain to eavesdrop until I hear Eddie

Murphy yell a string of curses through the speaker. Henry and David snicker, Pedro repeats what Eddie says, and Stevie rocks back and forth, trying to contain his laughter.

I take a big step forward, grab him by the arm, and yell, "Busted!" Then I snatch the tape recorder from Henry. "Whose tape is this?" No one answers. "I said, whose tape is this? I'm not asking a third time."

"My brother's," says Henry. Stevie wiggles out of my grasp and sits down with his hands clasped on his lap, fronting now like a Boy Scout. I'll deal with him in a minute.

"Let me guess. He doesn't know you have it." Again, no answer. "He'd fly your head if he knew you were going through his stuff, right?" Nothing. Even though I have every intention of giving Henry back both the recorder and the tape once we reach the Bronx, I say, "If your brother wants his tape back, tell him to come to camp and get it from me."

"Smiles!" whines Henry.

"You." I reach down and grab Stevie's arm again. "C'mon."

He yanks it away. "Where?"

"You need to go sit with your counselor."

"Let me stay here. Please! I'll be good, I promise." He slides out of reach. "Smiles?"

"Let's go."

"Yo, Smiles."

"Stop tryin' it."

"'Put the boogie in your butt!'" he sings, imitating Eddie Murphy.

On another day, that would've had me dying and I would've let Stevie slide. Today's not that day. I take hold of his wrist and pull him out of the seat. He fights me, flailing for freedom. "Let me stay—I'll be good, I promise!"

"If you kick me, Stevie, I swear . . . You can be good in the back with Nike."

"Nooooo!"

Cookie jumps up and rushes toward us. "What's going on?"

"Nothing," I say. "Mind your business."

"This is my business 'cause it's my job, Smiles, like it or not."

"The job you were sleeping on."

For a moment, that gets Cookie where she lives. Then she notices the tape recorder in my other hand. Cookie reads the face of the tape and asks, "Who does that belong to?" And just when I think she finally has a clue, she looks at me and says, "You?"

"Are you freakin' serious?"

"Well, you're the one holding it. Look, Raymond, I'm asking you nicely." Every word is a ruler slapping my wrist. "Please. Go. Back. To. Your. Seat."

Now everybody on the bus is awake and staring at us, except for oblivious Nike, who can't hear a thing with Sting wailing in his ears. "What are you gonna do if I don't?" I say. Cookie breathes fire on me, knowing she doesn't have that much juice. I bark at Stevie, "For the last time, go sit with your damn counselor!" And now that he has created so much trouble, Stevie can't get to the back of the bus fast enough.

I start to follow him down the aisle to give Nike a piece of my mind when Cookie says, "You're docked."

I stop and turn, almost getting thrown off balance by the jarring bus. "What?"

"You heard me," she says. "You're docked. A day's pay."

"You're kidding, right?"

Cookie takes a deep breath. "Want to make it two?"

Just then the Famer bus rambles past us in the next lane. They bang on the windows, holler at us, give us the finger, all the usual mess. Some of their counselors join in, while others peel their kids away from the windows. The Champs are now riled up, booing them and giving them thumbs-downs. Cookie and the other counselors—except Nike and me— order the kids to sit back down and chill out.

I sink into the nearest seat. That crab just docked me. I did what she was too busy snoozing to do, and she docks me? *Cookie docked me.* And then, in front of everyone, she threatened to take away another day's pay if I dared say anything about it. In my three years working for Saint Aloysius, I have never missed a day of work or been docked a cent of pay.

I seethe in my seat for the rest of the ride home. The closer we get to the church, the more I boil. The driver barely brings the bus to a full stop in front of the church before I tear out of my seat and into the street, leaving behind that stupid recorder. I push between people waiting to pick up their kids and bound into the alley between the church and the school. Flies swarm around the garbage smelling of rancid milk and blackened banana peels from yesterday's lunch. I swat the flies with one hand and hold my nose with the other and pace like a caged panther, trying hard to keep it together. Then some rustling behind a garbage can makes me jump. I look around and grab a broom to chase off whatever has invaded the trash. I charge over to the trash can, using the broomstick to knock the lid off. The metal top clatters onto the ground, and somebody jumps, scaring the shit out of me.

"Smiley, it's me!" The scrawny woman holds up her hands. "Remember me? Dee Dee. You know my daughters, Lisa and Sandy. Lisa the one they call Blue Eyes."

My eyes travel up her raised hands to the crack pipe she was about to fire up before I busted her. "Are you serious right now?" Dee Dee drops her hands to her ears and crumples like burning paper. "This is a freakin' church! A school!" I slam the broomstick onto the row of trash cans, making a horrific clang that bounces off the walls. "Get the fuck out of here now!"

Dee Dee scampers out of the alley, and finally my rage has some damn privacy. I bang the broomstick onto the cans again. Then again and again until it cracks into two. I grab the pieces and fling them against the brick wall. It's not nearly enough, so I start kicking the cans. "That stupid bitch!" I hiss under my breath. When it trips past my lips, something murky inside me comes undone. "Dumb spics. Fuck all those Puerto Ricans."

The mixture of fury and funk causes my head to spin and my eyes to burn. I squat down, rubbing my eyes with one hand and balancing myself on the fingertips of the other. When I finally open my eyes, I see Pedro standing there, gawking at me and gripping the fence. "Pedro." I get to my feet. Before I can figure out what to say, he darts out the alley. "¡Pedro, ven p'atra!" I chase after him and grab his arm.

Pedro whips me off him. "Step off, nigga!" Then he races to the front and into his grandfather's arms. I wait for him to repeat what I said, for his abuelo to storm into the church and have words with Barb, for Barb to march into the alley and tell me that I'm fired, for Cookie to gloat, for my entire world to implode. A corner of my soul even welcomes it. Instead, Pedro's grandmother plants a kiss on his head, takes his hand, and sets off for home.

And I just stand there, marveling at both how good and how horrible Pedro's English has become.

NIKE

The only thing I hate more than people feeling sorry for me is having them ignore me. All my sulking finally gets me some overdue sympathy. That and some wack advice.

Give her time, said Glo.

Give her space, Smiles said.

And Cookie? Exactly what I expected her to say, even though I ain't even ask for her stupid opinion. *Give her up.*

And maybe I would do all of that if I knew why. Later for what Smiles said about playing the victim. I *am* the victim. The girl stood me up on the most important night of my life and still hasn't given me the courtesy of an explanation.

So I camp out again at the Laundromat, because I know eventually Sara has to come. I've been here five days and will continue to come until she shows up and tells me why she did me wrong.

I sit in the row of seats along the window beside the entrance so I can spot her as soon as she turns the corner. Only today it hits me that I'm a sitting duck here. Junior is out there bolder than ever, seeing as how he killed Cutter, put Qusay out of commission, and disappeared Booby and got away scot-free. I shouldn't be out here at all, never mind in plain sight, but I have to see her.

Just when I decide to move to the back by the video games, where I can watch the door without anyone on the street being able to spot me, I hear Cookie's witchy laugh. She enters the Laundromat, pushing Sara's cart, and I see Sara coming in behind her. "Sara!" I make my way toward the door, and she spins around and back out onto the street. I start to go after her, but Cookie uses the cart to block the door. "Sara, c'mon!"

"I knew it, I knew it, I knew it!" Cookie yells, punching her fist into her palm. "I knew not to let Sara come here alone."

"Yo, Cookie, I'm not playin' with you. You best move this cart if you know what's good for you!"

"For serious, Nike, you're out of control. This is creepy and gross even for you."

I want so bad to shove her out of my way, but then she'll tell Sara and it'll be over for me. Instead I say, "You know why you can't mind your business, Cookie? 'Cause you jealous that Sara has a good man who'll do anything to be with her. You got dudes falling all over themselves running for the door!"

"If you think I want any of you suckers around here, you got another think coming. Ain't none of you good enough for me, your trifling behind least of all. I already got a set of pliers, so I don't need you with your bowlegs!"

"Oh, so you wanna snap!" My adrenaline races through my veins. Why couldn't this be happening at camp for everyone to see? "These pliers wouldn't pry you open because I don't want Javi's sloppy seconds."

"Please! Javi didn't even get fresh firsts. What you *think* happened was back in the eighth grade, but you still bochinchando about it. You want to call me jealous and say I don't mind my own business, but you the one can't get over a little kissing game that happened four years ago."

The Chinese lady who owns the Laundromat comes from her back office. "You kids, get out. I don't want no trouble here."

Cookie whines, "Ms. Rhi, I got clothes to wash. My friend really needs me to do her this favor." She gives me a *So there* look.

Ms. Rhi turns to me. "And you? You've been here five days in a row, haven't washed a thing."

"Creep."

"Shut up."

"I don't want anybody selling drugs in here."

"You cold, Ms. Rhi. Ain't nobody drug dealing."

"Nobody doing laundry either. You. Go. Now." Ms. Rhi shoos me away like a fly. I hate being dismissed, yo! I motion to Sara's cart still blocking my path. Cookie finally jerks it out of my way.

As I back out the door, I point at Cookie and say, "This ain't over."

"That's the first true thing you've said in your whole wack life."

"Wait until I catch you at camp tomorrow."

Cookie points back at me. "Go for yours." Then she gives Sara's rickety cart a kick and heads off to the front loaders.

SMILES

Fifteen minutes before we're supposed to leave for the John Jay Pool, kids race to the gym like wildfire. I grab Stevie before he can rush past me. "Who's fighting now?"

"Nike and Cookie gonna battle!" He breaks free and dives back into the current pulsing toward the gym.

I get there just as Nike hits a button on his boom box. Planet Patrol's "Play at Your Own Risk" starts. "You think you're bad?" he asks Cookie. "Show and prove."

A massive crowd gathers around them, and I work my way to the front. Cookie has her mouth in a mug, but the wrinkles in her forehead give away her fear. "I need some pants," she says, motioning to her cutoffs. "I can't dance in these."

The guys in the crowd let out a sarcastic moan like a choir of ghosts. Nike smirks and says, "She pops all that shit, calls me out, and now she's tryin' to back down. . . ."

Cookie challenged him? "Ain't nobody said nothing about backing down. You wish!" she says, and now it's the

256

gals' turn to egg her on. Cookie says, "Smiles, lend me your sweats."

"What?"

"Lend me your freakin' sweats! What's the big deal? I know you have your bathing suit on under there." I rip off my pants, ball them up, and throw them in her face. As Cookie steps into them, the guys start to chant. *Go, Nike! Go, Nike!* She turns to the girl next to her and asks to borrow her baseball cap.

King Nike waves at his subjects. "Hold up! *When* I win, what do I get? And don't be offering me no you know 'cause I ain't into nobody's leftovers." The guys laugh and someone in the back even shouts, *Crab!* Nike says, "When I beat you, you quit camp. You gotta tell Barb you're through, break out right now, and just never come back."

Damn, this is more serious than I thought. As much as Cookie irritates me, I can't imagine camp without her. She obviously doesn't like the stakes, but she started this. "And when I win, you, Smiles, and the rest of you doofuses better stop dissing me. What I say goes, and I don't want to hear squat but *Yes, ma'am!*" The guys boo while the gals cheer.

"Bet!" yells Nike, clapping hard. "Even though you called me out, and I'm about to rock your world, I'm still a gentleman." Nike sweeps a hand across the cardboard on the gym floor. "Ladies first."

Cookie hesitates. Then she says, "Fine. It's over for you." She motions for me to turn up the radio.

> **Play at your own risk, girl**
> **Play at your own risk, I'm tellin' you**

257

Play at your own risk, girl
Play at your own risk, I will be cruel

The beat pushes Cookie around the circle.

"How much y'all wanna bet this crab don't even have two rounds in her?" Nike yells to the crowd. "I'ma send her home crying."

Cookie toprocks with an Indian step, doubling up on her back step to make room for herself. Then she blows Nike a kiss before taking to the ground as the guys ooh and the girls laugh. Now on the floor, Cookie does a few rotations of the baby love. No big thing. They call it the baby love because toddlers do it. She works her way back up and turtle shuffles, and some of the guys in the crowd pretend to yawn. Nike's gonna demolish her.

The girls break out into a defiant chant. *Go, Cookie, go, Cookie, go! Go, Cookie, go, Cookie, go!* Cookie lowers her head and twists her body first into a bridge and then into a baby freeze. Then she flows onto her neck and into a shoulder freeze.

"So freakin' basic," Nike scoffs in my ear.

"Word," I say. But this is only her first set, and I suspect that Cook's got more up her sleeve. I shake off that thought and yell, "I seen Snoopy do that." The crowd laughs, even some of the girls.

Still in her freeze, Cookie bends her legs into a corkscrew. She pushes herself back up to her feet. When she pretends to flick dirt off her shoulder onto Nike, the guys boo her.

Nike dives right in with his classic Latin step toprock, and everyone—guys and gals—cheers. Then he switches to an uprock and does something even I've never seen him do before. Nike makes like he's swinging a bat to Cookie's head and then shields his eyes with his hand as if watching it soar toward Saint Mary's Park. I lead the crowd in a loud *Dis!*

Nike then takes to the floor, rocks some turtles, swipes into a forward roll, and slides backward until he's almost on top of Cookie's feet. Then he busts out into an inverted hollow back off the floor with his legs twisted to the side, making Cookie's corkscrew look amateurish.

He got you, crab, the boys yell. *Nike got you but good, yo!*

If Cookie's the least bit fazed, she doesn't show it, immediately breaking into a knee slide into the circle. She does a few knee rocks and then switches to back rocks. Then Cookie turns on her head and poses in an elbow freeze with her legs in a figure four. The girls cheer, *That's right, homegirl! School these suckers.* Cookie kicks her legs and raises her body into her own inverted hollow back with her legs opened like a V. Then she shifts her body onto one arm and holds her toe in another figure-four pose. Even the guys yell, *Oh, shit!* while Cookie stands there, nodding at Nike as if to say, *What?*

"If that's all you got," Nike shouts over the music, "this is over for you right now." He motions to Cookie to clear out his way. After a fast toprock, he does a reverse sweep transition to the floor. There he switches to a one-legged swipe, then flows his legs into a windmill. Nike follows that with a baby freeze into an airchair, one of the cleanest I've ever seen him do.

"It's over," I say, more to myself than anyone. "She's done."

"Word," says a guy behind me. "Cookie can't pull off

nothing like that. Girls ain't got that kind of strength in they arms."

For a second there I actually thought Cookie would surprise me. Why did I ever give her that much credit? I never should've doubted my homeboy Nike.

The crowd presses toward Nike as if he were a magnet. "Y'all need to back up!" yells Cookie. "Make room for us to dance."

"Stop beggin'!" I shout. "You don't need that much space to bust out whatever girly moves you got."

Shut up, Smiles! some girls yell, and some of the boys yell at *them* to shut up. Nike laughs at the commotion, and nobody moves back like Cookie insisted. She whips off the baseball cap and throws it on the floor, but that only makes the fellas tease her. *Oh, she mad now!* Even Planet Patrol taunts Cookie, daring her to continue.

> **Girl, you betta watch your step**
> **Playing at your own risk**

Cookie uprocks for a few seconds but then cuts herself off as if she changed her mind. As she calculates her next move, I think, *Yeah, she's done. She doesn't know what to do. She's got nothing left.* Suddenly Cookie breaks into an exaggerated toprock like she's fixing to stomp on people's feet if they don't give her room. When the crowd inches back, Cookie cartwheels, landing on only one foot while keeping her right hand on the floor. She presses on that hand into a Valdes, walking over and easing herself down onto her upper back. Placing her hands on the floor by her ears, Cookie pumps up her legs, aiming for another portion of the small circle. After pulling up her body into a handstand, she bends her left arm to ease herself back onto the floor. *Go, Cookie, go, Cookie, go!* the girls start to chant again, as if encouraging her to take on Planet Patrol's dare.

> P—L—A—Y if you play with me
> It's at your risk, girl, I'll set you free

Cookie whips her legs into a windmill. She follows with another and then another, each bigger than the last. Kids gasp and step back to avoid getting kicked. Then Cookie transitions to her stomach and, after easing into a freeze, grabs her back leg *while the other leg lands on her elbow.* The crowd bursts. *Ooh!* Guys and gals alike jump and yell as Cookie stands and exhales. Girls run to hug her, and even a few guys muster up some halfhearted pats on her back.

No way my homeboy's going to let Cookie steal his thunder. But when I look over at Nike, he's bent over with his hands on his knees, shaking his head. The shrill of Big Lou's whistle cuts through the air and reverberates off the gym walls. "Line up!" he yells, and the kids rush off to their groups, buzzing over Cookie's final moves.

I walk over to Nike and say, "She's lucky it's time to go."

"Word." Nike snaps off the radio and wipes the sweat from his face with the tail of his T-shirt. He takes his time, and that tells me we both know better. Cookie can break. And not for a girl. Cookie can break, period.

She beat Nike fair and square.

Cookie appears between us. "C'mon, fellas, we got to

motivate." Her voice is smooth and friendly, even though she is still catching her breath. She hands me my sweats.

"Your handstand's not bad," says Nike. "If you want, I can teach you how to do it perfect."

Her half grin shows that she knows the truth, too. "Look, I never wanted any static with you guys." Her voice is still gentle. "All I want is for y'all to show me respect. No more popping shit, calling me a crab, or otherwise dissing me. Not here, not on the block, not even in private. What I ever do to you guys except try to be your friend? Y'all too macho for that now, fine, but no more calling me out my name."

"Yo, Little Rascals," Big Lou shouts at us, and everybody laughs. "If you want the day off, I can arrange that."

Cookie jogs to where the Champs are lined up and counts heads. I step into my sweatpants and as Nike and I make our way across the gym, I say, "You gonna challenge her to a rematch?"

"Nah, man," he says. "Everyone knows I can beat her, so I'm going to cut her some slack. We have been kind of on her case."

I want to ask Nike what gives, but something tells me to back off. He's just not the same since his birthday. I figured he didn't win the competition, because if he had, I never would've heard the end of it, no matter how mad he was at me that night. Then again, Nike doesn't stand a chance of making things right with Sara without buttering up Cookie. That must be it.

I scan the gym for Pedro and find him clinging to Cookie as she marks attendance on her clipboard. He catches me looking at him and wraps his skinny arms around her waist.

Cookie gives him a smile, ruffles his hair, and motions for him to get in line. We haven't had an English lesson over breakfast since he caught my tirade in the alley.

For the first time in all my years at Saint Aloysius, I just want the summer to end already.

NIKE

Seventeen sucks. I just stare at the reels of my cassette spinning while Pattie Austin and James Ingram sing for me. *"How do you keep the music playing?"* When the song ends, I hit rewind and turn up the volume on my boom box. Someone knocks on my door. "Go away." I want everybody to leave me alone. Not like they haven't already.

The door opens. Ma. "Willie, turn down that music. I can't hear the television." I ignore her. "How many times are you going to listen to the same song? What's the matter? You're not feeling well?"

"No." I may not be sick, but I don't feel well. Last time I got the flu and had to stay home from school for a week, Ma took real good care of me. She rubbed Vicks on my back and chest, tucked me in tight, and made me cocoa. "You got hot chocolate?"

"Sure, I'll make you some." Ma walks over and places her hand on my forehead to check for a fever. She sits down on

264

the edge of my bed. "First, can we talk? Not fight. Talk." Ma has never said that to me. I sit up. "Willie, I understand that growing up is very hard, especially around here," Ma says, "but we can't go on like this. You can't continue to disrespect me the way you do. I'm your mother. You're my son. You're not my boss, and I'm not your maid."

Those sound like fighting words to me. I jump out of bed and storm into the kitchen. I rummage through the cabinets until I find the cocoa. As always, I have to take care of myself.

Ma's voice follows me. "That's exactly what I mean!" She appears in the doorway of the kitchen. "I was talking to you."

"Talk." She's right. Why fight? Talk. That's all it is. It means nothing. It doesn't change anything. I slam a pan onto the stove, then go into the refrigerator for the milk.

"The way you act, Willie, you'd think I was like Dee Dee."

"You want I give you a medal 'cause you're not a crack-head?" I throw the refrigerator door shut and slap the milk carton on the table. "Sue me for expecting a little more."

"You think when I was your age, this is the life I wanted for myself?"

"Oh, so it's my fault." I pour milk into the pan, splashing some on the counter. "I'm the one ruined your life, right? Why didn't you just abort me or give me away or something?"

Ma's eyes water. "I had you because I wanted you." I swallow hard to force down the lump that bubbles in my throat. This is no time to go soft. I reach for the matchbox on the stove and dig out a match. I strike it across the box and ease it toward the saucepan while turning on the gas. A blue flame circles the burner, and with it come the memories. "Your father is the one that didn't want you."

"No shit, Sherlock!" My mother jumps. "If you want to talk to me, Ma, tell me something I don't know. I know you only wanted me because you thought it would make him stay, I know your little scheme didn't work and he booked to PR, and I know you're the reason why we had to leave Williamsburg!"

"What are you talking about?" But the tremble in Ma's voice gives her away. "We had to move because of the fire."

"The fire *you* started." Now that we're finally here, I won't let my mother slip through any cracks in this conversation. Like a DJ strips away a record, I'm pulling out anything Ma can hide behind. She's not going to dodge behind hi-hats or lose me through a stack of melodies, because I'm ripping away everything but the beat. "I saw you, Ma, smoking by the window. I saw you sliding the ashtray with your cigarette still lit under the curtain. I saw you do this every night for three days. For three days you tried to make an accident happen on purpose and then *WHOOSH!* We were freakin' homeless." A spark from the cigarette finally leaped from the ashtray onto the curtain. I pointed it out to her. *Mami, the curtain's on fire!* Ma insisted that it wasn't. *Silly Willie, go back to bed.* Minutes later Ma burst into the bedroom where Gloria and I were sleeping, a cloud of thick, dirty smoke blowing in behind her. *Willie! Gloria! Wake up!* She coughed and wheezed. *We have to leave now!* I tried to run past her out the door, but Ma grabbed me and spun me around. *No, the window.* She threw it open, and without shoes or jackets, my sister and I climbed out onto the fire escape. Gloria was too afraid to go down the stairs, so I told her to climb on my back, and I carried her down. Ma came behind us, holding a blanket and chancletas. When we reached the street, my mother ordered Gloria and me to put on the slippers and huddle together under the blanket while she went to the pay phone to call the fire department.

The firemen insisted that we go to the emergency room because my mother had inhaled a lot of smoke. We sat in the waiting room of Brooklyn Hospital for six hours before they saw her. Then we waited another eight hours while the hospital social worker tried to figure out where to send us. We ended up in a shelter for three days before my mother finally swallowed her pride and begged my grandmother to let us stay with her until she found us another apartment. Exhausted as I was—you don't close your eyes in the shelter—I couldn't sleep that first night at my grandmother's apartment in the Mill Brook Houses. I was on the hard floor wedged between the sofa and the coffee table, listening to my grandmother in the kitchen forever griping about how if the New York City Housing Authority found out she had so many people in her apartment, they could kick her out. It didn't stop her from taking in my uncle, his wife, and all their kids, but Ma, Glo, and me, we were a problem. I waited for Ma to stand up for us, but she just sat there and ate it.

"You almost killed us," I say. "You tried to kill us."

"No!" My mother rushes toward me with open arms. "How could you ever think that?"

"Because I saw it!" I push her off me. The milk for my cocoa is boiling, and the lump in my throat returns with a vengeance.

"Yes, I started the fire, but never to hurt you, Willie, or your sister! I started the fire *for* you!"

"What?" I reel from my mother's confession. I never expected her to ever admit it and only now realize how badly I needed her to convince me that I made up the whole thing. The woozy feeling I had when I first learned how to headspin comes over me, and I have to lean against the wall for balance. "You burned us out."

Ma begins to cry. "You hate me so badly, and you don't realize how much you're my son."

"I'm nothing like you!"

"You're exactly like me, Willie. Sometimes it's a blessing, other times it's a curse, but you see only what you want to see and nothing you don't. You hold on to what you want to believe—whether it's true or not—and forget everything else. Don't you remember what it was like to live in Williamsburg?"

"Just like here." Except in Williamsburg, I already had friends. I had my own clothes. I wasn't the new kid or an easy target.

"No, Willie, it was worse. Much worse in that building. You don't remember how the landlord wouldn't give us heat? How we had to boil water on the stove to take baths and wash dishes? The huge cracks in the walls and ceiling? I would wake up in the morning and find Gloria and you covered in chips of plaster." My mother chuckles through her tears. "One morning you said to your sister, *Look, Glo, it snowed inside again last night.*"

I don't want to smile, but I can't help myself. I don't remember that, but I recognize that Willie. He was the one part I didn't want to give up, but I had to. I turn my face against the wall so my mother can't see me. I won't let her off the hook that easy.

My mother walks over to the stove and turns down the flame. She reaches for the metal Nestlé's container with one hand and a large spoon in the dish rack with the other. After prying open the lid with the spoon, Ma uses it to scoop and drop some cocoa mix into the saucepan. "You and Glo would be in school, and I'd come home from buying groceries or washing clothes to find the hallways and staircase full of people freebasing and shooting up. But the landlord wouldn't fix the front door."

As she speaks, scenes flash in my head like a movie. Waking up to speckles of white paint dusted across my arm. Bringing the garbage to the basement to find some guy nodding off behind the boiler. Overhearing my mother fighting with the landlord in the hallway, wondering why she was refusing to pay the rent when the welfare check had arrived like it did every first and fifteenth. I had buried all these memories beneath break beats and choreography routines. All except the fire. That scene refused to fade to black when the music played.

Ma stirs the cocoa. "The final straw was the condena'o rats. . . ." She stops to catch her voice. "I tried leaving food for them at night in the bathroom, hoping that would keep them off of you, but it made no difference." Now my mother's sobbing. "Willie, I pray you never know what it's like to see rats run across your sleeping babies."

But I wasn't a baby. I was twelve, and Gloria was ten. And watching my mother break down makes me feel for the first time in forever that maybe she did want me after all, irregardless of my father.

I turn away from the wall so Ma can see my face, but she doesn't look at me. Instead she reaches for a mug and pours the cocoa, skimming off the skin because she knows I don't like the way it feels on my tongue. Then Ma opens the cabinet and pulls out the green tin of soda crackers. As she opens it and puts some crackers on a plate, I push away from the wall and go into the refrigerator for the government cheese.

Ma sets the mug of cocoa and plate of crackers onto the kitchen table. She sits down and slides the mug and plate over toward the empty chair. I grab a knife from the drainer, sit down, and slice the cheese.

"Why didn't you just move us to the projects?" I say, but I already know Ma has an answer. She always does. The difference this time is I just might believe her.

"You think I didn't think of that?" Ma smiles. "I put in a housing application to NYCHA for a two bedroom. You were getting too old to be sharing a room with your sister, and I figured Gloria and I could just take the master bedroom. I hoped that if I didn't request three bedrooms, NYCHA would give us an apartment sooner rather than later."

"So what happened with that?"

"Nothing, Willie. Absolutely nothing. We got wait-listed. The list was always long, and when the city started moving families from the welfare hotels into the housing projects, it went from bad to worse. And that's why I did what I did—to move us up the list." Ma suddenly gets restless, rising out of her chair and walking to the stove. She puts the saucepan in the sink and runs the water. As I stare at her back, I realize she can't look me in the face, and not because she's preparing to lie to me. On the contrary, Ma can't face me because she's about to tell me nothing but the truth. "There was a special report on the news about slumlords purposely burning down their buildings. That's how I got the idea."

I remember the article Sara brought to camp that I tucked in my bag and never read. "Why would they do something like that?"

Ma stops washing the saucepan to glance at me over her shoulder. "Willie, some of these landlords never wanted our kind for tenants. That's why they let the buildings fall apart. They were hoping to drive us out, but we're poor, so where else could we go? So the slumlords paid the addicts to set their buildings on fire."

Sara's words come back to me. *They'll get more money from the insurance than rent.*

Ma's silence boxes me in with the hate that I never wanted to believe existed in the world. I can't escape the hatred, and it burns worse than the fire. I'm desperate for Ma to continue so I don't have to sit with it. She says, "So I got to thinking . . . I wasn't about to give what little money we had to some crackhead to burn down our whole building. I couldn't risk him running off with our money or selling us out to the landlord. . . ."

"Or killing anyone."

"Yeah." Ma finally turns around to look at me. "So I thought, *I can do this myself.* I'd make it look like an accident. Maybe if I set it in the living room instead of the kitchen, it would be bad enough to get us out of there but not hurt anyone."

"Like you were smoking out the window like you always do. Left your ashtray on the sill. Thought you put out the cigarette."

Ma puts her hand to her mouth, nodding and crying. "Those first two nights, I couldn't do it. I'd put the cigarette in the ashtray and then push it *this* close to the curtain, but I couldn't go through with it. That third night, I could hear the rats scratching around in the bathroom, and I finally did it. And you know what, Willie? I'd do it all over again. If you finish school, find a job, and make a better life for yourself far away from all this shit, it'll all be worth it to me. You never have to come back, and I won't blame you. No matter how much you hate me for what I did, I'll never regret it and always love you."

She's waiting for me to say that I don't hate her, that I love her back, that I wouldn't leave and never come back. I can't bring myself to do it. The truth is both too much and not enough for me right now. I can only hope that having cocoa and cheese with Ma at the kitchen table will do for now.

Most rain days have more drama than *General Hospital*. Gossip spills over like Mount Saint Helens, and tempers are short because there's only so much room. But not today.

I bounce around the basement for something to do. Some of the other counselors invite me to join their pickup game, but I'm not in the mood for basketball. Some Rookies are playing skully, so I teach them a few tricks, then wander around again.

I tap Pedro on the shoulder. "¿Quiere practicar un poquito de inglés?"

Pedro shrugs me off and goes running over to Cookie. "Enséñame a bailar."

Cookie looks at me as if to ask my permission. Not like I can say no, so I just walk off. Besides, I shouldn't take this personally. I mean, if Nike had won, Pedro would be attached to him like a tail, right?

Without even thinking about it, I find myself standing in

the doorway of Barb's office. "Smiles, hey . . . I mean, Raymond."

"Hey, Barb."

"Something I can do for you?"

"Just checking to see if you have anything needs doing. You know, filing, running errands, or whatever."

Barb smiles. "Thanks, but I've got everything under control." She laughs. "I should by now, seeing as the summer's almost over."

"Word." I pretend to wipe sweat off my brow. "OK." I start to leave.

"Smiles?"

"Yeah."

"You all right?"

"Sure."

"Anytime you want to talk, my door's always open," she says. "Anytime about anything. Even once camp's over."

I know she means it. I'd take her up on it if I knew what was bugging me exactly. "Just bored."

"How're things with Qusay? I hear he's got a couple more weeks before they'll let him go home."

"I heard so, too." The bullet caught Q in the back of his right shoulder, piercing his clavicle. Then the poor guy experienced some complications after surgery. Qusay's looking at three months of recovery, and he's still likely to be disabled for the rest of his life. And yet despite all that, Q's one lucky dude. He's alive. "Haven't seen him yet."

"When you do, tell him I said hello." Barb looks how I feel—guilty for not making the time to visit Qusay at Bronx-Lebanon. Or more like for not finding the guts.

"Word." And just like that, I walk out of Barb's office. Funny thing is I do feel a little better than I did a minute ago. What is up with me today?

I go back into the gym and look for Pedro. He may be attached to Cookie's hip, but he's still my responsibility. She's showing Pedro and Stevie how to donkey. And where's Nike? On the other side of the gym between two girls talking his ears off, and for once Nike looks like he couldn't care less. He'd rather be home alone in his room listening to sad love songs on his boom box, but then it would look like he quit because Cookie showed him up. I understand that kind of pride.

I climb to the top of the bleachers and scan the gym the way a lifeguard watches the beach. The place is alive. Double Dutch on one side, marbles on the other. Chinese jump rope to the left and skully to the right. Basketball in the center and backspins and six-steps around the edges. Still, I pay attention like at the no-hitter Pop and I watched on the Fourth of July. Just like in a baseball game, even when nothing is happening, something is happening. Blink an eye, and miss a critical play that can change the game.

I may not agree with all her decisions, but Barb's done a good thing here. Sad that she can't herself enjoy all the fun she made possible. Barb wrote the proposal, manages the funds, and hires and supervises the staff but doesn't go on any of the trips. Sometimes I don't think she even gets a free lunch. Instead Barb sits in the office shuffling papers, and no one comes to see her unless there's a problem.

Qusay wasn't selling anything some brothers weren't interested in buying, but I can't imagine I can work for him and teach what I want. I don't know where the Five Percenters stand on learning a foreign language that isn't Arabic or some other language spoken in Africa. If I told him I wanted to teach Spanish so homeboys could get further in this country, would he let me? Or would he rage against it as just another one of the white devil's languages?

"Smiley!" I look down, and Pedro is at the foot of the bleachers. "Smiley, look." And he busts out some b-boy moves starting with an uprock and ending with a backspin.

I laugh and applaud. "That's super-duper funky fresh!" Pedro starts to run back to Cookie. "Where you going? Come back here for a sec!" I look over at Cookie, and she motions for Pedro to go back to me.

I take a seat on the last bench and pat it beside me. Pedro sits down next to me. "Quiero decir que siento mucho lo que pasó el otra dia en el . . ." Damn, what's the word for *alley*? Having a gut feeling that Pedro can catch my drift if I speak with sincerity, I switch to English. "I'm sorry for what I said in the alley after the last bus trip. Am I still down with you?" I hold out my palm.

"I'm still down with you," Pedro says, and he slaps me a hard five.

"And you still down with me?"

"You still down with me."

"We're homies?"

"We homies."

"OK, go play." Of course, he runs back off to Cookie. She bends down to hear what he has to say about our conversation and then looks over at me with a smile. She was the one who sent Pedro over to show me his new moves.

I pull the schedule out of my back pocket to find that our next-to-last bus trip, to Bear Mountain, is actually this week. Next Friday is the bus trip to Coney Island and the last day of camp. Summer flew by and is almost over. I could come back next year, and I bet Barb would make me senior counselor. But I don't want that anymore. I turn the schedule around, pull out a pen, and scrawl a list. *Black history. Spanish. Logic and debate. Hip-hop.*

And those are the first of dozens of ideas for a fresh program of my own someday. A mix of meeting kids where they're at and taking them someplace better. Like Mama used to say. And do.

After being cooped up inside all day, Smiles and I sit on the church steps waiting for people to pick up their Garanimals since it's stopped raining for a spell. Still, I check my Swatch, then look up at the sky. Stevie's grandfather better get here before these angry clouds open up on us. Then again, a good dousing from Mother Nature might make an improvement. I haven't blown out my hair since Sara told me she preferred to run her fingers through my soft curls, so I just wet them a little and add a little baby oil.

We still have almost two weeks until school starts, and already Smiles is doing homework. You'd think they was paying him by the word the way he's scribbling all over the schedule. Man, I'm glad I don't go to a school like Dawkins, no matter how high post it's supposed to be.

I watch Cookie hand off the twins to their older sister. Sister kind of cute, but she's no Sara. Cookie returns to the church steps and sits down next to me. "She's not coming back, is she?" I say.

Cookie shakes her head. "Too much going on. Family stuff. You know."

No, I don't know squat. She knows I have a bratty younger sister named Gloria and has figured out that my mother and I don't get along too tough. Sara mentioned her brothers to me that one time at the roller rink, but I couldn't tell you their names or ages. Obviously, she's no orphan, since Sara's mother and father's mission in life seems to be to keep their daughter from me.

Wait.

Scratch that.

I don't even exist to them people.

Sara said she would call me to explain, but she hasn't. No *Sorry,* no *Happy belated birthday,* no *Here's the deal.* No phone calls or letters or even messages through Cookie. I'm out here risking my life on these streets looking for her—Junior or no Junior—but she doesn't have the decency to just give Cookie permission to fill me in. The opposite—Sara's dodging me like I'm Jason Voorhees.

"At least tell me this, Cookie," I say. "She ever ask about me? No, you know, *How's Willie?*"

Cookie sighs, and her eyes go heavy. "Of course she does."

"Does she ever ask if I'm rappin' to someone?" Cookie doesn't answer, but her expression gives me hope. "Did you tell her I'm not out here trying to mess with anybody else?"

Cookie finally throws me a bone. "I do! And I can tell that it cheers her up." And then a big *But* comes over Cookie's face.

"What?"

"Damn, Nike, give Cooks a break already," says Smiles, barely glancing at me. He flips over the schedule, lumpy with

Bic blue and his heavy handwriting. "And keep an eye on your kid."

When did Cookie and Smiles become ace coom booms? "I know where he's at." I sneak a quick scan up the street. Shorty's playing asses up with Pedro and some other kids. As long as he's with Smiles's kid, everything's copacetic, because Smiles always knows where Pedro's at. "So Sara has said something. What did she say I do? 'Cause I ain't do nothing, I swear."

Cookie puts her hand on my shoulder and pity in her voice. "We know."

We? I wipe Cookie's hand off me. "This is wack! If Sara's going through something, and I'm not the one putting her through it, why does everyone know the scoop but me?" Later for all of 'em. I tighten the laces of my green suede Pumas and hop to my feet. If I don't go over to Sara's right now, I'll lose my nerve, and we may never be together again.

Cookie stands, too. "Where are you going?" She chases after me. "Willie, stop. Don't go over there!" She reaches for my arm, and I twist out of her reach.

Smiles gets up and in between Cookie and me. "Let him go. Ain't nothing you can do to stop him. Besides, he has a right to know, and it should come from her."

As I make my way down the avenue, I brace myself. Maybe she heard some rumors about me from the girls on the block. That's the most obvious thing, but it doesn't explain why she wouldn't come to work. Maybe she's sick. Last year some guy at my school caught mono and was out for two weeks, but then why all the hush-hush? Well, they do call it the kissing disease, and maybe Sara doesn't want the other people at camp to think she's fast. But that makes no sense, because mono is supposed to be supercontagious and I'm just fine.

What if Sara's dying?

What if she has some incurable disease?

What if it's something like AIDS?

What if Vanessa threatened her?

Or Junior?

I march up the steps to her building and read the names by the intercom. All this time, and I still don't know Sara's last name. She lives on the third floor, and five of the six apartments have labels.

3A   RODRIGUEZ

3B   MILLER

3C   GARCIA

3D   JABIR

3E

3F   MARTINEZ

Miller's probably a Black name, and I don't know what the heck Jabir is. It sounds kind of Muslim, so I'm guessing those are Black people, too, who converted like Smiles's uncle Naim. I take a chance and buzz 3E. No one answers. I buzz two more times and still no response.

I start at the top and buzz 3A. An old lady answers in Spanish. "¿Quién es?"

"¿Se encuentra Sara?"

"Ay, no, m'ijo, t'equivoca'te."

"¿Sabes en qué apartamento ella vive?"

"No, lo siento." And before I can thank her, she disconnects. I move on to Garcia in 3C, and again no answer. She must be Sara Martinez and live in 3F.

Some smart-ass kid imitating Boom Boom Washington from *Welcome Back, Kotter* breathes into the intercom, "Hi there." I can hear other kids snickering behind him. Damn, did I sound that corny when I did that?

"Yo, Sara there?"

"Who this?"

"Tell her it's Nike."

"Mikey?" Another brat in the background jokes, *Hey, Mikey likes it!*

"No!" Even when I break out of camp, I can't get away from these wiseass kids. "Nike!"

"Puma? Adidas?" More stupid giggles. "Converse."

"Stop playin', yo, and tell Sara that Nike's looking for her."

"There ain't no Sara here, homeslice." I can picture the little jokers, cracking up and rolling all over the floor. I hope they wet themselves.

God punishes me for that thought, because it starts to rain again. One of those deceptive drizzles that make you think you have a shot at getting home only to blow into a full-fledged storm when you're inches from your stoop. Still, I bang on the intercom a few times, but the kids don't answer. I lean on the buzzer and yell, "I'ma come back and tell your mother you be playin' with strangers on the intercom. . . ." I'm so loud they must hear me from wherever their apartment is.

I run to the corner, praying that the pay phone works. Just when I think that at least I can chill in the booth until the storm passes, the stink of piss and alcohol slaps me in the face. Even though I should clear out of this one-man-sized petri dish, I call the camp office. Big Lou answers. "Good afternoon, Saint Aloysius's Day Camp."

"Hi, Lou, it's Nike."

"Hello, Guillermo." I can't catch a break today. "Where you calling from? I thought you were outside with Smiles and Cookie."

"I had an emergency. Look, Lou, what's Sara's last name? Garcia or Martinez?" Those smart alecks could've been her brothers.

Big Lou laughs. "Neither. Sara's last name is Jabir."

"Ha-beer?" I say, pronouncing it in Spanish. "Or Javier?"

"No. Jabir. Just the way it's spelled."

"What kinda Spanish name is that?"

"It's *not* Spanish, knucklehead. It's Arabic."

"This is the first time I ever heard of a Puerto Rican whose last name was Arabic," I say. I've known a few Boricuas whose names were not Spanish. Like that kid in junior high school, Herman Wu, whose parents owned a hardware store on Third Avenue. They were Cubans who fled to Puerto Rico when Castro took over and then eventually wound up in the Bronx. But they were straight-up Chinese! And I once had a girlfriend whose last name was Laporte or LaCourt or something like that, but she wasn't French or Haitian or nothing. But this Arabic thing's a first. That's not even a Latin language. Is it? Where's Smiles when you need him?

"Puerto Rican? Sara isn't Puerto Rican. She's Palestinian. From Lebanon, to be exact." Now Big Lou laughs even harder. "Yo, Guillermo, as bad as Port Morris might be, stay your ass in school."

Despite the cramped quarters and awful smell, I stand in the phone booth for a long time with the dead receiver to my sweaty ear. That cloudy day where I went off on Arabs, and Sara got so upset, haunts me as I head back to her building and stare at the intercom: 3D JABIR. The cold raindrops cut into me, each a reminder of all the nasty things I said about Sara's people. And she gave me so many hints and clues.

But she never came straight out and told me. Only when I remember how each time she had the chance she never chose to tell me the truth do I hit the button. No answer. I reach for it again when static comes through the grate. "Who?"

Through the scratching I can't tell if it's her or not. "My name's . . . Guillermo," I say. "Is Sara home?" Silence. I know better than to buzz again, but I won't give up. If Sara doesn't want to speak to me anymore, then let that be the last thing she ever tells me.

I run down the steps and look up at her window. A light flickers behind the closed pane. Is she looking at me through the curtains? If I call her, will she answer? Will she at least give me a chance to say I'm sorry?

Out of control. Cookie's voice rings in my head. *Creepy.*

I dig into the front pocket of my Lees for change. I've got three coins—a quarter, a dime, and a nickel. Three chances. First, I have to get her attention. Then I have to get her permission. Finally, I might be able to get Sara's forgiveness.

I take a few steps back, rolling the nickel between my fingers and praying everything I learned in Little League comes back to me. I wind up and pitch the nickel at Sara's window. It hits and bounces back down to the street. This time I toss the dime, nailing the pane once more. Nothing. "C'mon, Cutter," I say to one of the thunderclouds. "Be my backup." I make the sign of the cross with the quarter and fire it at the window. It clanks against the pane, and I run to catch it as it falls back toward me. Just as I do, a shadow moves behind the curtains. *Please be Sara, please be Sara, please be Sara . . .*

It's Sara.

Between the rain in my face and the drops on her glass, I can't see her expression. I make a receiver out of one hand and point to the pay phone with the other. Then I drop to my knees right into the middle of the wet street, clasp my hands together, and plead. A moment later Sara disappears from the window.

Where did she go? Is she coming back? Is it OK to call?

The only way I can find out is to take that chance.

I head back to the pay phone, drop the quarter into the slot, and dial Sara's number. If no one answers, that means it's over for me. "Hello."

It's Sara!

"Sara, thank God!"

"May I ask who's calling?"

She's covering up. "Look, if you can't talk on the phone right now, just hit a button. Not the hook, though!"

Beep!

"So somebody's home."

Beep! "Mr. Jabir's not available. Would you like me to take a message?"

"Sara, I know the truth. You're an Arab, and I'm an idiot. If you never want to go out with me again, I won't hold it against you, but please, please, please, talk to me at least one last time so I can tell you how sorry I am to your face. You deserve that."

"Could you spell that, please?"

"Can you pretend you're going to check the mail and come downstairs?"

Beep!

"The supermarket?"

Beep!

"The Laundromat?"

Beep!

"Not even camp?"

Beep!

Please deposit ten cents for an additional five minutes.

"Aw, man, Sara! I just got scammed by this stupid pay phone. You think you can call me at home? Please!"

She hesitates, then says, "Oh, sir, I don't think my father would be at all interested in that."

"Damn, let me think."

Please deposit ten cents for an additional five minutes.

"I just did, yo!" I jiggle the hook. "This phone tryin' to rip me off!"

Please deposit ten cents for an additional five minutes.

"Sara, just go to your window, OK?"

"I will. Thank you. Good-bye." Then she hangs up.

I walk out of that wack phone booth into the worst downpour of the summer. No matter. This could be acid rain. I'm on a mission. When I get back to Sara's building, she is standing in the window like I asked. Permission.

The ladder to the fire escape hovers about six feet above my head. With a good running start, I can make it. Walking backward, I count off three squares of concrete, the emerald suede of my soaked Pumas now a forest green that stains my white tube socks. I race forward, then leap for the ladder. Not even close, but before I hit the pavement, I still know I can do it. The second I land on the ground, I leap back farther, and try again. This time my fingers graze the cold, wet metal of the last rung. I land hard on the concrete. My legs vibrate from the shock, and it takes me a minute to recoup. That has never happened to me, even when I danced.

As I walk back six full squares, I rub my hands on the front of my damp hoodie, my drenched sneakers clomping through the puddles on the concrete. I look up at Sara's window and wait for the light to flicker as if signaling *Go*. After the flash, I burst forward, take flight, and finally clutch the wet rung. No sooner do I wrap my fingers around it than my weight rattles the ladder toward the ground. I grasp for the rung with my other hand and hold on. The ladder clangs to a hard stop, leaving me dangling several feet off the ground. For a few seconds I twist in the rain, and I'm hanging there laughing because, once again, it pays to be a b-boy.

Hauling myself up the wet ladder is no piece of cake, though. Just as I manage to plant one foot on the bottom rung, my other sneaker, heavy and bloated with rain, slips off and lands in a puddle. For a moment, I think about jumping off the ladder to go get it, then I feel the rubber of my other sneaker slide against the wet rung. I kick it off, and it drops to the ground and bounces into the gutter. Some poor kid who's braving the rain to run an errand for his mama will probably find them and take them home, hoping all they need is a tumble in the dryer. They were slippery and slowing me down. No matter. There are more important things than kicks.

I ease my way up the ladder, fighting the urge to look down. When I reach the first landing, I feel a little better. *If I take my time, I should be all right,* I'm thinking. But then I start worrying that someone's going to see me and call the police.

And that's when Sara opens her window and sticks her

head out. "Willie!" She says my name, and I like to fly up this last set of steps. "Be careful, please."

I get to her window, and Sara steps back so I can climb into her bedroom. Once my wet socks hit her hardwood floor, I look at her. Her dark eyes are red and watery, and she wipes her runny nose with the back of her hand. Sara flails her arms toward the room. "Home, sweet home." And then she starts to cry. She lets me take her into my arms, and while Sara cries on my shoulder, I look around her room. It's the same size as mine, with three twin beds, which is two too many. A large crucifix hangs on the wall against the same red-and-white scarf that Arabs wear. A small black-and-white TV sits on a dresser, and right above it hangs a flag that looks both strange and familiar. It looks kind of like a Puerto Rican flag, except it has only three stripes and no star. The triangle is red instead of blue, and the three stripes are black, white, and green. On the TV, the tail end of a jingle for Double Stuf Oreos gives way to an afternoon newsbreak.

French paratroopers and Italian soldiers have joined the United States Marine Corps in Beirut, forming a multi-national effort to assist the Lebanese army in maintaining order as the Palestine Liberation Organization evacuates the nation's capital, Beirut.

Sara pulls away from me, taking a pillow off the bed and kneeling onto the rug in front of the TV. She hugs the pillow to her chest as the newscast continues. *Although a cease-fire was arranged, Israeli troops remain in southern Lebanon while Syrian troops and PLO forces hold fast to the north and east of Beirut.* Then the same flag as on Sara's wall quickly flashes on the TV screen. *Israel has agreed to withdraw its forces from Lebanon on condition that Syria and the PLO retreat as well, but PLO leader Yasser Arafat instead has called for renewed warfare against Israel.*

When she hears this, Sara buries her face into the pillow, sobbing as if she wants to flood the room with her tears. I lower myself beside her, shivering more from the truth than the wet cold. I have the urge to put my arm around her and pull her to me, but I don't want to push myself on her. "Sara." Even if I knew what else to say, I can't imagine it would help. First time I truly care about a girl, and I have no lines to make her feel good. "Sara, what can I do?"

"What do you care?" she snaps at me. "You're getting what you wanted. Bomb all the Arabs off the map, right?"

"C'mon, Sara, Cookie done warned you," I joke. "I'm ignorant, remember?"

"Then you should shut the hell up."

At least this isn't new. Usually when I see a girl angry, it's me who's done pissed her off. If my jokes don't work, I snap back right at her. At first, the girl will go toe to toe with me, but eventually I get her wondering if maybe she is at fault. That's when I try to break out so she'll come running after me. This won't work with Sara, and not just because I have God knows how many years of history against me. I don't even want to try to play her like that. "OK."

"You *are* ignorant."

"I know."

"If you had half a brain, Willie Vega, you'd be dangerous. All the money you spend on your expensive sneakers and name-brand jeans couldn't buy you the first clue."

"Word."

"Stop patronizing me!"

"I'm not, I swear. I don't want to fight with you anymore, that's all," I say. "I'm sorry for all those things I said, and I admit I don't know nothing about no world affairs."

"Then how can you have such strong opinions?"

I just shrug. I'm glad Sara's asking me questions, even if I have no good answers. It beats her furious name-calling. "Even if something is hard to understand," I say, gesturing toward the television, "it's not hard to figure out how you're supposed to feel about it."

I expect Sara to tell me how stupid that is and why don't I think for myself and blasé, blasé, but she doesn't. She just nods and drops the pillow into her lap. "Right."

I reach over and take her hand. "Maybe you can explain it to me."

"If you truly want to understand what's going on," she says, "turn off your stupid boom box and read the newspaper for a change."

And I just stay shut up because not only does Sara have a point, she's still holding my hand.

SMILES

"Man, you're moving like an old man," I say. I dig a stick into the hillside and plant my foot on a flat rock. "I thought I'd be the one dragging up this mountain."

"Don't try me," mutters Nike. "You know I ain't get no sleep last night." Like Barb predicted, Sara won't be returning to camp, but at bedtime she sneaks the phone under her covers and whispers to Nike until all hours of the night. Homeboy's lucky the rent on the phone isn't tied to the minutes he's on it.

"How is she?" After Nike told me what happened, I did some research to make better sense of it. When the Israeli military took over the land and forced them out of their homes in Beirut, Sara's family scattered all over the globe. Some fled to other parts of the Middle East and she came to the United States, but most wound up in refugee camps. And now that Lebanon is in the midst of a civil war, with one side wanting to fight the Israelis to get their land back and the

291

others siding with the Israeli agenda for continuing to expand into Palestine, refugee camps have become prime targets. The night we were all supposed to go to the Roxy with Nike, they decimated the refugee camp Mar Elias in Sara's hometown. No one can verify the number of people massacred. One side says it was a few hundred. The other insists on thousands.

The only thing we know for sure is that several of Sara's relatives who were living in that refugee camp—including two cousins no older than the Champs—were slaughtered.

"Not good." Nike shakes his head. "No wonder she was so afraid of fireworks. Can you imagine living in a war zone like that?"

I bite my tongue. You would never think only three weeks ago a man died on his knees here or that every other night we hear gunshots in the distance and thank God we're blocks away. Poor Sara only traded one kind of war zone for another.

As I wait for him to catch up to me, I check on Stevie and Pedro ahead of us. "Y'all need to slow down now!" I yell. Shorty thinks he's Indiana Jones, the way he's running up this mountain. "Yo, I said—"

"I ain't wanna come up here anyways," Stevie says. "I wanted to go to the lake."

Nike says, "If I told you once, I done told you a thousand times. No lake. Quit bellyachin' about it." With the rash of drownings at city pools, Big Lou decided that the lake was off-limits.

Even Pedro tells Stevie in Spanish to chill out. Then he sits down to rest. "Yeah, good idea," I say. "Vamos a descansar un poquito."

I find a patch of dirt free of rocks and take a seat. "Land is important the world over, B. Look at these gangs shooting up the block trying to get control of turf. It's why Qusay had to rent the storefront and why families save to buy their own homes. Control the ground beneath your feet, control your destiny. And maybe that of everyone else living on it, too."

Nike finally reaches me and plops down beside me. "I thought Sara's situation had to do with religion or race or whatever."

"It does. People usually use something like race or religion to justify why they have a so-called right to take over some land. Remember learning about Manifest Destiny?"

He shakes his head and holds up his palm like he can't take anymore. That is so Nike. Dude can only stomach reality in doses. It makes him charming and pathetic at the same time. "Yo, why you ain't tell me about Sara? Shoe on the other foot, I would've told you."

"I know." But for some reason, I can't bring myself to apologize to him. I wouldn't have done anything differently. "You really should've heard the truth from Sara, and I promised Cookie a chance to convince her to tell you herself." I give it some more thought, then add, "I do feel bad that it didn't go down that way and messed up your birthday. But you have to admit, B, you be illin' sometimes with the things that come out your mouth. You be tryin' it."

Nike snickers and grabs a twig. He starts scraping it across the dirt. "Yeah, I know."

"So what really went down at the Roxy?"

He shrugs. "Nothing. Hardly nobody was there. Breakin's going out of style."

293

Even though I'm not a b-boy, I don't want to believe that. I love my nana, but she has to be wrong on this one. A few years back, she walked in on Nike and me tripping over the "Rapture" video on MTV. She took one look at the Man from Mars and Blondie and said, *By this time next year, this rap nonsense will have gone the way of beehive hairdos and lava lamps.* Nike always had faith, but at the time, I believed Nana. It put me in a funk, thinking that something that made me so happy could just disappear one day. It's one thing to outgrow my Saturday-morning cartoons or my Aurora racetrack. It's another to have something taken from me just because some dudes in a conference room flip over an hourglass. Now that Mama is gone, what would Pop do if he couldn't break out his 45s and listen to the Four Tops and Sam Cooke? Pop had them, Nana had Nat King Cole and Frank Sinatra, and now I have Grandmaster Flash and Michael Jackson. Come to think of it, I have them all. Still, it's cool to have something that's only mine, and that's hip-hop.

When I saw that Dawkins kids bought Sugarhill records and went to the Roxy, I began to have faith that hip-hop— the music, the dance, the language, the clothes—was here to stay. It could change. After all, Run-D.M.C. sounds nothing like the Furious Five, but it feels good to think that I'm a part of something that is going to last and connects me to all kinds of people.

Malcolm went to Mecca and thought Islam was the answer to racism. But maybe it's hip-hop. When I create a program of my own, it's going to be one of the things I teach. Even in the worst-case scenario that hip-hop doesn't last, it will always matter like rock or jazz. Despite Reaganomics, crack, AIDS, and all the other things that should have knocked us down for the count, we stood our ground and created something so, so def. That's something that should never be forgotten.

"So does that mean you're no longer going to Hollywood?"

Nike laughs. "I don't know. I mean, maybe. Not to dance, though."

"How about college?" I ask. He snorts, and I elbow him. "Nike, there are all different types of colleges. Bound to be one that'll take a sucker like you."

"You so funny I forgot to laugh."

"Major in dance."

"Ha! Can you see the diploma? Instead of Gothic letters and that hear-ye Old English, it be printed in bubble letters." He frames his fingers in the air as if to hold up his degree. "To Guillermo Vega Jr., bachelor of arts in dance with a concentration in breakin'. I mean, if people can major in history . . ." He laughs again, then drops his hands and goes back to his twig. "And where you going? Harvard, right?"

"Nah, B. I'm going to a Black college. Howard or Morehouse or someplace like that." I'm ready to defend my decision, but Nike nods like he already understands and accepts it. It hits me that this is probably our last summer together, and we're not going to have the *Grease* ending at Coney Island next Friday. Funny thing is that as different as we are, that's probably something Nike and I both wanted.

"Yo, it's too quiet out here," interrupts Nike. He looks over his shoulder up at the mountain. "Oh, shit!" He scrambles to his feet. "Where'd Shorty and Pedro go?"

I jump up, too, shielding my eyes as I look toward the top.

"Don't trip. They're up there somewhere." I scale the mountain. "Pedro!"

"Yo, Shor-tay!"

"Stevie!"

They don't answer, and when we reach the top, not a soul. I look around and spot other hikers in the distance, but no sign of Pedro or Stevie.

"Aw, man," say Nike. "Smiles, we done lost our kids."

NIKE

"Chill out," says Smiles, but he's panicking, too. "They couldn't have come back down past us without us seeing them, so we gotta go this way." We head down the opposite side of the mountain, praying that any second now Pedro and Shorty will pop into our line of sight. No luck.

I check my watch. "We need to find them kids now, Smiles. We're supposed to be back at the bus by three, and it takes at least fifteen minutes to get to base camp."

"That's where they are!" But Smiles sounds way more confident than he looks. "They already headed back."

I can't believe he said that. "All this time, B, and you still don't know my kid? Shorty done dragged Pedro deeper into these damn woods." I slap my hands to my face. "Them kids is lost and don't even know it!"

"Calm down." Smiles turns in the direction we just came. "Cross your fingers that Shorty took him that way back toward the bus."

I make the sign of the cross and yell for the hundredth time, "Shorty!"

"Pedro! Stevie!"

I cringe at the thought of other counselors hearing us wail for our kids, but we ain't got no choice. "Shorty! I swear, Smiley, when I catch the kid, I'ma kill him. You think I won't . . . SHORTY!"

We walk and call their names for ten minutes. Then I spot some other counselors and kids from Saint Aloysius in the distance. Smiles cups his hand around his mouth to holler again, and I yank at his arm. "Don't! We got to play this off. We got to stroll back to base like everything's copacetic and pray that they're there like you said."

Cookie sits on a blanket playing gin rummy with a few kids. Sure enough, the second she lays eyes on us, she asks, "Where are Pedro and Stevie?" I swear she got a sixth sense for opportunities to stick it to Smiles and me.

"They right back there," I say, quickly tossing my hand over my shoulder to no place in particular. "We got any more juice? I'm thirsty." My throat feels like sandpaper. I head over to the table where the cardboard lunch boxes are stacked and look for something to drink. There are some extra sandwiches and fruit but no cartons of milk or juice. "Damn."

A few moments later Big Lou blows his whistle. "We're breaking out in five minutes, people. Pick up your garbage. Like Smokey the Bear says, *Keep America beautiful.* And make sure you have all your stuff, because once that bus starts moving, we're not turning around."

Cookie yells, "Motivate!"

Smiles and I gawk at each other like two pooh-butts as

counselors and kids scuttle around, dumping their trash and collecting their bags. Nowhere in the crowd is either Pedro or Shorty Rock. "What we're going to do, man?"

"I don't know, B." Smiles lets go a deep breath and tosses up his hands. "I don't know."

"Shit!"

And here comes Cookie. "What's up, guys?" Her voice sounds friendly and unsuspecting. I wonder if she knows something we don't. What if this is just one big prank on me?

Smiles blurts out, "Our kids are lost, yo!"

"Smiles!"

"What, B? They are. This isn't the time to play the role."

Cookie laughs. *She laughs.* "Stop lyin'." She thinks *we're* playing a joke on *her.* It only takes a second for her to realize that Smiles and I aren't kidding. "Oh, my God. Wait. For serious?"

"Like a heart attack."

I say, "We went hiking up that mountain over there, and we all sat down. . . ."

"All four of us together," Smiles adds, to prove that we're not total fuckups. "And at one point, they took off. . . ."

"Without permission!" I say. "They just broke out without telling nobody. Cookie, you know how Shorty be!"

I wait for Cookie to yell that we do, too, which is why we never should have taken our eyes off of him. Instead she says, "OK, this is what we're going to do. Nike, you go back to the bus. If anyone asks where Smiles and I are, you tell them that you saw us near the bathrooms."

"And that Shorty and Pedro are with Smiles."

"Yeah, we took them to make one last trip before getting

299

on the bus," says Cookie. "And you make sure all my kids get on the bus."

"Bet." I break into a run toward the parking lot.

"Wait!" I stop in my tracks for more direction from Cookie. "If we aren't back in fifteen minutes, come clean to Big Lou. Pray to God it doesn't come to that." I've started running again when Cookie calls out, "And don't say anything in front of the kids! We don't want to upset them."

If Cookie ever wanted to show and prove, this is the time, and as I run toward the bus, I think she just might.

SMILES

"We went this way," I say, and Cookie and I break into a jog toward the mountaintop. As we run, I explain that they had to have gone down another side because they didn't pass Nike and me on the path we came. When we reach the foot of the hill we had climbed, I start to hike up, but Cookie grabs my arm.

"Let's just step back a few yards and see if we can spot them first," she says. "If they're still up there, we might be able to see them."

"Good idea," I say. "You go over that way. I'll go over there."

We separate, both of us calling out for Stevie and Pedro. I go for five minutes, and I don't see anyone, let alone my kids. Could they have covered that much ground already? I turn back toward where I left Cookie, and soon enough she reappears, alone but excited.

"Smiles! I saw some people from another camp, and they

301

said they saw two boys with orange T-shirts on the other side." Cookie waits for me, and when I reach her, we break out into a sprint to the other side of the mountain.

"Pedro!"

"Stevie!"

As we call their names, I keep my eyes peeled for a patch of orange amid the brown and green. "Pedro!" She stops, grabbing my arm.

"Wait, Smiles, I just thought of something. Isn't the lake this way?"

"I think so."

Cookie hop-skips into a run again. "Shorty made a big deal about wanting to go to the lake, 'member? How much you wanna bet that's where they're at?"

My stomach knots up into a braid of relief and fear. Relief because I already know that Cookie is right—the kids are at the lake—and fear that the worst has come to pass. Always spending time in a public pool where the waters rarely run deeper than three feet, lots of city kids tend to think they can swim when they can't.

"Pedro!"

"Smiley!"

Just when I think I can't go any faster, both Cookie and I ramp up our speed at the sound of Pedro's voice. We race toward the lake, leaving the competition between us in the dust. I spot them. Shorty sits on the ground with his right leg resting on a big rock. Shirtless Pedro sits beside him. He sees me and comes running. "Smiley, Smiley, Smiley!" Pedro leaps into my arms, and I hug him tight, the Spanish flooding over my tongue as if it were my first language.

"Chico, ¡me asustaste!" I try to scold him, but there is too much relief in my voice. "Why did you take off without telling me? You know you're not supposed to do that." I carry him over to where Cookie kneels beside Stevie on the ground.

Pedro says, "Stevie, he fall and get hurt."

Shorty's snot and tears have left streaks across his dirty face. Every few seconds, a sob bursts out of him like a hiccup. I have never seen the kid so beaten. I hate seeing him like this, yet wish Nike was here. My mom would say, *A quick mouth often guards a soft heart,* and Cookie was right—there's a lot of Shorty Rock in Nike Fresh.

I put down Pedro so I can kneel beside Cookie as she wipes Shorty's face with the gentleness of a mom. Pedro's camp T-shirt is knotted snugly around Shorty's ankle, which is wedged between two sticks into a makeshift splint. I smile proudly at Pedro. "¿Dónde aprendiste cómo hacer eso?"

"Yo estaba en e-boyscaut en Puerto Rico."

Cookie scolds, "¿Cuando él fue herido, por qué tu no viniste a buscarnos?"

"Porque él no quería que yo le dejo solo. Puso a llorar y llorar y llorar." I can hear the break in Cookie's heart at the picture of Shorty Rock pleading for Pedro not to leave him alone to come get us. "Y yo sabía que Smiley no me dejara." And that breaks open my heart. Of course I wouldn't leave without him, and not because it's my job. "Pues, decidé a esperar aquí con el." Cookie and I nod at him. Pedro was right to wait with Shorty.

"OK, buddy, we need to get you back to the bus." She pivots on the balls of her feet so Shorty can climb onto her back. And even though he's just fine, I hoist Pedro onto my hip and carry him, too. "It's been over twenty minutes, but hopefully Nike chickened out and didn't tell Big Lou what happened."

"From now on we shouldn't come on these trips without walkie-talkies," I say.

"That's a fresh idea, but can you imagine how much it would cost to have one for every counselor?"

The second Big Lou spots us, he yells, "What the hell happened?"

"Stevie got hurt while hiking." I wait for Cookie to throw Nike and me under the bus, but that's all she says. Big Lou looks to me for some kind of confirmation or denial, but I have nothing to say.

He's not having it, though. "Go on." Big Lou fumes as he steps aside and watches us carry the kids onto the bus. "We'll deal with this when we get back to the Bronx."

NIKE

When Smiles carries Shorty Rock onto the bus, some of the other kids applaud, while a few counselors mumble sarcastically, *'Bout time.* Me? I almost die. No one has a clue yet how serious this could have been. They just think Shorty and Pedro zoned out during their adventures and lost track of time.

And that's what the kids are supposed to do at day camp. Our job as counselors is to keep track of them and time so they can lose themselves without getting lost. I failed at my job today.

Big-time.

A few kids spot the splint on Shorty's leg, and the buzz starts. As the bus driver pulls out of the parking lot, Big Lou heads to the back where I'm hiding. Without raising his voice, Big Lou says, "You're docked for the rest of the week."

What am I going to do? Jump bad? Instead I nod twice, look down at my Nikes, and say, "Yes, sir. I'm sorry."

I watch Big Lou make his way to the front of the bus.

305

Cookie, Smiles, and I look at each other. I can tell we're thinking the same thing. Are they next?

But Big Lou walks right past them. When he reaches his seat, he claps his hands and starts a chant. "Everywhere we go-oh . . ."

"Everywhere we go-oh . . . ," the kids repeat.

> People want to know—oh
> People wanna know—oh
> Whooo we are—ah
> Whooo we arrah
> And we tell them
> And we tell 'em
> We are the Champions!
> We are the Champions!
> The mighty, mighty Champions!
> The mighty, mighty Champions!
> Your leeeft, your left
> Your leeeft, your left . . .

While Big Lou and the rest of the campers continue the chant as if it were still an ordinary day, I get up and head toward the front of the bus. I find Shorty Rock sitting by himself, hiccuping sobs. He looks up at me and throws his arm over his head, trying to block the oops upside his head he's expecting from me.

But that's the last thing on my mind. "Scoot over." For the first time all summer, Shorty does as I ask him without first giving me any lip. "You OK?"

Shorty Rock sniffs and nods.

"Good. I'm glad." Then I put my arm around his shoulder and stroke his hair. Within minutes the rocking of the bus puts him to sleep.

Maybe he's not such a demonio after all.

SMILES

The second we get back from Bear Mountain—fifteen minutes late and to a crowd of worried relatives—Big Lou hauls the three of us into Barb's office. "What happened?" she asks, her voice already assuming trouble.

"Once again, this knucklehead wasn't watching his kid." Big Lou swats Nike's baseball cap off his head. "This time when Stevie wandered off, he took Smiles's kid with him and got hurt."

"Please don't tell me that," says Barb. "I don't want to hear that." She looks at me, hoping I can explain how Big Lou got it all wrong.

With my eyes fixed on my shell-toes, I say, "Shorty, I mean Stevie, must have tripped and fell, because when we found them, his ankle was sprained or something."

"Oh, shit." Barb puts her fist to her mouth. After a few seconds of silence, she begs for another explanation. "We sent this kid home hurt?"

Nike blurts, "You should've seen him, though. Once we

got back to the Bronx, he was laughing and jumping around like nothing happened. He's OK, Barb."

"But something did happen," yells Cookie. "And just because he's bouncing around doesn't mean he isn't really hurt."

Nike is about to sass back at her, but Big Lou says, "If I were you, I'd keep my mouth shut."

"You know what?" says Barb. "He can tell his story walking."

"I'm way ahead of you, Barb. Knucklehead already knows not to expect a full paycheck next week."

"A full check next week? I'm talking don't bother coming in Monday." Barb turns to Nike and says, "You're fired."

That doesn't surprise me, but I had hoped it wouldn't come down to that. A sprained ankle isn't just a sprained ankle. A sprained ankle is a potential lawsuit. A sprained ankle can make the city decide to pull the Summer Youth Employment Program from Saint Aloysius, costing all of us our jobs. A sprained ankle can shut down the camp and leave the kids in this neighborhood on the streets. Like Qusay said, *This is not Mecca.*

What does surprise me is that Nike doesn't fuss about it. Instead, he hangs his head and says, "Sorry." And I know I won't hear any rants from him later blaming Shorty Rock or about suing Barb. He means it. "Can I go?"

"No," says Barb. "I'm not done with you. Go outside and wait until I deal with these two." Nike leaves, and then Barb turns to me. "So Pedro took off with Stevie, is that right?"

"Yes, ma'am."

"That means had you been watching him, this might not have happened."

If I had been watching Pedro, it definitely would not have

309

happened. Those two are thick as thieves. A month ago Stevie might've taken off on his own, but now Pedro and he are inseparable, the way Nike and I used to be. They're homeboys, and where one goes, the other follows. "Yes, ma'am."

Barb turns to Cookie. "And your involvement in all this?"

"I just helped Smiles look for them, that's all."

And that's the shocker of the day. Here's Cookie's chance to rub in the fact that not only did we lose our kids but she was the one who found them, and she doesn't take it.

Big Lou isn't about to let her off the hook, though. "Don't fall for it, Barb. She was in cahoots with Frick and Frack."

"No, she wasn't," I say. "She wasn't even with us when the kids got lost."

"I don't believe that," says Big Lou.

"Don't then." I don't mean to disrespect him, but now he's busting chops for kicks. "But it's the truth."

"She didn't try to help you cover it up?"

"No, she didn't," I say. "She just went with me to look for them. It was Cookie's idea to go to the lake, which is how we found them."

"You realize how bad this could've turned out, Raymond?" Barb stands up and points her finger at me. "Those kids could've drowned."

"I know," I say. "And I'm sorry." I almost wish she would fire me already. I couldn't possibly feel worse. Getting my just deserts might actually make me feel a tiny bit better about the whole fiasco.

"You're both docked for the entire week." Barb retakes her seat. "Now get out of here."

Cookie is too ready to leave, but I say, "She didn't do anything wrong, Barb. Why dock her?"

Barb straightens up. "Are you talking back to me?"

"No disrespect. I've got it coming, but Cookie didn't do anything but help us. She doesn't deserve to lose a week's pay." At twenty-five cents more an hour, she would pay a lot more for doing a lot less than I did.

Big Lou says, "She does deserve something, because as senior counselor, her job is to help me make sure the counselors are doing their jobs. I don't know where she was at when y'all were acting the fool on the mountain, but obviously it wasn't where she was supposed to be. Probably playing around with some kids." Cookie drops her head and sniffs hard. *Don't cry, Cookie,* I say to myself as if she can hear me. *Stay tough or they'll fire you.* Her biggest mistake was wanting to prove herself to Nike and me.

"I told you, Barb, anybody who's young enough to qualify for SYEP is too young to be a senior counselor," says Big Lou. "It's a job for some college kid."

Cookie sniffs again, and I tug at the hem of her shorts to get her attention. She glances toward me, and I give her a slight nod. *Don't cry.*

Barb finally says, "Two days, because I'm not buying you weren't involved in the attempt to cover it up." She motions for us to leave, but just as we're halfway out the door, she mutters to Big Lou, "I should just close down this damn camp. Too much responsibility, too little money, no respect, no appreciation. What's the point?"

Cookie and I walk out of the church basement and onto the street without saying a word. Nike's sitting there on the

311

church steps, waiting for us. "You still here, B?" Not like him to stick around to take any more licks from Barb since he doesn't work for her anymore, but I'm glad he stayed and lower myself beside him. "Better break out while you can. Barb's fixing to yank Jesus down off the cross so Lou can crucify you instead."

"Ha." Nike pulls off his cap and wipes his forehead with the back of his hand. He glances at the church and starts to make his way back. "Let me get this over with."

"We'll wait."

"Good luck, Willie," says Cookie. She plants herself on my other side. I bet it makes her feel good to be included, even if she's in deep trouble. On the one hand, she showed and proved. On the other hand, Cookie's a dummy for wanting to be down with two suckers like us. The Mod Squad: Bronx Division? More like the Three Stooges. That cracks me up.

"Man, you laugh at everything," Cookie says. "That's why we call you Smiles."

NIKE

I've been reading the newspapers and watching the news for a few days now, and I still don't get it. When I ask Smiles to help me understand, he goes off on one of his Black militant tears, talking about *occupation* and *oppression,* confusing me some more and scaring me to boot.

"Smiles, not for nothin', do you even know everything you're saying?"

"You cold, B."

"Not to dis"—yes, just a little—"you be sounding like a Qusay Jr."

Smiles laughs. "Call me Smiley X."

That got me dyin' like old times. Then I ask, "Yo, what went down between y'all, anyways?"

Smiles pauses. "We were both at fault. I was looking for a way to make a bigger difference in the neighborhood, I guess. Like what we do at camp is medicine, but I wanted to find a cure. And to some extent, Qusay took advantage of that, but that's because he wanted to do the same thing.

313

"And you know what?" Smiles says. "Maybe I don't get everything. But if anybody did, all the problems would be solved, right?" Then he adds, "Here's the thing, though. A lot of folks don't want to get it. We confuse complaining about things with really wanting to change them. The reality is we're more comfortable with the evil we know."

Smiles didn't do squat to help me understand what's going down in the Middle East, so while he made me feel a little better, he made me feel a little worse, too, to be honest. On the one hand, I'm not an exception. On the other, I'm part of the problem.

Then I call Cookie. "You know how not all Muslims are Arabs, right?" she says. "Well, not all Arabs are Muslims. Some are Christians like Sara. And you know how during the Holocaust in Europe, Jews either fled or were expelled? The same thing happened to Palestinian Christians during the Arab-Israeli War a few years later."

"Yo, how do people who got that much in common beef so much?" Confusion makes my head pound. "And if Sara's Greek Orthodox, that's something completely different than Roman Catholic, right? Is she Palestinian or Lebanese?"

Cookie exhales. "Willie, why don't you just ask Sara? There's so much history involved here. No one is going to know it better than she does."

"'Cause . . ." *How much more ignorant do I have to look in front of this girl?* "Forget it."

"C'mon, don't be like that."

"Nah, it's all right."

"I feel for you, Willie. For serious I do. You always be trying so hard, just in all the wrong ways."

"So what's the right way?" I say, all frustrated. "At least tell me that."

"Just listen, Guillermo."

I hang up the phone. Then I smack all the newspapers off my bed and stare at the cracks in my ceiling until my room grows pitch-black. I must've fallen asleep, because I don't even hear the phone ring. Gloria knocks on my door, and a beam of light from the hallway cuts into the darkness.

"Oh, wait, he is here," she says into the phone. Gloria carries it over to the bed as I squint so my eyes can adjust to the sudden light. "It's Sara."

And for once I'm glad Cooks meddled. No way Sara would be calling me if she hadn't pushed her. I take the phone. "Hi, Sara."

"Hey, Willie."

"How you doin'?"

"Not so good."

I remember what Cookie says. "You want to talk about it?"

"You wouldn't understand."

"Try me. Keep it basic, though. You know I ain't some foreign correspondent."

A whisper of a smile flows through the receiver. "OK, let me think." I let Sara take her time. She finally says, "So you have this home, right? This beautiful place where you have always lived. In fact, your family has been there for centuries. It's full of traditions and memories for you. This place is a major part of who you are. Then one day, Javi moves in across the street—"

"Uh-oh . . ." I know I'm supposed to be listening, but I can't help myself.

"It's not bad off the bat. Although he's been around to other parts of the world, he's got ties to the land, too. Javi and his people come back because things were horrible for them everywhere else."

Something clicks. "You're talking about the Jews in Europe. The Nazis and the Holocaust and all that." Reading the paper and watching the news is paying off. Only one or two things I took in referred to that history, but I got the gist.

"Right. Javi's people were running for their lives. The United Nations decides, *OK, since they have ties to Willie's land, let them return there. In fact, we'll give them more. This one block. And that one. Oh, and this one, too.* Next thing you know, Javi is at your doorstep, telling you, *Get out. This is my house now.* All that you have ever known he is now claiming is his for the taking."

"I wish he would try it."

"So you would defend your home."

"Hell, yeah!"

"Remember when we first met, how Javi and his buddies were chasing you? How it wasn't safe for you to go home? Remember how you said to me that you could take them in a fair fight but they like to gang up on you?"

"Yeah." My body tightens as if I'm wedged between Pac-Man and the wall again. I have this sinking feeling that no matter how much time passes, it's always going to feel like it happened yesterday. In the middle of all this tightness, though, is an oasis of light because Sara remembered, too. She felt for me in that moment. She still does.

"Whether you want to talk things out peacefully and come to some kind of compromise or just duke it out and let the strongest man win, it's not just Javi you have to face down. It's Javi and his friends."

"Junior. The Barbarians."

"And they have friends. Or at least people who are afraid of them because they have money and guns. You don't have the same things at your disposal." Sara's voice cracks. "They come push you out of your home and force you into camps. You fight back, but they have money and weapons and allies. . . . It's just not right. It's not fair."

Then it clicks.

Junior and the Barbarians aren't some foreigners. He's our president. The Barbarians are our government, army, and all that.

I would accuse Smiles of being Qusay's parrot, but every time I boasted about being patriotic without knowing the whole deal, I was cheating and acting like a Barbarian, too.

This is devastating.

And confusing. The news is filled with stories about terrorists killing innocent people and sometimes even suicide bombers who check themselves out in the process. They're so big and bad that they've started bringing their fight here. We supposed to just let them do that?

Before I can find the right words to ask that without further upsetting her, Sara continues. "The news keeps calling this a conflict or a war, but that's a lie," she says. "How is this a war when one side has no army, no navy, no air force?" She breaks down sobbing. "This is a genocide. They're wiping us off the face of the earth."

Somehow I understand that Sara doesn't mean to throw my words back at me to make me feel guilty. Still, that's the moment I realize that there's no winning her back. Even if I understood and agreed with everything she said—which I'm not too sure I would—I could never give Sara what she wants most in the world.

Sara doesn't want my buckle or the latest fashions or a night out at a hot spot.

She wants to go home.

She wants to be safe.

She wants her people to be saved. Or at the very least to not be labeled criminals for doing whatever they can to save themselves.

But I can't give Sara what I myself never experienced.

I never really had a place that I could call home. I've never felt safe. And while I know I'm part of a people, I've been so disconnected from them I had to be told that they may need to be saved, too.

I stay losing for not having.

Right now I do the only thing I can. I stay on the phone and listen to Sara cry. She wails with a grief a lot older than she is, and a few times I think I won't make it. I have to fight the urge to, for the first time ever, be like, *OK, Sara, I got to go.* My love and sympathy for this girl help me to hang on the line for her. I stay on the phone with Sara until she cries herself to sleep. It was my way to, for once in my life, do good and throw it into the sea.

"Bye, Sara," I say for what I know will be the last time, and then I hang up.

SMILES

I jiggle my knee as I wait for Cookie to answer the telephone. Why am I so nervous? It's not like I've never called her before. It's just been a while.

"Hello?"

"Hey, Cookie. It's Smiles."

"Hey . . ." She sounds surprised to hear from me. "Everything OK?"

"Oh, yeah, everything's chilly most."

"So . . . what's up?"

"I came up with an idea." I switch the phone to my other ear. "And I thought you'd be down with it. A way to make it up to Barb."

"OK."

"You know how she never gets to go on any of the trips, right?"

"Yeah."

"Well, I was thinking this year maybe you and I stay

319

behind and watch the office or do whatever needs doing, you know, so she can go to Coney Island."

"Smiles . . . that's a fresh idea." I notice a difference in Cookie's voice. It's relaxed and deep. She sounds like a woman. "You think she'll trust us?"

"I know Barb. If we go to her together, she'll agree to it. And appreciate it a whole lot, too."

Cookie says, "We can really hook up the space for the fall. Take inventory, organize the supply closet, throw out junk . . ."

"Maybe we can paint!"

"We won't have time for that, Smiles, but we'll Spic and Spade the hell out of it!"

I laugh. Cookie can be funny sometimes. "Word. Cooks, can I ask you something? And you won't get mad."

"Sure. But it depends. Take your chances."

That is so Cookie. "And you can tell me the truth. I won't judge you or talk behind your back or anything like that. I promise."

"My God, Smiles, ask already!"

"You and Javi . . ."

"Not that again."

"I kind of already know."

"Know what? That we made out? When he tried to feel me up, I kneed him in the nuts, and that was that."

"Oh, snap." I crack up at that. "For real?"

Cookie laughs. "C'mon, Smiles . . . you know me."

"I knew all along he was exaggerating."

"Then why did you act like you believed him?" Her usually shrill voice goes soft and shaky. "Calling me a crab and all that?"

"I don't know. Immature guy stuff. I'm sorry, Cooks."

"Forget it." We share a breather. "Now can I ask you something?"

"Sure."

"Did your mom really die of sickle cell anemia?"

I've been dreading the day when someone would come straight out and ask that. Now the moment is here, and without saying a word, I already feel like I finally dropped a wheelbarrow of bricks that I've been pushing around for too long. The right person asked. "She died of pneumonia, but her doctors are starting to think that maybe it wasn't the sickle cell that made her vulnerable to it, because Mama . . . she contracted HIV." I brace myself for a big, uncomfortable reaction, but Cookie is as silent as stone. It's the only response that would have let me continue unloading. "Her hematologist now thinks she may have gotten the virus from one of her transfusions."

"I'm so sorry, Smiley." Cookie sounds as if she's holding back tears, and I appreciate her trying to be strong for me. "I'm so, so sorry."

I start speaking at the speed of light. "And Pop and Nana won't talk about it. They say, *It's just speculation. It was the sickle cell. No one really knows. It was the pneumonia. Don't tell anybody. It wasn't that, OK, so there's nothing to discuss. It doesn't change anything.* And if we can't have a conversation about it in my own family, I'd probably get disowned if they knew I was telling you." Now I wish I hadn't said anything. I just betrayed my family. Nike was right to question my loyalty. Qusay was right not to hire me. Barb was right not to promote me. The way people vilify people

321

who have AIDS, and my own mother couldn't trust me to protect her good name.

"I'll never tell a soul, Smiley. Who knows how people gossip and judge more than me, right?" says Cookie. "And even though it bothers me in the moment, it never lasts, and you know why? Because eventually I remember what Ms. Netty always used to tell me." Then, in the worst Jamaican accent ever uttered in the history of the world, she says, "*Time langa den rope.*" I must laugh for a good five minutes. The pounding in my temples and cramp in my belly hurt so good, and I fall off my bed dyin'. Cookie just snickers into the phone and waits until I compose myself. "Anyway, that's just my way of saying that nothing could ever come to light to hurt your mother's reputation, that's all."

Clutching my aching stomach, I crawl back into my bed. The hard laugh doesn't distract me from the sadness in Cookie's voice. "How's your mom, Cooks?"

"She's good. Not ready for the school year yet," Cookie chuckles. "Said the summer went way too fast."

"Word. It did." Should I ask? "And your dad?"

Cookie sighs. "If you ask him, he's just fine, you know, 'cause now he only drinks on the weekends. But you know the deal, Smiles. He's the same. They call it dry drunk syndrome."

"Yeah, my mom explained that to me once." She's revealing all these painful things, yet I feel good. Not that I'm glad Cooks is having problems, I'm just happy she feels she can trust me with them, especially after all the static between us this summer. "I'm sorry about that."

"Ah, don't be sorry. He just sits there and stares at the TV.

Could be worse, right? He's not in a bar getting into fights or whaling on us or anything like that, the way some dudes do." Even over the phone, I sense the force behind Cookie's chuckle. "And how's your dad, Smiley?"

"Pop's good."

"Cool. And Nana?"

I smile at the way Cookie refers to my grandmother as Nana. "Nana's no joke. She's gonna outlive all of us."

"Right? I have to come by and see her."

"She'd like that. Nana and Pops, they always asking, *How's Carolina?*"

"Really?"

"For real."

We're both quiet for a moment, and funny that it feels normal. Cooks and I could always just chill. That's how our friendship was different from the one I had with Nike. When we went to a movie or watched TV, he was always so restless, but Cookie and I could do homework together, ride the subway reading our own books, and even watch a ball game on TV, quiet and cozy.

Then Cookie says, "I don't know why I've never told you this before . . . I mean, it's not like it's bad or anything. . . . Whenever I go to Woodlawn to visit my abuelita and bring her fresh flowers, I stop by your mom's grave and leave her some, too." The ache in my heart has a twin in her voice. "Not for nothing, Smiles, you know I love my mom to death. . . ."

"I know, Cooks."

"She's a good person."

"Your mom's real good people."

"But your mom, Smiley? She was just . . . When my dad

was really bad, and my mother could barely cope herself, never mind be there for me, Ms. Netty helped me so much." Cookie's voice breaks, and she stops to sniffle. "I love my mom with all my heart, but it's your mom I wanna be like when I grow up."

"You will, Cooks. I can already see it." Even though my voice gives away that I'm crying, it's cool. After all, she's my oldest friend. "You will."

NIKE

A yo, Nike!

Nikeee!

Nike, oh, Nike, wherefore art thou, Nike?

That sucka's wherefore art upstairs, that's where. Yo, Nike, why don't you come down here and face me like a man, homeboy?

For the past fifteen minutes, I've been acting like I don't hear Junior and his court jesters taunting me. Gloria busts into my room and bum-rushes the window. "Get lost."

But Glo looks worried. She stands off to the side, peeking through the *Star Wars* curtains. "What you gonna do, Willie?"

"Find out if Archie chooses Betty or Veronica," I say, rolling onto my side toward the wall. I already know that this time Archie chooses sweet Betty over conniving Veronica, even though I've been stuck on the same page ever since those clowns showed up under my window. If I had made the same choice, I might not be in this wack situation. "*Get* away from the window already!" The last thing I need is for any Barbarians to see the *Millennium Falcon*s on my curtains. The second they're gone, I'm taking down those damn things. *Niiikeee . . . come out and plaaay!* I make out five different cackles, although I'm sure there's a full crowd in front of my building by now.

Gloria makes a beeline toward my door. "I'm calling Vanessa," she says.

"What the hell for?" I shoot up in bed. "She's the reason he's down there."

My sister runs out of my room. "That's why she's the one who has to put her stupid brother in check."

I chase Gloria into the hallway. I can't have my little sister fight my battles, but Gloria has grabbed the telephone and locked herself in the bathroom. "Gloria, you're making things worse!" I bang on the door.

"Can I speak to Vanessa? . . . Yo, why you send your brother over here to pop shit with Willie? Don't deny it. My brother quit you, get over it!"

I pound on the bathroom door. "Gloria, stop!"

"I swear to God, Vanessa, if you don't put Junior in check, I'm not going to be your friend anymore. And if I'm not your friend, you can forget about Judy and Monique and them being your friends, too."

"Gloria!"

My mother tears out of the living room into the hallway. "How many times do I have to tell you to leave your sister alone?"

"I didn't do anything!"

Ma pushes me aside, grabs the doorknob, and rattles it. "Gloria, I'm going to count to three, and if you're not off the phone and out of this bathroom . . ."

"You don't got no one to blame but yourself," Gloria tells Vanessa. "What I tell you? *My brother's a playboy!* But you ain't wanna listen."

"One . . ."

"And it ain't like you the Virgin Mary either, so stop playing the role."

"Two . . ."

"Let me tell you something, Vanessa. Stop sending Junior and his boys to jump Willie. If my brother gets beat down, I'ma kick your butt good for you. Y'all don't scare me." My mother doesn't even say *three*. She grabs the telephone cord and yanks it out of the jack "You hear me, Vanessa? Vanessa? Hello? What happened to the phone?"

"Ma broke it 'cause you wouldn't get out the damn bathroom!"

"I did not break the phone, I only disconnected it." Then she growls into the bathroom door, "Gloria Marie Vega, if you do not come out of the bathroom this second, you will not leave this apartment until school starts." Two seconds later, Gloria opens the door. "Give me the phone now." My sister hands Ma the phone. Ma wraps the cord around the receiver and tucks it under her arm. "You kids think that because I don't say anything, I don't know what's going on, but I know everything." She makes her way to the door, grabbing her pocketbook off the table. "I'm putting an end to this right now!"

"Ma, where you going?"

"Mommy!" Phone still under her arm and keys in fist, my mother makes her way out the apartment and toward the stairwell. "Oh, my God, Willie, she's going outside to tell off Junior." In her bare feet, my sister takes off after her.

"Oh, shit!" I run into my bedroom and scramble around looking for my socks and sneakers, because I can't throw down in chancl'as. Whatever beef I may have with her, that's my mother, and nobody is going to disrespect her. Nobody.

When I get outside, everyone on the block is surrounding my mother and Junior. "My son don't want your sister anymore, OK? Punto final. Just leave Willie alone already y todos los Melendez que se vayan pa' carajo!"

Vanessa rushes into the crowd just in time to hear my mother send her entire family to hell. Ma moves toward her, fixing to repeat the message, but Junior steps between her and his sister. "You females stay out of this and let me talk to Nike, man to man."

"If you want to talk to him, man to man, then why you bring these entrometi'os to yell things at his window?"

My guts jerk every time Ma emphasizes a point by jabbing her finger inches away from Junior's face. I keep waiting for him to warn her to knock it off, but he takes it like it's nothing. "I just wanna talk to your son," he calmly repeats. "Tha's all."

"You walk around here like you're Mr. Mucho Macho, but I've seen how you do. My son gets up early and goes to work. He comes home, he hangs out with his friends, talks on the phone with his girlfriend. Willie minds his own business. All you do is stand across the street and do your dirt, ruining families vendiendo drogas."

The Professor yells, *Oooh!* and some of the younger kids join him.

"No disrespect, Doña Alicia," says Junior, his voice getting thinner by the word. "But this here is between your son and me, because he's been doggin' my sister. Good boy, my ass. You ain't got nothing to say about that?"

I wish the sidewalk would crack open and swallow me whole. But then the word on the street would be *not only does Nike get his mother to fight his battles, he leaves her flat.* I don't know what else to do except first get my mother to leave. I grab at her housecoat and say, "Forget it, Ma."

She swats my hand off of her. "You want to fight my son?" Damn, who does my mother think she is? Cus D'Amato? "You fight my son fair and square. One on one. Like a man." More *Oooh!* and *Dis!* from the crowd. "Don't send your little spies across the street to pretend to be his friend and trick him into saying bad things about you behind your back so you can come over here and start something." Ma gives Javi a dirty look. I had no idea she was hip to his double-agent ways! All this hood I never knew she had in her is on display, and it'd be kind of cool, if I weren't the reason.

Then Gloria puts in her two cents. "This is between my brother and your sister anyways, so why don't you just mind your business, Junior?"

"Yo, my sister is my business!" yells Junior, taking a step forward.

My instinct takes over, and I step in front of him. "And my sister's my business, so don't even think about jumping bad with her. You want to talk to me? Here I am."

Pooh hollers, " 'Bout time, nigga!"

329

"I've always been here," I say to him. Then I tell Junior, "What is it that you think I did to your sister?"

"Stop playin' stupid." He gets into my face. "You know what you did."

I take a step back. "First of all, don't be gettin' all up in my face, B. You need some Certs, a Tic Tac, or something." I'm as loud as I am scared, but I can't let him pop shit in front of all these people. Otherwise it'll be open season on Nike until I move or die.

"Oh, you want to snap?" Junior steps back into my face again.

"I'm just sayin'." Man, I'm glad that my throat isn't quivering like my knees. "Stop playin' me close."

"You the one who need to stop playin'. You got your mama out here talkin' 'bout the dirt I do. What about the dirt you doin' my sister?"

"I ain't even going out with your sister no more!" Now I'm really mad, and I don't care what happens. Everybody knows Vanessa will go all the way with any dude who spends a little money on her, and I know for a fact that's she gone out with more than one dude at a time, too. I'm just one record in her jukebox. The worst thing I did to Vanessa was love her and leave her before she played me. "I been quit your crab of a sister."

"Nigga, I'll . . ." Junior takes another step closer, and this time, instead of backing up, I meet him halfway. Now we're nose to nose. This is it.

That's when my crazy mother pulls an ice pick out of her pocketbook. "¡Mátalo, Willie!" she screams while trying to press the pick into my hand. "¡Mátalo!" Folks yell, *Oh, shit!* and start to back up.

"Ma, are you crazy!" Kill him? *She's* killing *me!* I swear to God, I'ma die of embarrassment right here.

"Junior, you promised me!" Vanessa finally steps in between Junior and me. "You just made everything worse. Take a chill pill."

"All you people leave my son alone!" Ma screams, waving the ice pick as my sister pulls her back inside the building. "You mess with my kids, you answer to me!"

Vanessa says, "I told you I wanted to talk to Nike in private."

I suck my teeth crazy loud at that one. Vanessa knows her brother. She blabbed all our business precisely because she wanted him to create a scene.

Junior says, "Yo, I'm tired of putting up for you, Nessa. You be runnin' these streets like a little sucia and then gonna whine when niggas disrespect you. What I told you when he first started rappin' to you?" Vanessa just stares at her jelly sandals. "I said stay away from Nike 'cause he a dog, right?" The crowd that's left oohs, and I wish I had a dollar for every time someone called me that. It'd be better than winning Zingo. "And did you listen to me? No! You went and spread ya legs for him and now you wanna come cryin' to me about how he played you dirty." The crowd uh-huhs. "You know what?" Junior swipes his palms across each other. "Se 'cabó. I'm not sticking up for you no more. The next time some dog plays you or some female out here calls you a ho, I'ma say shit." He motions for the Barbarians to follow him.

The crowd is still crowing *Damn!* and *Word!* as they break out, too, and I suddenly feel sorry for Vanessa. Her own brother just dismissed her in front of the entire block. It's one thing for Junior to accept the way she be carrying herself and decide he can't do nothing about it. But to come down on her like that for everyone to hear? He might as well have stuck a KICK ME sign on Vanessa's back. What a punk. Gonna put an innocent man in the ground but leave his own sister defenseless. Glo works my last nerve, and I sure be going off on her behind closed doors, but no matter what my sister says or does, I'm not gonna give the block permission to dis her like that. Just like when push came to shove, she ultimately sided with me. My mother, too. If you can't count on your family for backup, you don't got nobody.

I don't have everything I want, but at least I got them.

"C'mon," I say as I reach for Vanessa's hand. When our fingers touch, she starts crying a flood like I pressed a button to make the tears flow. "Let's go to our spot."

We walk across the street and into an alley between the buildings. As we cross, I look over my shoulder to shoot a nasty look at any averigua'os even thinking about shadowing us. It feels odd to be in our alley with her again. Vanessa and I have been here a hundred times, sometimes to make out, sometimes to fight, but always alone and together. This is the first time we've been here since we broke up, and now I realize how dark, narrow, and smelly it is. I can hardly breathe and want out ASAP. "So what's up?"

"The reason why my brother was so mad at you is because he thought you got me pregnant and broke out." I hold my breath. "I'm not. You can chill."

I sigh. "I was gonna say . . ."

"Say what?" Vanessa locks her arms across her chest. "That you're not the father? It ain't like we used anything."

The conversation I had with Smiles after the first time

332

Vanessa and I did it flashes through my mind. After getting all the juicy details out of me, he asked if Vanessa was on the pill. When I told him I didn't know, Smiles shook his head, patted me on the back, and cracked, *Congratulations! It's a boy. Guillermo the Third.* "C'mon, Nessa, you sayin' that I'm the only guy you've been with?"

"I'm not saying ever, but when I was with you, Nike, I wasn't with anybody else. What you take me for?"

"You didn't mess with Pooh? Or Flex?"

"I went out with them, but I didn't *do it* with them."

I scoff at her. "Yet."

"You know what, Nike?" Vanessa charges me until her head is right under my chin. She practically shoves a chipped nail into my nose. "I'm tired of you saying that like you're better than me. Yeah, I mess around. So what? At least I admit it. Unlike somebody I know, if I feel I gotta hide something, then I don't do it."

"Yo, get your hand out my face." And like brother like sister, Vanessa practically stands on my shell-tops and jabs her finger into my forehead. I shove her to get her off my dogs and drop down to clean them off. "You are so lucky you're a girl, man!"

"Lucky?" says Vanessa. "When I wasn't ready to do it, I was a tease, so you cheated on me, and that was cool. For you, anyway. *Oh, Nike's a playboy. He's such a Casanova. What a Don Juan.* No matter what you did, you were so high post. Meanwhile, when you were out there messin' with whoever, I stood home alone crying, and what did that make me? A pendeja. Una estúpida. A big dummy. So I say, *Two can play that game,* and go and have some fun. And what happens then? People call me a ho or a crab or whatever just for doing the same thing you were doing. You're the hero and I'm the villain, even though I'm the one telling the truth."

Now Vanessa is sobbing so hard I'm afraid she might have some kind of attack. I reach out to her. "C'mon, Nessa, calm down."

"Don't touch me, you stupid jerk!" She slaps me upside my head and then runs down the alley. "And don't tell me I'm lucky I'm a girl!" And just before Vanessa disappears, she pulls something out of the pocket of her shorts and throws it hard on the ground. It makes a loud clang and pops into two pieces as it hits the pavement. I go to see what it is. My buckle. I finally got it back, with the frame and the letters N, K, and E in one hand and the letter I in the other.

SMILES

I take a deep breath and walk into Qusay's hospital room.

"Raymond?"

"What's up, Q?"

"Wow." He offers me his left hand. I take it, and we have an awkward shake. Then we lean into each other for a short hug. "It's good to see you, G."

"I'd rather see you back on the block, though."

"You and me both," he says, sitting up in his bed, careful to lean only on his good arm. "Doctor says a few more days and I can go home."

"And home is . . ."

Qusay gives me a big smile. "You really think I'm going to let some kids run me out of my own neighborhood?"

"I don't know, Q," I say. "That kid had a gun."

He nods. "Any word on Mark? Have they found him?"

The hard part came so quickly I didn't even have a chance to butter him up with Nana's coconut drops. She had me

335

thinking I was dicing all that coconut for her friends at the community center, only to hand me the bag as I walked out the door. Nana shrugged and said, *Howdy an tenk yu nu bruk no square.*

"Yeah, Q, they did." I shuffle my feet, and that broadcasts just how bad the news is. "They pulled his body out of the Harlem River."

Qusay knows how these things go down. "He didn't drown, though."

I shake my head. "He was shot and fell off the Willis Avenue Bridge." Or more likely was tossed off.

"The cops," says Q.

"C'mon, G." I was actually surprised that Junior chose to handle it that way. I kept waiting for Booby to resurface long enough for an addict to wild out on him during a hand-to-hand or another Barbarian to drop him in an alley over a made-up girlfriend. Junior took care of this one personally. And because every block has a drug lord cutting down folks who are Black and poor, the cops will knock a few heads—maybe even score some kills of their own—and then throw their hands up. "You know it was Junior."

"You don't think Junior has some fuzz in his back pocket? If he didn't pay them to do it, he paid them to look the other way."

"I don't doubt it, but . . ." I stop arguing. I didn't come here to do that, and it doesn't matter anyway. Qusay and I agree on one thing. The cops don't have to be on Junior's payroll to decide to ignore Booby's murder.

Qusay puts his hand over his eyes and takes a deep breath. When he drops his hand, his eyes are full of tears. "He didn't want to do it, Ray. Mark was close enough to kill me if he wanted to, and I'm still here."

"What are you saying, Q?" Even though we're in the room alone, I lean in closer to him. "You saying Booby missed you on purpose?"

"I was running into the school for cover, and Cutter got in front of him. I heard Mark beg Cutter to get out the way, with Junior behind him yelling, *Do it, Boob. It's him or you. Finish him already.*" Qusay finally looks me in the face, tearful eye to tearful eye. "That's why I have to go back. My work there is not done. Cutter knew it. Mark knew it. And you know it, too, G." I nod, and Qusay puts his hand on my shoulder. "Come back to the academy. I need you to help me convince the other brothers to return. I'll pay you."

I step back away from Qusay, his hand sliding off my shoulder and back onto his hospital bed. "I admire you, Q. Words can't describe how much I do. And the homies need a brother like you. But it's not the place for me."

"Get this straight, G." Qusay squints at me. "You belong anyplace you see fit to be."

As much as I appreciate Qusay's words, I don't believe him. Maybe I can bend myself to fit somewhere, but that doesn't make a place right for me. It's the block, but it isn't, and so I still live there. It isn't Dawkins, but it is, so I still go there. It is and isn't Saint Aloysius, which is why I'll give Barb this last year in the after-school program before moving on to something else. That's probably why I wanted to be part of the academy so much after I didn't become senior counselor. That was supposed to be my place—or so I thought—but it wasn't. For a moment I believed I had finally found my own bridge between Mott Haven and Dawkins at Hebron. Now I know I have to build my own bridges, and I can do that anywhere. On the block, at Dawkins, at Saint Aloysius. I just have to find people who want to build with me. Not for me or around me or despite me. *With* me. It's not where I'm at as much as who I'm with. "But you were right. Not that I regret helping you get a jump start, Q, and I'll still back you up. I just have to go for mine."

I expect Qusay to give me the hard sell. Instead he just holds out his hand. "Show and prove."

I take his hand, and we shake. "I got to break out. Pop took the day off. We're going to catch a game at Shea." Qusay laughs as I steal one of Nana's coconut drops, pop it in my mouth, and head out the door.

I step out of the hospital and onto the boulevard. At the first mailbox, I drop my letter to Russell at Princeton. I hope he answers, but it felt good just to write it.

The sun warms my head as I stroll down the Grand Concourse, admiring both the architecture and the graffiti. Beneath the siren of fire engines and patrol cars, kids are playing kick the can and Aretha Franklin is singing, "We won't stop, not until we get it right . . ." This street was designed to be New York City's Champs-Elysées, and there is no reason why it can never be. Grace can come through grit, Mama used to say, which is why no one is disposable. Look how we turn litter into toys, abandonment into abandon.

For all the hardship here, and maybe even because of it, this can still be Mecca. I don't have to know how right now. I just have to keep the faith and play my part.

WILLIE

For the first time in my life, I want to give one girl all my attention, make things right, and otherwise be the guy she hoped I was, but she doesn't need me. On the contrary, I finally accept that what Sara needs most is for me to leave her alone. I miss being with her—it doesn't matter that we didn't do anything but talk—but Sara needs space, and even though it's killing me, I'm going to give it to her. I guess this is what they mean when they say if you love someone, let 'em go.

It sucks.

Still, I stop calling her and trying to cross paths with her on the block. I don't bring her up when I bump into Cooks. Sounds so simple, but it's the hardest thing I've ever had to do.

It really sucks, yo.

Sometimes I can't help myself, though, and I go to that spot on the roof where I first saw Sara. I never see her, but it turns out to be a good thing. One thought leads to another,

339

and I make some decisions about my life. Good decisions, I think.

First, I'm going to talk to Big Lou about enlisting in the military. I need to see the world, be on my own, the whole nine, and as scary as it is, I don't know another way. Plus I used to think that because I manage to survive in such a tough neighborhood, I'm all worldly and whatnot. Truth is, though, I don't know squat. And maybe I could ask Big Lou about other things in life.

But I'm not going into the army or navy or whatever until after I graduate from high school. No way am I going to drop out for that. Uncle Sam ain't going anywhere, and I want to see what happens in the world first before signing away four years of my life. As much as I want to travel, learn some skills, and grow up, I ain't trying to go to war to do that if I can avoid it.

I haven't ruled out college, but I don't know. That may have to come later. I really want to get my own place after high school, but I can't afford to do that without working full-time. The other day I was chillin' on the stoop with Ma, and I told her she should think about becoming some kind of teacher because she's good at explaining things. That got her excited, and she wrote away for catalogs from the different CUNY schools, like Lehman and Hunter. I started browsing through them, too, and was shocked to realize that public colleges aren't free like high school.

It's a vicious circle, yo. I have to get an education to make enough money to be on my own without scraping by, but I need to make money to go to school, even with financial aid. Now I have a better understanding of how hard it was for Ma to reinvent herself after Glo and I were born and our father broke out. Even though we're getting along a little bit better, I don't want to push it. That means moving out after graduation and, in the meantime, helping her with the bills. No leather bomber or sheepskin for me this winter. Whether I get a full-time job or enlist in the military, I'll still send a little bit of money Ma's way.

I head up to the roof to do some more thinking about life, and I find the Professor playing with his Frogger Coleco-Vision. Usually, I don't like sharing this spot, but instead of chasing him off, I sit down on the tar beside him and watch him play for a while. Over the game's audio, I hear a bunch of kids running through a pump on the street below. "Afraid those pooh-butts will get your game wet, huh?" Jerry just shrugs, squinting at the screen as he jogs the joystick. "You should be down there getting wet, too. You can play Frogger all winter long, but summer's gonna be over soon."

After he finishes his game, Jerry says, "You want to play?"

"Nah, I'll just watch you." I do want to play, but I can't take Jerry's toy away from him. "Although if you want someone to play against, there are bound to be some takers downstairs."

With a game like that, the Professor should be Mr. Popularity. When Booby got the new Atari, Smiles, the homies, and me used to be in his apartment for hours every day after school and before *Kung Fu Theater* on Saturdays, playing Missile Command, Defender, Centipede, you name it. It wasn't as cool as the game room, but we could save our quarters for snacks and avoid Don Silvio's hawk eye.

The Professor says, "Yeah, but then I never get to play."

"What you talking about? It's your game."

"I always have to fight to get it back, even when it's time for me to go home. Last time I came home late, my dad went off. Said I shouldn't bring my stuff outside anyway. That if it breaks or gets stolen, don't come crying to him expecting to buy another one."

I get where his father's coming from, but he doesn't need to be so hard on the Professor. It's not easy for a kid like him to make friends, so how can you blame him for using his things to break the ice? Still, your friends should like you for who you are and not what you rock. I start to wonder why the Professor never went to day camp. It would've done him some good. He can be a know-it-all, but I would much rather've been Jerry's counselor than Stevie's any day. Even though sometimes I find myself missing that brat.

And if the Professor's parents have the money for telescopes and video games, surely they could afford day camp. Hell, they could probably send him to one of those sleepaway camps where Jerry could visit another part of the state and learn cool things like how to fish or ride a horse. The toys go out of style, but the experiences last forever.

"Professor, wait right here," I say, crawling to my feet. "I'ma be right back." I run to my apartment to get my boom box and linoleum. Then I decide to drop the mat, keep the radio, and grab my Little League mitt and an old baseball. When I return to the roof, I put on the boom box. I motion for Jerry to come over and stuff his hand in the mitt. "So who do you like? I mean like a girlfriend." Jerry's cheeks go pink, and I laugh. "You can tell me. I promise not to say nothing to nobody."

He grins at me. "You know who."

I shake my head. "Nah, B. Vanessa too old for you. You need to be realistic. There's got to be some girl you know who's into history and video games and all that stuff that you like." Jerry goes from pink to red. "Ah, see! Don't pretend to not like that stuff to impress some girl who's not into those things. There's nothing wrong with you. Or her. Y'all just don't fit. Stand over there." Jerry backs up. "What's her name?" I roll my shoulders and set to pitch.

"Tasha."

"Tasha? Wait. Booby's little sister?" Jerry nods. "Wow." At first, I want to warn him to stay away from her. But instead I say, "She could probably use a friend right now." I pitch and Jerry's arm shoots up, the baseball landing squarely in the mitt.

Who would've thought the Professor had athletic skills? Not always a bad thing to let people surprise you. It inspires you to try to surprise yourself.

If you want more from Willie and Raymond,
visit sofiaquintero.com.

ABOUT THE AUTHOR

Self-professed "Ivy League homegirl" Sofia Quintero is a writer, producer, activist, educator, and speaker. Born into a working-class Puerto Rican and Dominican family in the Bronx, where she still lives, she holds a BA and an MPA from Columbia University. She also recently earned an MFA in writing and producing television at the TV Writers Studio at Long Island University in Brooklyn.

Sofia is the author of another novel for young readers, *Efrain's Secret,* and she has written several hip-hop novels under the pen name Black Artemis.

When not working on her next young adult novel, Sofia runs an after-school program in the Bronx for a girls'-empowerment organization and is a teaching artist for the National Book Foundation. You can learn more about Sofia and her projects at sofiaquintero.com.

Crete Public Library
305 East 13th St.
Crete, NE 68333
Established 1878